The Corpse Played Dead

Georgina Clarke has a degree in theology and a PhD in history but has only recently started to combine her love of the past with a desire to write stories. Her Lizzie Hardwicke series is set in the mid-eighteenth century, an underrated and often neglected period, but one that is rich in possibility for a crime novelist.

She enjoys running along the banks of the River Severn and is sometimes to be found competing in half marathons. In quieter moments, she also enjoys dressmaking.

She lives in Worcester with her husband and son, and two extremely lively kittens. For more information please visit her website https://www.georginaclarkeauthor.com/

Social media: Twitter @clarkegeorgina1

D1639045

Also by Georgina Clarke

Lizzie Hardwicke

Death and the Harlot
The Corpse Played Dead

GEORGINA
CLARKE
THE
CORPSE
PLAYED
DEAD

🜊 CANELO

First published in the United Kingdom in 2019 by Canelo

This edition published in the United Kingdom in 2021 by

Canelo
31 Helen Road
Oxford OX2 0DF
United Kingdom

Print ISBN 978 1 78863 794 7
Ebook ISBN 978 1 78863 454 0

Look for more great books at www.canelo.co

Printed and bound in Great Britain by Clays Ltd, Elcograf S.p.A.

1

For Sebastian

Chapter One

'There's little point in being famous if you don't make the most of it, Lizzie.'

Mrs Sarah Farley, owner of the finest brothel in Soho, leaned out of the theatre box and waved to everyone she knew in the audience. Being the sort of woman who was generous with her charms, she waved to everyone else as well.

'I'm not certain I want the fame, Ma,' I said, shrinking back into my seat. We all called her Ma, those of us who lived with her.

'Nonsense. You just have to know how to milk it.' She sat down heavily, the jewellery jangling in her bosom. 'You can learn a lot from me.' She patted my arm. She had taken to patting me now that I was famous, as well as declaring that she had always been fond of me. We both knew that she was fonder of the money that I brought into her house, but neither of us was so impolite as to mention it.

There were four of us in the box. Ma Farley had decided that we were celebrating my new-found notoriety by parading ourselves in the most public way possible: taking a box in the theatre at Drury Lane.

The play happened to be *King Lear*. This is not one of Shakespeare's cheeriest efforts, but, as Ma said, we were not here to watch it – we were here to be seen. So here we were, me and Mrs Farley, with two others from our house, Polly and Lucy, each of us dressed, powdered, and made up in our harlot's best. We had brought a hamper of food and wine to sustain us through the evening of preening and flirting that stretched ahead of us. Ma would make sure that we left in the best carriages with the wealthiest gentlemen.

I took a sip of wine and closed my eyes for a moment. I had been in London for nearly nine months. Once a gentleman's daughter, a clergyman's daughter even, I had fallen spectacularly from grace and landed in Ma Farley's bawdy house on Berwick Street. The change of circumstance had brought me an income, but not, until recently, the sort of notoriety that had Ma reaching for enough of her own coins to buy us the best box in the theatre.

'It's not every day that a girl gets her name chanted all the way from Newgate to Tyburn,' said Polly, pouring herself a glass of wine and knocking it back. 'Everyone knows you now.' Her face was already flushed, and a strand of blonde hair had fallen loose at the temple.

Two months ago, I helped to catch a murderer. Yesterday, they hanged him along with five robbers. I did not go to see it, but my dear friend Polly, like most London harlots, loves a good hanging, and had given such a spirited account of the bodies twitching on the ends of their ropes that my stomach had twisted with horror as if I had been there. Crowds had turned out in their thousands, she told me. Three people had been trampled to death in the crush.

The murderer had gone to his death raging.

He had tried to kill me, but this was insignificant in the light of three other deaths. My name had been mentioned briefly at the trial, and I had enjoyed a modest increase in attention as a result, from the sort of gentlemen who read trial reports and fancied the thrill of associated danger. They had satisfied their curiosity, and I had charged them handsomely for it.

But the murderer had travelled to Tyburn in his cart yelling abuse all along the road at the one person in London who had chosen not to watch him die; the vicious whore who had sent him to his doom.

Me.

And now, everyone knew my name. Lizzie Hardwicke: London's finest.

—

We could see the whole audience, even without leaning out. We were near enough to the stage that, should we ever wish to cast our eyes on this evening's play, we might do so. The sconces were bright on the walls, the large chandeliers – the girandoles – were full of candles, and the whole theatre glimmered and glowed, giving us full view of everyone as the musicians began their pre-performance offering.

'The pit's nearly full already,' said Lucy. Lucy Allingham, who by established custom in our house barely acknowledged my existence, except to pass a disdainful comment, was, for the time being, also basking in my reflected glory. Lucy Allingham, whose dark eyebrows were permanently arched into an expression of surprised innocence, would never stoop to entertaining a man who sat in the pit, so I assumed she made the remark for my benefit. It was kind of her to offer me the poorer scraps.

'Perhaps they knew we were coming,' Ma said to me with a wink. She rose from her seat, smiled benignly at the crowd below and waved to a box on the other side, as though she were the queen.

I thought, perhaps, that the crowds had come to see Mr Garrick, rather than us, but held my tongue. David Garrick, the manager of the Drury Lane theatre, and also its finest actor, had given the world *King Lear* earlier in the year, to great acclaim, so this was something of a reprise. On the raked seats of the pit gentlemen sat gossiping like market girls. Lawyers, lately well-fed and well-watered at their Inns of Court were seated alongside newspaper men, clergymen, would-be playwrights, and other gentlemen about town. Had they been so moved by *Lear*'s final scenes in March that they had returned for the thrill of it in May? Every newspaper and journal had spoken of grown men reduced to tears, after all. Or had they caught the rumour, as we had, that Susannah Cibber – so affecting as Cordelia – had given way to Lucy Hunter? There's nothing like a change of actress to bring out the gentlemen. The hacks would, no doubt, be sharpening their pens, poised to offer their judgements and, even before the next performance, she might be toasted in the taverns and hailed in print as a goddess, or else damned as a pale imitation, unworthy to tread the boards. Much would depend on the name of her patron, of course; even the poorest actress can claim success if she has the right friends.

Neither of the two galleries was full. It was only six o'clock and, unlike the gentlemen, the working men who would fill those seats had not had leisure to eat. Many would arrive after the third act, on their half-price tickets, bringing baskets of bread and cheese and bottles of porter to share in companionable fashion with wives and children. I envied the conviviality and the anonymity of the lower gallery but knew that the likes of us would be unwelcome there.

Far above us was the upper gallery. I couldn't see much of it, and I didn't care to. No one wants to spend an evening watching the common sort jostling for space, but we could certainly hear them. They hadn't started throwing fruit at each other yet, although I had seen a curl of orange peel fly through the air into the pit. They were making a tremendous noise, but I couldn't catch the words of the song they shouted out.

It was the people in the other boxes that we had really come to watch, just as they watched us. Polly nudged my elbow and nodded to the box directly opposite. Three gentlemen were arriving, laughing with one another as they took their seats. A servant emerged from the shadow behind them and placed a large basket on the floor. He began lifting out the contents, wine and food, and laying them on the cloth-covered table. The men – young, wealthy and ready to be parted from their money before the evening was out – raised their glasses to us in salute. We knew far better than they how to play this game and gave them our prettiest looks and returned the salutes before coyly turning away. My smile, Ma tells me, can charm birds from trees; it certainly earned a response from a man whose diamond pin was so large and bright that I could see it from across the theatre. We had attracted their attention early in the evening, now we needed only to wait until the first interval before beckoning them over. A few teasing fondles while the dancers and tumblers entertained the galleries and we could be certain that they would drive us back to Berwick Street for the night, ready to lavish their affections – and their guineas – upon us. We were content to enjoy the theatre's entertainment – being certain of how the evening's sport would end.

The chairs on the apron of the stage were beginning to fill with the privileged members of the audience; those with enough money or connection to mingle with the players in the green room and sit nearest to them as they performed. Some of these were noblemen, charmed by the latest pretty actress, wanting to sit so close that they could smell the scent of her gown as she moved, or gentlemen of letters keen to breathe the air that Garrick exhaled, ready to be overcome by his majestic presence.

I swept a glance over the theatre, this vibrant house of play and illusion. We were all playing, in truth: the jovial fellow, the serious critic, family man or coquette. But, for a moment, in company with other players, we could lose our daily reality and give ourselves up to the fantasy that all was well and that we were gods or kings.

A man in the lower gallery caught my eye; a gentleman I knew well was looking up at our box. He was sitting at the edge, near to the balustrade, his wig pulled back into a low tail with a simple black ribbon. He was wearing a brown coat with unfashionable loose-fitting shoulders. The coat, I knew, enabled him to run and climb and to fight, if fighting were called for. He had a slender frame, but he was strong and wiry, like a cat. Yesterday's hanging would have been a duty. He would have had no choice but to attend and would have taken no pleasure in it. This was one of the magistrate's men. I wondered what he was doing here. From our previous acquaintance, I thought it unlikely that he nursed a secret passion for theatre.

He was watching us. I tilted my head to acknowledge him.

He held my gaze for a moment, gave the smallest of nods, and then turned his eyes back to the stage. The players had arrived.

'Good evening to you too, Mr Davenport,' I said, under my breath.

Chapter Two

There were two incidents of note in the performance – beyond anything that happened to Lear and his daughters.

After the third act, during the long interval, the audience numbers swelled as those bearing half-price tickets made their way into the auditorium. There is usually a moment of tension when this happens, as those who paid the full two and six for a place on the pit benches are forced to squeeze in for the latecomers who have parted with smaller coin. There is always some grumbling. Those on the cheaper tickets are deemed to be philistines by the serious-minded critics in the pit. They have come only for the end of the main play and to see the after-piece – the frivolous little play tacked on to the performance. After-pieces are usually nonsense, but they draw the crowds. We, who had not come to see either play but rather to parade ourselves, did not judge.

The greater noise came from above, where the galleries now began to fill. The mood was cheerful. Garrick had already demonstrated his magnificence, and there was a general sense of satisfaction with the performance. Lucy Hunter was proving very nearly equal to the task of stepping into Mrs Cibber's shoes with a sweet, if slightly garbled rendering of Cordelia. Indeed, she was so pretty and delicate and she flashed her eyes so adorably that the gentlemen of the pit were happy to ignore a little stumbling over the words. I decided that her patron must be either wealthy or very notable.

The interval entertainment, by contrast, was miserable. A man was standing on stage, trying to coax a small monkey to jump between poles and ropes in time to music provided by the orchestra. Half of the orchestra. The other half had decided to disappear to the tavern next door for a beer and a pipe. The monkey was not interested in being entertaining. It sat on top of a pole and washed its face, looking up occasionally to stare at the audience before resuming its meticulous cleaning. If the monkey was not interested in us, then neither were we interested in the monkey. Its handler was growing increasingly anxious as we became restless. The noise from the audience began to drown out the music.

The people in the upper gallery began to throw fruit on to the stage – which did interest the monkey. It leapt from the pole and began gathering up apple cores and orange peel, to the exasperation of his owner and the amusement of the crowd. Finally, it gave us all a withering look, showed us its arse, and then scampered off the stage into the wings, the owner running out after it, mortified with embarrassment. We cheered loudly.

Polly, who was bored with the Shakespeare but jolly with wine, shoved her fingers into her mouth and whistled her appreciation – much to Ma's disapproval. Despite her profession, Ma disliked vulgarity. The whistle had the effect of causing one or two of the men in the pit to look up, so Polly began to blow kisses, to their evident enjoyment. One man, a lawyer a little to their left, glanced up and saw me. He began waving enthusiastically and shouting my name. At some point, since the trial,

I must have entertained him, although his face was only dimly familiar. He, though, had not forgotten me.

Ma gave me a sharp poke in the ribs and nodded for me to acknowledge him. I played my part, waved back and favoured him with what I hoped was a warm smile.

But my name was, as of yesterday, known to the whole of London, thanks to the murderous man sent on his way to Tyburn. A few others began to shout it out, delighted to see the woman responsible for the downfall of a notorious killer. And then, suddenly it seemed as though the whole of the theatre was shouting, every head was turned in my direction while my name was chanted across the galleries.

I ducked my head down, praying for them to cease.

Ma was having none of this and hauled me out of my chair so firmly that I nearly tipped over the balcony.

'Wave!' she hissed at me. 'Smile at them!'

'Blow them kisses,' Polly advised, giggling, 'they'll love it.'

I waved and smiled and nodded as best I could. The crowd went wild.

'Lizzie Hardwicke! I think I'm in love!' Someone yelled.

'My wick's gone hard, that's for sure,' shouted another, standing up on a bench and rubbing his crotch. This set off roars of laughter.

'Careful lads,' another voice rose up from the pit, 'from what I've heard, if she falls in love with you, you'll be on your way to Tyburn within the month.' The man who shouted was fat-faced, wart-covered, and the wrong side of forty. He thought it funny to lay the blame for a hanging at my feet. That was unfair. I glanced across to the gallery and saw Davenport's scowl. He knew what that death had meant to me.

'Don't you worry about it, sweetheart,' I said, now leaning out over the balcony and addressing the joker below, 'I only ever fall in love with men who are very rich or at least middling handsome. You, dear sir, have nothing at all to worry about.'

The crowd roared with laughter and the man, now a dark shade of red, sat down – to be slapped on the shoulder by his friends.

Davenport had covered his face with his hands.

I did not like the attention, even though Polly, Ma and even Lucy were revelling in it.

Mr Garrick could not have appreciated it much either, for the orchestra members were being harried on to the stage. The music drowned the laughter and shouting and heralded the final act.

I sat down and handed my glass to Polly.

'I need another.'

I drank it in one gulp and held out the glass for more, desperate for the play to resume.

Mr Shakespeare, I am reliably informed, gave *King Lear* a miserable ending. Garrick, having a much better idea of what pleases the crowds, re-wrote it to make more sense. Why would anyone want to see Lear die in grief, after all? Far better to know that the traitors would be punished, Cordelia and Edgar would rule in prosperity, and that Lear would enjoy a tranquil retirement.

We were just coming towards the final scene, and the wrongs were being beautifully righted. Mrs Hunter had found her confidence at last and the quaver in her voice now seemed almost deliberately designed to tug the hearts of her audience. Mr Garrick was beginning a tender speech in praise of filial piety when suddenly, off-stage, there was a scream.

This gave rise to the second incident of note – a more devastating one for the performance than my own repartee with the audience.

The scream might not have been heard at all had the audience not been so gripped – and thus nearly silenced – by the closing lines. Above Garrick's intense, whispered words we all heard it. Then it came again; louder and shriller. A woman was screaming murder.

I saw the back of Davenport's coat as he sped from the gallery.

Garrick faltered. The screams continued. There was nothing he could do but stop speaking, gesturing to the orchestra to play as he and the actors ran into the wings.

There was uproar in the pit, and in the galleries, as everyone began to talk at once.

From our box, Ma and Lucy chatted amiably to our neighbours, discussing the merits of the performance so far as though nothing had happened. Their interest lay less in the acting and more in the fact that Mrs Hunter had worn different jewelled necklaces for each act. This was a sure sign – according to Ma – that she had more than one lover on the go.

'Perhaps they came from her husband?' the neighbour ventured with a titter. Ma's laugh turned into a cough when she snorted her wine.

Polly nudged me.

'Something's happening. Look.'

On the stage, Garrick had appeared. He was no longer Lear; he was the theatre manager, with a look on his face that lay somewhere between anxiety and anger. He waved his hands in the air to quieten the crowds.

'Honoured guests, ladies, gentlemen, please I beg your attention. I stand before you, no longer a king, but your servant.'

There were mutterings in the pit. Garrick stepped forward again.

'It is my unhappy duty, as manager of this fine theatre, to inform you that we cannot continue with tonight's performance.'

Someone booed noisily from the gallery, as Garrick cut in, 'There has been an accident. A most unfortunate accident.'

A ripple of excitement ran around the audience. The men on the stage, more privileged than us and closer to the wings, nodded to one another, knowing, perhaps, what he meant.

'What about our money?' a voice yelled from the gallery. 'We paid for a whole play, not half of one.'

Garrick's face wrinkled in annoyance. The players had reached the closing scenes of an immaculate perform-ance – everyone knew it had been so. But the audience, this rabble of critics and philistines, would squeeze their pennies out of him for the sake of an after-piece. Anyone could see the conflict in Garrick: he had bared his soul as Lear, and now he was going to have to refund the audience for some nonsense full of lurid innuendo – or risk a riot. The manager weighed his options; the actor delivered his line.

'Gentlemen, we have given of our best and have suffered a shock in the dying moments. If our play has displeased you, or if you feel that you have not had a spectacle worth your coin, then we will, of course be pleased to offer you a refund. I would only hope that we may be glad of your generosity, if you have been glad of our energies in bringing Shakespeare's genius to life.'

Some clapped. I clapped. I had no desire to have my money back, even if it had been my money – not when I had secured several guineas for the rest of the night. I'm always careful with my coins, but Garrick was right: they had given us a treat, very nearly. I respected those who worked hard, and the labourer is worthy of his hire, as my father might say. Others, though, were deciding to claim their money, and began bustling to the doors, looking for someone to claim it from. Ma, without a doubt, would have gone with them, but for the fact that the gentlemen in the box opposite, being men of adequate means, were gesturing to us that they were ready to leave without worrying after shillings. They were keen to continue the evening at Berwick Street.

Lucy, Polly and I nodded and waved, exchanging, behind our smiles to them, our private observations on their likely preferences.

Laughing along with the others, I soon found myself on the arm of a pleasant creature with a neat face and merry eyes. The elegant cut of his coat, the diamond at his neck, and the bright jewels on his fingers were even more pleasing to see, as they promised a lucrative night.

Even so, as I giggled and flirted with him in his carriage, I wondered what had happened behind the scenery of Drury Lane. What was the shock that had cost Lear his final embrace with his cherished daughter?

Chapter Three

The gentleman sitting in my room at noon the next day was not the one I had brought home.

My evening guest had been full of gratitude for the hours he spent in my company – and he had spent many hours. He had left in the morning kissing my fingers, after dropping his coins on my table, assuring me that he would return. The diamond pin that I had admired in the theatre was also now mine for a service that, in the harsher light of day, made me queasy to recall. But everything had been done, as it was always done, to build up my private treasure store: my retirement fund. The contribution to Ma had been given faithfully, as usual in our house, but the rest – the coins and gifts I had never declared – were hidden away under one of the floorboards.

This new gentleman was sitting stiffly, his body tense, even though he had chosen my more comfortable chair. He was also scowling. Scowling was his expression of choice, I remembered.

'I hope you've brought me news from the theatre, Mr Davenport.' I perched on the second, less comfortable, chair, wishing that I was wearing more clothing. 'I've been desperate for news all night.'

He looked around the room. Over to my bed.

'I imagine you've kept yourself busy, even so.'

I had done my best to tidy up. 'Even so.'

William Davenport was not quite thirty years of age, barely more than ten years my senior, although his manner made him seem older. He had trained as a physician but had set that profession aside after the death of his wife and child and had latterly become one of a small band of men in the employ of Mr Fielding, the magistrate of Bow Street. Fielding's men were charged with hunting down robbers and murderers as swiftly as possible, and overturning vice and corruption where they found it – mostly among the lower orders. They had done a good job in harrying and disrupting some of the worst criminal gangs, but ordinary brothel keepers like Mrs Farley also fretted at their presence. Davenport was grave, sharp-witted, and he disapproved of my way of life.

He intrigued me.

We sat in silence for a moment.

Most men visit my room to deal with the lusts that are not satisfied at home. Most men do not sit frowning at me. Most men, by now, would have thrown back a glass of wine and shed their breeches.

Davenport was different. He liked pretty women – I had noticed that – but he was not interested in me. He had once thought me a murderer, and a thief, but I had given him cause to cast that judgement aside when I had caught the killer for him. That was two months ago, and I hadn't set eyes on him until last night at Drury Lane. He didn't need to know that I was glad to see him. Or that it irked me to discover that I was glad.

He unclasped his hands, clasped them again, and cleared his throat.

'How good are you as an actress, Miss Hardwicke?'

I laughed.

'My dear Mr Davenport,' I said with a dramatic sweep of my arm, 'I spend the whole of my day pretending. In this room, I am able to make any man believe that he is the finest lover in the world and that I am dying for his love. But please don't ask me to recite lines of Shakespeare, like Mrs Hunter – or even to do it as badly as her. I'd be dreadful on the stage. Why do you ask?'

'I need you to act for me.'

I raised my eyebrows.

'What do you mean, act for you?'

'Mr Fielding sent me. He wonders if you'd like a role in the theatre.'

'I've just told you, I can't recite lines.'

He hesitated. I wondered what was coming next.

'He doesn't want you on the stage. He wants you behind it. The manager is looking for a second seamstress.'

'Why on earth would I want to be a seamstress?' I gave him my haughtiest look. 'It's a pity that you know so little of my real talent, sir. Perhaps you should enquire of the gentleman who left here not an hour ago, as happy as he was exhausted.'

He shifted in his seat. 'Nothing to do with me, of course,' he said, giving me the impression that it had a lot to do with him, 'but Mr Fielding needs someone inside the theatre to find out what's going on.'

Maddeningly, my curiosity was aroused. He knew it would be, and this made me madder still.

'I thought you wanted to know what's happening.' he said, stretching out a leg and smoothing a crease over his thigh. 'Don't you want to know why Mr Garrick has come running to Bow Street? Would you like me to tell you all about it, Miss Hardwicke?' He paused and looked over at me. 'Ah, but of course you would. And when you

17

find out, you'll want to be at the heart of it, I'm sure. So, would you like to play at being a seamstress for a day or two?'

I folded my arms, unwilling to give him the satisfaction of getting the better of me, but wanting to know what was going on. There was also the matter of income. Davenport had hinted to me before that the magistrate might pay for my work – and a decent sum had, indeed, arrived when I had led his men to a killer.

'Is Mr Fielding going to pay me? I don't want to find that Ma has let my room while I'm scratching for farthings on the floor of the pit. I have to make a living and Ma's keen to make the most of my new notoriety.'

Davenport knew that I had not chosen this life. He knew, or believed he knew, the circumstances that had brought me to Berwick Street. He knew that I was carefully saving my money in order that I might leave one day. He also knew of my desire for adventure; but adventure doesn't keep a girl in food, let alone in hats.

'I can speak with Mrs Farley. It's only for a day or two and Mr Fielding is prepared to pay you.' There was a touch of hesitation in his voice.

'How much will he pay me?'

He pulled a face. 'Enough to keep your landlady happy, I'm sure.'

There would be nothing extra for me then.

'It's the best I can do,' he said. 'Mr Fielding is willing to pay informers, but even the money I receive has to be squeezed from the government.'

He was inviting me to exchange a life of comfort, albeit shared with any man who walked through my door, for a couple of days of labour, dodging the groping hands of many other men and running to the beck and call of insufferable actresses. If I made better use of my wits, I would surely reject his invitation. But my interest was piqued, and curiosity has long been my undoing.

'I'll do it,' I said, standing up from my seat and holding out a hand. 'You know I can't resist. As long as Ma's happy to let me go, and she gets paid, you needn't worry about me. I'll get by. I'm sure I'll manage without my jewels and ribbons.'

He rose from his seat and shook my hand.

'Thank you. Mr Fielding will be pleased.'

'Never mind that. How about we find some food and wine, and you can tell me what's going on at Mr Garrick's theatre?'

Chapter Four

'David Garrick is a remarkable man,' said Davenport, helping himself to several slices of meat and some bread. 'The trouble is, he makes a lot of enemies.'

'I've heard.' It was common knowledge that the man who was so brilliant in communicating the full range of human emotion on the stage could be capricious, moody and tight-fisted when off it.

'At the smallest criticism, he takes to his pen and dashes off letters to the newspapers, choosing to air his disagreements in public. He would be better served by trying to soothe his critics, I think.' Davenport would rather cut off his arm than play out an argument in the press.

'His letters suggest that he's a man who doesn't like to let matters rest until they're resolved in his favour; a man thoroughly convinced of his own approach and opinion,' I said.

Davenport looked up, surprised.

'I do read the newspapers, Mr Davenport. I don't spend every hour of the day on my back.'

'Forgive me, I meant no slight.'

I poured him a glass of wine. 'And what you're going to tell me now,' I said, ignoring his discomfort and helping myself to a glass, 'is that some of these critics and enemies are making life unpleasant for him?'

He nodded, took a sip from the glass, and settled himself in the chair. He had, by now, decided to unbutton his waistcoat.

'Exactly so. The problem is, no one knows which of his many detractors is causing the unpleasantness. This wine is excellent.'

The wine was good. French wine was over-taxed and expensive, so I settled back into my chair to appreciate it. If I was going to spend days away from the better comforts of Berwick Street – decent wine and the opportunity for quiet conversation in my own room – then I needed to know more. A second seamstress was unlikely to have much chance to sit down, let alone indulge in such luxuries as eating and drinking.

'Burgundy. I've no idea where Ma bought it. But tell me about the unpleasantness. What happened last night?'

'A number of fusses about nothing; that's what we thought at first. Mr Garrick, as you observed, is like a dog with a bone when he thinks he has cause, and he strongly believes that someone is out to ruin him and his theatre.' He paused. It sounded as though he had not been convinced, initially. Garrick, dramatic, flamboyant and obsessive, was the antithesis of the taciturn Davenport. The thought of them meeting made me smile.

'He began pestering Mr Fielding some weeks ago. Fielding's not a great lover of theatre – his blindness means it's of little enjoyment – but he knows a great deal about it and is much admiring of Garrick. They have connections in common, of course.'

Wealthy, well-known, self-made men working in Covent Garden: naturally they would move in similar circles.

'There were a few incidents of theft and petty destruction. A costume or two torn, a piece of scenery slashed, an important item of furniture for a play missing and then found broken. It was, by and large, unimportant stuff, but taken all together it began to look like a deliberate and calculated attempt to unsettle the theatre people. They're all prone to fantasy and superstition. These things were making them skittish. Garrick called almost every day last week – as if we don't have enough to do. Then, two days ago, he claimed that one of his actresses had been poisoned.'

'Poisoned? Not Susannah Cibber? She was supposed to be playing Cordelia last night. Lucy Hunter took her place.'

'Mrs Cibber became unwell in the night. Complained of stomach cramps. Garrick says that she's been poisoned.'

I snorted with laughter. 'She's notorious for falling ill. Why did he think she was poisoned this time?'

'Is she? I didn't know that.'

'You should pay more attention to the gossips and scandal sheets, Mr Davenport. One may learn a lot from tittle-tattle – even more than from the newspapers, you know.'

He rolled his eyes. 'This is why we have need of you, Miss Hardwicke. I knew there had to be a reason for my being here, other than this excellent wine.'

'This is a house of pleasure, sir. We like to please our guests in every way, as you know.'

He took another mouthful of wine.

I wondered, as I watched him relax, what his own particular pleasure would be, if he were to pay for it, or ever seek it with me.

I pulled my mind back to our conversation. 'Tell me more about Mrs Cibber's poisoning.'

'Well, Garrick believed she had been poisoned, at least. That's why I was in the theatre last night. He was extremely exercised about it. I was to be in the audience, to watch for anything suspicious.' He smirked. 'You put in a very good performance, by the way. You were even better than the monkey.'

I saluted him with my glass. He was, slowly, becoming better company. 'Perhaps I'll pick on you next time I spy you hiding behind a pillar. Why was there so much screaming at the end of the play? A "most unfortunate accident", Mr Garrick called it, I think.'

'You've a good memory.'

'I know.'

'It turns out that was all it was, an unfortunate accident. One of the stage hands fell from a ladder. He's broken a leg but is otherwise perfectly fine.'

'So why all the screaming? Why stop a performance when it's nearly ended just for a broken leg?'

'At first I thought it was just an actress getting over-excited – I told you they were skittish. The man had fallen badly, twisted his leg and knocked himself on the head as well. When she found him, it looked to her as though he was dead.'

'Poor woman,' I said. It's not pleasant to encounter violent death. 'That still doesn't explain why—'

'When I reached him, he was beginning to come to. His leg was causing him a lot of pain, but he didn't seem to have damaged his head too badly. Even so, next to where he lay there was a note.'

'Ah.' Now I was truly interested. I leaned forward, the fabric of my gown slipping a little at my shoulder.

Davenport looked away, concentrating on his plate. 'The note was a threat to Garrick and his players. It said that more accidents would happen until Garrick left the theatre.'

'What does that mean?' I asked, hitching my gown back to a more modest position.

'I have no idea. Garrick had no idea, either, but the players refused to continue. There was something close to mutiny behind the scenery. Thankfully, the audience members were talking so loudly I doubt anyone heard the arguments back stage.'

I hadn't heard them, but then, I had been in a box with Ma, Polly and Lucy. I would not have heard the roof falling in.

'That explains the expression on Mr Garrick's face,' I said. 'He was furious.'

'He was, although whether he was furious with the note-writer or the players, I couldn't tell.'

I drained my glass and set it down. 'So where do I fit into this pantomime?'

He laughed. He didn't laugh often, which was a pity. His brown eyes twinkled when he was cheerful, but the grief he carried, and the murky aspects of his work made him far too serious.

'Yes, I was coming to that. Once he had dealt with the audience Garrick strode off to Bow Street to find the magistrate, demanding that Mr Fielding do something. Fielding was in an imaginative frame of mind and suggested that he might put a man into the theatre, behind the scenes, to see what was going on.'

'A man?'

He scratched his cheek and pulled a face. 'I suggested you.'

'I knew it. Why did you suggest me? And as a second seamstress, for heaven's sake? You don't even know whether I can sew on a button.'

'I made a guess,' he said. 'An educated one. From what I know of your life before this...' he nodded to my room, my bed, '...I imagined that you would have learned to sew, or at least know how to hold a needle.'

I thought back to my attempts to sit quietly and embroider, when my father had tried, unsuccessfully, to contain what he had called wilfulness, and I had called a desire for liberty. Davenport was right: although I had no idea how to create the gowns I wore, I could embroider. I could stitch and mend.

'A reasonable assumption,' I said, shaking away the thoughts of home. 'But why put me in the theatre, and not one of the men you use as informers? One of them might act a stage hand?'

'Because women can come and go unnoticed. A seamstress gathering mending can poke about in dressing rooms in a way that would attract attention if a man did it. You'll be insignificant, beneath notice. Besides,' he said, looking me square in the face, 'you pay attention to things. You're probably the best eyes and ears we've got. I'd sooner have you in there than any of the men I know.'

I am not averse to flattery. This is a serious flaw in my character and I really should excise it.

'When do I start?'

Chapter Five

Davenport escorted me to the theatre the next day. It was mid-morning and Covent Garden piazza was full of people buying and selling spring flowers and vegetables. The air was fresh, and I could smell roses and sweet peas as we walked through the market. It was a different place in the daytime; full of natural colour and vibrancy. It was pleasant and wholesome. In the evening, the square turned into an arena of artifice, filled with people dedicated to the pleasures of the flesh and the pursuit of vice.

By the time we reached the theatre, the sounds of market bustle were behind us. Last night, the streets had been thronging, but now I saw only a few scrawny children, more interested in picking up scraps of discarded food from the ground than waiting to glimpse the leading players or argue about Shakespeare. There were three entrances to the theatre. The main door at the front was used by the grander sort of audience member, making their way to the boxes. We had used it last night, displaying ourselves to the people of consequence. The large door that opened out from the pit was always the busiest. It gave access to the pit benches as well as to the galleries. The passageway to the pit door was, at opening time and at the long interval, a heaving mass of noisy play-goers, all pressing to find the best seats. At the rear of the theatre was the stage door, used by the members of the company.

This was where we found ourselves now. The door was closed, as I'd expected at this time of day. Players, like harlots, begin their work late. Davenport banged with his fist and we waited.

I hugged my possessions. They were wrapped in the dullest shawl I possessed; a few small items that Davenport had allowed me – after much arguing – to bring. A hair brush, two ribbons, and a large slice of apple pie that Sarah, our cook, had given to me. I contemplated the parcel, pressed close against the most dismal gown that I'd ever worn.

After Ma had been persuaded to let me leave for a couple of days – Davenport had made use of Mr Fielding's name more than once – the whole house had taken a perverse delight in dressing me like a drab. Emily, older than the rest of us, hard-faced and spiteful as a rule, had been so enthusiastic about this that she had exchanged one of her own gowns with a street walker to 'help' me. It fitted badly and had been worn, in my most conservative estimate, by ten others before me. I could smell their lives in the fabric. The shade of this gown lay somewhere between brown and grey – the colour of Thames mud. Meg, the girl who was employed as our maidservant, but who dispensed her fashion advice to us for free, brushed my hair into dullness. The powdered curls had disappeared, and I was left with limp red strands tied in a dirty length of string that Meg had the audacity to describe as a ribbon. I wore no jewels and no rouge, obviously. Polly, usually the kindest of the girls at Berwick Street, had laughed so hard at the sight of me that tears had run down her face. When at last she caught her breath, she slipped me a penny for luck. It was the only coin I carried – and I'd hidden that from Davenport.

Davenport had suggested that I changed my name. I was playing a part, after all. This was less of an injury: I had abandoned my family name of Vessey when I came to London, taking my mother's name of Hardwicke instead; changing it again caused no hardship and it was wise, given that my name had lately become so well-known. We decided on 'Lizzie Blunt' – an amusing choice for a girl with a needle. Meg had found a small needle box for me, reasonably equipped, that gave me the tools for my supposed trade. My real tools, as Davenport had said, were my eyes and ears.

'This gown is itchy,' I said to Davenport as we waited for someone to let us in. 'And it smells.'

He banged on the door again, louder than before, and gave me a withering look.

'Lizzie Blunt, I'm afraid you'll need to learn to keep your complaints to yourself.'

I growled at him, already beginning to regret the adventure.

'No one will look twice at me dressed like this.'

'That is the idea, remember?'

A heavy bolt was drawn back and then the door swung open. A man stood looking us up and down with a surly expression. He was stocky, broad-shouldered, and covered in dust. Under the dust, he was swarthy; the sort of cull who needed his barber almost hourly.

'I'm here to meet Mr Garrick,' said Davenport, already playing his part by ignoring me. 'I've come from Bow Street.'

The man was carrying a lamp, even though it was broad daylight.

'Aye, he said someone was coming.' The gruff voice matched his dusty appearance. 'Who's this?' He nodded to me.

'New seamstress, I believe,' said Davenport.

The man wasn't interested in me. He shrugged and gestured that we should follow. We made our way into a dark passage where the need for a lamp became apparent. There were no windows here and it was poorly lit. We were, I imagined, somewhere behind the stage.

After a while, we emerged from the dingy corridor into a room. It was generously proportioned, comfortable and bright, lit with a few sconces, but enhanced by the sunlight that was shining through the windows. Paintings of theatrical scenes hung on the pale green walls and dotted around the room were small plinths carrying marble busts of eminent men. This was the green room, where actors mingled with favoured members of the audience, even as they waited to appear on the stage. It was a mess. I could see remnants of food and drink, empty bottles, glasses and discarded pipes strewn over tables. There were sundry items of clothing left over couches and on the floor. More than one chair had been knocked over. There was a faint smell of vomit in the air, mixed with stale tobacco. It was like Berwick Street after a lively party.

'I'll take you to Mr Garrick. His office is upstairs.'

I looked at the man, but he was speaking to Davenport, not me.

'What should I do, sir?'

He stared at me, as though the answer was obvious. 'Put your goods down, girl, and start tidying up,' he said, waving a hand at the chaos in the room. 'Gather up the clothes and see what needs mending. I'll send someone over to you shortly.'

I nodded and looked for a clear surface where I could lay my possessions. There being none, I shoved the bundle under a chair and wondered where to begin the task.

The man was already disappearing through a door. Davenport, with a measure of sympathy in his expression, mouthed 'good luck' before turning to follow. I pulled a face and mouthed something obscene to the back of his coat.

I stood and surveyed the devastation for a minute, assessing the worst of it, and then did as the dark-eyed man had ordered and picked my way around the room collecting up stray hats, handkerchiefs, shawls and gloves. I found seven discarded stockings – not an obvious pair among them.

I was standing with a pile of clothing in my arms when a solid and capable-looking woman entered the room and asked who I was.

'Lizzie Blunt,' I said, with a little bob. 'New help for the seamstress.' I made my voice sound like the servants at home; trying to recall the girl who used to light the fires, and her slightly breathy country tone.

She stood, arms folded, head on one side, regarding me. 'Well at least you look like help. The last girl was useless. I'm Molly Bray. Head seamstress,' she added, because I needed to know my place.

I ducked my head again, acknowledging my subservience in all matters needle-related.

She was twenty-four or twenty-five; taller than me, and a great deal stouter. She had wide shoulders and, with her sleeves rolled up, I could see strong forearms. I could imagine her wrestling both of my brothers at the same time – and taking the honours. She was not what a seamstress should be; not neat and delicate, but sturdy and robust with a frizz of pale hair under her cap. Her face, doughy and round, was friendly enough.

'Is it always like this, miss?' I twitched the bundle of fabric in my arms and glanced at a pile of broken glass.

'This?' The laugh was sharp, but hearty. 'This is nothing, Lizzie Blunt. We closed early the day before yesterday – you might have heard – and we didn't open yesterday at all. This is nothing compared with what it's like normally. The mice have had most of the food I see. That's a shame.'

She sighed and collected a bonnet, brushing dirt from the brim and rubbing the ribbon with her sleeve.

'Has anyone shown you around yet?' she perched the hat on her own head and picked up a coat that lay on the floor.

I shook my head. 'Just arrived, miss. A man covered in dust told me to clear up. He took a gentleman to see Mr Garrick.'

'That'll be Joe. Mr Sugden, I mean. Stage hand. Second only to the stage manager.'

'And the stage manager is Mr Garrick?' I said, keen to demonstrate my ignorance, being a spy.

She laughed again, a playful chuckle this time. 'You've got a lot to learn. Mr Garrick's the theatre manager, lead actor, director and writer of plays and the reason this theatre is still standing. Mr Garrick's whole life is about being seen – on the stage, in clubs, on the streets, talking with polite company. The stage manager, Mr Dinsdale, and his assistant, Mr Sugden, on the other hand, spend all their time trying not to be seen. Joe's work is behind the scenery, making sure that everything runs smoothly for

Mr Garrick and his cast whenever they decide to step out on the boards.'

'He looked to me as though he'd been under the scenery, not behind it,' I said.

'That'll be Joe. He'll have been crawling about in the store, finding the set of backdrops for next week's play.'

'Oh.'

She smiled again, which I took to be a good sign, given that she was going to be giving me my duties. 'Come on, I'll show you where we live.'

Chapter Six

We carried the clothes back down the passageway I'd come along with Davenport, and then turned into another. This one was also badly lit by a meagre number of tallow candles.

I could hardly see Molly ahead of me when, suddenly, there she was, leaning out of a doorway with light streaming behind her.

'This is us,' she said, holding open the door at the very end of the passage as I struggled through with my load. 'This is the costume room, where we sit and mend for most of the day.'

We were standing in a room lit, astonishingly, by daylight. I could not immediately work out where I was and Molly, sensing my confusion, pointed out what I had failed to notice: there were windows at the top of the walls on two sides of the room. Molly's working space was in the corner of the building, but because of the uneven nature of the theatre layout it sat a little below the level of the street. I stood and watched legs and feet walk past the window at the same height as my head. I was separated from the street, from the life and daylight of Covent Garden only by thin glass and lead bars.

Molly laughed. 'You get used to it eventually,' she said.

'I'm not sure, miss. It's strange having people's shoes walking past the top of my head.'

But I could see why we were in this room. It was hidden from the prying eyes of the public when players came to try on costumes, but, at the same time, the light was very good. At this time of year we could work for most of the day.

There was a large table in the brightest part of the room, on which lay needle boxes, scissors, a jug, a plate of bread and four drinking pots stacked up together. There were clothes everywhere. Piles of garments lay folded on the floor, and on the corner of the table. The walls were lined with cupboards, wardrobes, and trunks, all filled with cloaks, gowns, coats, shoes and shawls. There were props too: cushions, curtains, feathers, books and swords. This room contained the costumes needed by the company, and probably more besides.

Molly took the clothes from me and shook them out, tutting as she tried and failed to pair the stockings. I sat cross-legged on a cushion.

'How can they lose them so easily, I wonder?' I asked as I took out a darning needle from the box in my pocket and began, as best I could, to stitch the holes. It was pretended innocence. I knew exactly the sort of situations in which stockings came loose.

Molly rolled her eyes. 'You're in for a shock, Lizzie, if you think theatre folk just enjoy drinking wine and chattering with one another after a performance. Only last week I saw—'

Quite what she saw I never discovered, as there was a sharp rap on the door. It opened, even before Molly responded. The man with the scowl and the dark stubble stood in the doorway.

'You found her then,' he said, nodding over at me. I jumped up from the cushion.

Molly put an arm around my shoulder.

'Seems I have a new assistant, Joe. This is Lizzie Blunt. Lizzie, this is Mr Joseph Sugden.'

I gave him a small curtsey, lowering my gaze meekly as I did so because I was a servant here, and not a brazen harlot.

'Mr Sugden.'

He eyed the grubby gown that was too large for me, the straggly red curls and the needle and thread in my hand. He had no idea who I had been only hours ago. If nothing else, his disinterest told me that my disguise was good. I wasn't used to disinterest. It was an odd experience, not to be desired.

'I've noted that you began to clear the green room, as asked, Lizzie,' Sugden said, unsmiling.

'Yes, Mr Sugden.'

'It's not clean, though. You'll need to go and finish what you started.'

'She's with me, Joe. You leave her be,' Molly said. 'Send Mary up, as normal. We've brought the clothes away to mend. That's our job.'

The look on Sugden's face told me that he was unhappy at being contradicted.

'Mary's not in. Her mother's having another baby and she's been called away to help. Lizzie will go up and do it. You can help her.'

'There's plenty of time to clean,' Molly said, her voice soft and soothing. 'They won't be in for hours yet. You know what they're like.' She pulled a chair for him at the table and poured a pot of ale.

'Garrick's in – and you know what *he's* like,' said Sugden, grumbling into the cup that she handed to him.

I supposed that 'they' were the players.

'When do the actresses come in, miss?' I asked, keen to avoid the chores and needing to discover more about the people around Garrick. 'I'm longing to see them, Mrs Cibber and Mrs Hunter especially.' I could play the excitable admirer easily enough. These two, who worked behind the stage, might supply some useful information about those who walked upon it.

Molly rubbed a hand across Sugden's shoulders, encouraging him to sit at the table with her. 'They're supposed to be in by two o'clock when it's an ordinary day,' Sugden said, as he acquiesced and sat down. 'They'll rehearse the evening's performance for an hour or two and then get themselves ready to greet their guests before the play starts.'

'They perform with only two hours of rehearsing?' I asked, easing myself back to the floor and picking up my needle. I was genuinely impressed. I had, after all, seen a performance the other night.

'Only if it's a play they've been doing a while,' said Molly. 'If it's new, or if there's a new player stepping in, then they should be here at eleven.'

'They never are,' said Sugden, frowning. 'Garrick shouts and stamps, but they drift in when they fancy.' He was not impressed by such casual behaviour, I could tell.

'There's stage hands know the lines better than some of them,' said Molly with a shrug. She picked up a soft cap from the floor and turned it in her hands, examining it for tears. 'I don't know why Garrick doesn't put us on the stage instead.'

'You'd be a wonderful Cordelia, Moll,' said Sugden, with a sudden look of genuine affection. 'Ophelia too. You should perform for him one day – show him what you can do.'

36

Molly blushed as she snorted.

'You talk such shit, Joe Sugden,' she said. 'I've got shoulders like a man's and arms like a bear.' She started to laugh. 'And that's before you get to my face...'

'It's better than mine,' he said. 'My face is just right for behind the scenery.'

Molly threw the cap at him, still giggling.

I asked again about the players, Davenport's instructions in mind. Sugden was not slow in his criticisms.

'You'll find out soon enough what they're like,' he said. 'The women are thought to be attractive, but it's a miracle what the paint can do to make plain girls look appealing. The men all hate each other. They're all jostling for position with Garrick.'

'That's true of the women as well, Joe,' said Molly. 'You don't see as much of them as I do.'

'I see plenty of them in the green room,' he said, rolling his eyes. 'You can hardly move in there without seeing them displaying themselves like whores on the streets.' He looked at me. 'I hope you're not easily shocked, Lizzie Blunt.'

'Shocked?'

'Poor girl, she's all anxious now Joe,' said Molly. 'She's only a little thing.'

If only she knew.

Sugden gave me a hard look, and for a moment I was worried that he had read my thoughts.

'I wonder now,' he said, setting his pot down on the floor and wiping his mouth with the palm of his hand. 'Where did you blow in from, did you say?'

I hadn't said. Davenport and I had decided on a story to explain my presence, though. It seemed an ideal opportunity to rehearse it. It was my turn to play the actress.

'I'm not from London,' I said. 'You can probably tell that, sir, but my mother was a mantua-maker, so I've been holding a needle for as long as I can remember. She's dead now; my pa too. I thought I'd come to London because there are more people needing clothes made and mended down here.'

'Why did you come to a theatre? There's plenty of women making gowns in London,' he asked. I took a deep breath, as if I was about to tell them something that troubled me, something I was ashamed of. I stared at the hands in my lap as I spoke.

'I got into trouble, see?'

'Oh aye, here it comes. What sort of trouble?'

I spoke quietly, keeping my head down. 'I was hungry, and I had nowhere to live. None of the mantua-makers wanted me, a girl from the country with no references. I...' I decided that adding a sob might sound too contrived, so merely hesitated. 'I took some bread, and a little cake, without paying for them. Only because I was hungry. I wasn't brought up to steal.'

They waited. I paused again, remembering my lines perfectly.

'I'd already eaten the cake when I got caught. The baker took me to the magistrate. I was so afraid of him I thought I would faint. He can't see – he's blind, you know – but he listened to my story and he took pity on me. Then he said that he had heard Mr Garrick wanted an extra needlewoman in his theatre. He even paid the baker for what I'd taken. I could hardly believe it, and I've barely stopped thanking God for my good luck since yesterday.'

Joe Sugden stiffened. 'You arrived with the magistrate's man earlier.' He said this as a statement. 'He didn't look too pleased about it.'

'He wasn't, sir. He said he had business with Mr Garrick, he didn't have time to bother with the likes of me.'

Sugden, who had encountered Davenport at his most high-handed and dismissive, was satisfied with my story. Perhaps I was a decent actress after all.

Even so, he stared down at me with a look that was not at all friendly.

'I'll be watching you, girl. I don't like thieves, and if anything goes missing, it'll be you I come to first.'

I swallowed hard, feeling a little less confident.

'There's enough going on in this place at the moment without us harbouring someone who takes things that don't belong to her. You'll do as you're told, ask permission to leave the theatre, and go where you're bidden, you hear me?'

Davenport had intimated that there had been thefts from the theatre as well as damage.

'I said, do you hear me?'

'Yes sir.'

Molly leaned across the table and cut me a slice of bread, giving Sugden a frown. 'Here you go, Lizzie. You'll be happy here with us. The wages are rubbish, but you won't go hungry.'

Chapter Seven

Sugden gave a derisive laugh. 'Wages? What wages would those be, Molly Bray? I haven't been paid for weeks.'

'We don't get paid?' I asked.

'We do get paid,' said Molly, giving Sugden another stern look. 'It's just that Mr Garrick is not so good at paying us regularly.'

'Or fairly,' muttered Sugden.

'How do you survive?' I asked. 'How do I survive?'

Molly shrugged. 'We manage. Some weeks are harder than others. It's easier for us, in the dressing rooms, we get the cast-offs from the actresses. Some of them will drop you a coin if you treat them right, or they'll let you have an old ribbon. I got a hat once that was nearly new. It's harder for Joe and the stage hands – they've no one to look out for them.'

'The players get paid?' I said.

'Depends,' said Sugden. 'The likes of Mrs Cibber can demand whatever wages she chooses. Garrick has to pay her, or she kicks up the most enormous fuss. The spare horses – that's the lot that makes up the crowds or takes the smaller speaking parts – they make extra in the best way they can. So the stage hands and the actors screw over the rich gentlemen at the gaming tables and the women screw them in the usual way.'

It was why theatres were as notorious as brothels. In the audience, women like me laid plans with gentlemen who would take us home in a carriage and then spend the night. Backstage, or out in the alleyways near the theatre, the lower orders of players were making their own arrangements. Garrick, I knew, was trying to raise the reputation of theatres, hoping to present them as temples to high art; he had a long way to go to achieve his aim. I wondered whether Molly made ends meet like that or whether she really did survive on hand-me-downs from Mrs Cibber and stale bread from the green room.

The door was flung open. A man entered, older than Joseph Sugden, greying at the temples, but similarly covered in dust. He was tall and thick-set, making him seem almost as square as he was high. He was a man used to lifting heavy objects, shifting furniture and stage equipment. A deep line had formed between his eyebrows, the result of years spent frowning with physical effort. His nose looked as though it had been broken long ago. The whole effect made his face look like a squashed pie. He spoke in a curt and self-important tone; like a man who had only recently been put in charge, keen to impose his authority over the underlings.

'I thought you might be down here,' he said to Sugden. 'I need a hand shifting the flats. Tom's still out, on account of his leg, and the others are all down in the hell.'

'My apologies, Mr Dinsdale,' said Sugden, not moving, and not looking especially apologetic, 'I wanted to make sure that the new girl had found her way to the dressing rooms.'

Mr Dinsdale turned the frown towards me. I scrambled up from the cushion and gave a polite curtsey. This was the stage manager – second only to Mr Garrick – after all.

'Lizzie Blunt, sir. New seamstress.'

I was unimportant, compared with the scenery that needed to be moved. Everything in his face told me that. He barely even glanced at me.

'Molly Bray, the stage area needs to be tidied, as does the green room. I'm also down a maid, so you'll have to do it. You can take...' he paused, having forgotten who I was already '... this girl with you. Save your mending until the afternoon.'

'The light is better now—' Molly began, but Mr Dinsdale shook his head.

'No. The light will be fine when you've cleared the stage and green room. You'll go now.'

He favoured us with a final scowl before striding from the room. Sugden rolled his eyes and pushed himself up from his seat to follow.

'Better get moving, Moll. He's not in a good mood at the moment.'

'Is he ever?'

'Watch your step with Mr Dinsdale, girly,' this was addressed to me as he sloped through the door. 'If you get the wrong side of him, you'll be out on your ear.'

Molly licked her fingers and dabbed up the last crumbs of bread from the plate, as if to make a point of dawdling. 'Don't worry, Lizzie,' she said as she tucked her arm through mine and pulled me towards the dismal corridor and the equally dismal task ahead, 'Dinsdale won't bother us, he's too busy running his little kingdom upstairs to make our lives difficult. Come to think of it, no one takes much notice of the likes of us at all, unless a coat sleeve comes loose.'

I was happy to hear that. Davenport had told me to remain out of sight as best I could, to be quiet and unnoticed, the better to observe what was going on. I thought that I was ready for the task.

But what, I wondered with a slight shiver, was 'the hell'?

Chapter Eight

Molly and I worked solidly for over an hour in the green room, clearing the floor of food, discarded pipes and spills, wine bottles and glasses. We wiped tables, reset chairs to their upright positions and put fresh wax candles in the wall sconces. There was vomit in the fireplace. It lay crusted on the hearth, dry but by now only mildly pungent. Molly dealt with it, while I scrubbed the puddle of piss that was next to the hearth – still sticky when I trod in it – where someone had aimed poorly and missed his target.

I was becoming too used to the ways of London's gentlemen to be bothered by their habits. No one was ever sick in Mrs Farley's fireplaces, of course – not those who wanted to leave the house with their limbs intact, anyway – but I'd spent enough time in taverns to know what even the most charming of men will do when they've had too much to drink.

I found my small bundle under the chair and took it back to the mending room; by now familiar with the direction. I laid out my needle box and hairbrush, hid the ribbons in my pocket and put the apple pie, wrapped neatly in its cloth, on the table with the ale, deciding to share it with Molly later.

When I returned to the green room, it had transformed again.

It was full of people. Now, at last, I could begin my real work. I hid in the corner by the door and watched them. After a while, I recognised one of the women: a lean, pointy-faced person with a black spot pressed high on her cheek. She had been in the performance of *King Lear*, I was sure. I recognised the nose. This would be one of the 'spare horses', as Sugden had called them: lesser players who made up the company, or who drifted in and out of it as they built their career by seeking out wealthy patrons. Here they were, off stage and preparing for the evening, greeting one another loudly, brightly painted women and men, not all completely dressed, who seemed excessively diverted by one another's company. I knew well what they were beneath the paint. I had been brought up to regard such people as loose in morals, and nothing I had seen in London had given me cause to doubt their tawdry reputation. They were all whores, pimps or gamblers, who were gifted in the art of reciting lines, and who looked tolerably attractive in dim lighting. They were as notorious for their immorality as they were for their lust for life. Any one of them could be thieving from Garrick.

The sharp-featured one was playing cards with another woman, while a third was pouring wine and stealing a cheeky glance at her friend's hand. Cheats and liars, all of them, I thought – from my lofty moral position.

A small crowd had gathered around a man who was reading something from a newspaper, but they were too far away, and the room was too noisy for me to hear what it was. From time to time they erupted with raucous laughter. Mr Dinsdale and another man were tucked in a corner, deep in conversation over pots of beer. Dinsdale was sitting forward and scowling while his companion talked, making small stabbing motions with his forefinger, as if pressing his point.

Across the room, two men were playing with pistols, examining the silverwork on the handles, turning them this way and that, cocking and uncocking them and pretending to aim them at the fireplace that we had recently cleaned and lit, surveying themselves in the vast gold-edged mirror that hung above it as they did so. Fresh baskets of food and jugs of wine and beer had been brought in and laid along a wide table at the edge of the room. Everyone helped themselves and already it was a merry company.

Molly was sitting with Joe Sugden and another man, who looked familiar. Her hands were moving quickly, rolling about in the air, but it was a moment before I realised that she was juggling. She was taking slices of apple from a small monkey and throwing them up, several pieces at a time, before pausing to feed them back to him as she drank from a glass of wine. Their companion was the monkey man who had offered such a dismal interval performance two nights ago. His forehead was large and bald, but his cheeks were thin, making him look like his pet. The small amount of hair that he had fell in long grey strands to his shoulders.

I felt a hand on the small of my back, then an arm snaked around my waist, as a ginger-haired man tugged me into his body. I was treated to an ugly leer, and the stink of his beery breath.

'Not seen you here before,' he slurred into my face. 'You're a pretty little bird; want to come and get to know me?'

I gave him the heartiest shove that I could and wrenched myself free, nearly falling over in the process, telling him to leave me alone. He staggered back and laughed, as if I'd paid him a compliment. If he'd groped me like that on the street, I'd have told him to go and screw his sister. But I wasn't on the street with an armoury of insults, curses and comebacks to suit every occasion. Men like him were going to be an occupational hazard for poor Lizzie Blunt. I sighed at this dispiriting thought and made my way to the safety of Molly's table.

The monkey jumped on his owner's head, apple piece in one paw, and sat there, chewing. It was an ugly thing.

'How did you learn to juggle like that?' I asked Molly as I sat next to her. 'You're very good at it.'

She grinned at me and winked at the monkey man. 'I've had years of practice, haven't I, Ketch?'

I picked up a glass and began to help myself to the jug of wine on the table. A frown crossed Sugden's brow, and in a heartbeat, I knew that I'd done something wrong.

'M – may I? Am I able to have some wine, Mr Sugden?' I stammered out the words, replacing the jug on the table. I had been too free in assuming that what was on the table was as much for me as for the others. It would have been, at home. I was not at home, though, and Lizzie Blunt shouldn't take such liberties.

'Or, may I pour you some more, sir?' I asked, lifting the jug to his own glass, which was nearly empty.

He held out his glass, not saying a word, but watching me, eyes narrowed. I refreshed the monkey-man's glass as well, while the monkey danced about on his head.

'What a funny little creature, Mr Ketch,' I said, trying to shift my unease with mindless chatter. 'Wherever did you find him?'

'Southwark,' he said.

I was disappointed. I had imagined somewhere a little more exotic.

'At the fair,' he said in a ponderous voice, cupping the glass of wine as the monkey curled its tail over his brow. 'And it's Ketch. Everyone just calls me Ketch.' He reached out and shook my hand.

'It was love at first sight for your friend, I think,' I said, sharing my own name and nodding at the monkey.

Ketch didn't smile. The monkey had not been a clever investment – if the performance on stage had been anything to go by.

Neither of the men wanted to talk. I turned back to Molly.

'Do you know the fair, miss?' I asked. 'Have you ever been?'

'Been?' Her eyes twinkled. 'I grew up with the fairs. Southwark was one of the best.' She laid a hand over Sugden's arm, but as she spoke, she was looking at Ketch.

'My family were travelling people. My father and mother both danced on the high ropes. My brother used to do the juggling. I wasn't so good, despite what you think of the tricks with apple slices. I wanted to walk the ropes too, I was better at that, but...' her voice dwindled a little and she turned her eyes to me '...but my father died, and then my brother and mother died, and I decided to come to London. A bit like you, really.'

I was silent. My real story was quite different from hers. My mother was, indeed, long dead, but that was the only similarity. My father had thrown me out of his house for behaving like a strumpet and told me never to return.

I didn't need to respond; the brightest of London's stars were entering the green room and all of us, including the unsmiling men at our table, turned to gawp.

Chapter Nine

Even when surrounded by such lively and attractive people, David Garrick commanded the attention of every person in the room. He was not especially tall, nor handsome. His features were large, too big for his face, but – as I knew from watching him on stage – so very expressive. His velvet coat was a rich shade of blue, the colour of sapphires, and his waistcoat was heavily trimmed with gold, giving him a flamboyant and glittering air, and yet he moved with small steps and quiet gestures, as though containing his energy for the evening's performance. He did not need to be expansive here; everyone who greeted him fawned, fluttered and twittered in front of the great man, so that the drama seemed to happen around him. And yet, his dark eyes flickered with light as he listened, or spoke.

A glass of wine was brought to him. He took a sip and moved towards the men who had been playing with the pistols. They were now nursing pots of beer, but Garrick was keen to examine the weapons. They were for the stage, I saw. Handing his wine to a man at his side, he aimed one at the large mirror and pretended to fire it, his arm flicking back at the imagined recoil. A dark-haired woman in a vibrant yellow gown gave a small scream and a mock swoon as he did so, causing the group to laugh. Garrick put the pistol down and began to fan the woman with his hand, as if rousing her from the faint, until she, like the others, gave way to laughter. He kissed her full on the lips before reclaiming his wine and moving away.

'Kitty Suckley,' said Molly in my ear. 'She's playing Goneril in *Lear* from tonight. Fanny Barton's just married and gone away with her new husband. Kitty's been called up from the spare-horses. God knows, but she's nothing more than a whore.'

I turned and raised my eyebrows. 'Really?' If she truly were, I had never met her or heard of her. She was the sort of woman I would have remembered: one who would always be the centre of attention because that is where she would, rowdily, place herself. Fanny Barton, I thought, had made a splendid Goneril.

'Look at her,' Molly hissed. 'Prancing and preening in the brightest gown she could find. Always showing off in front of Mr Garrick. It's no secret that she'd love to be the toast of Drury Lane.'

That alone didn't make her a whore. 'Can she act? She does a good swoon, I think.'

'She speaks prettily enough,' Sugden said, overhearing our conversation. 'She's playing some of the better parts now, especially in the after-pieces.'

Molly gave a small grunt. 'Course she is. Still, the longer she's fucking every friend of Garrick's, the sooner she'll be lying back and swooning as Ophelia.'

I failed to swallow a giggle.

'It's how most of them get the better parts,' said Molly. 'Some of them are good, really good, but it always helps to have a generous patron. Kitty Suckley, on the on the other hand, is no better an actress than Ketch's monkey, so she relies on her other talents.'

'Why does she want to be an actress, then, if she's not very good at it?' She wasn't a beauty, but she was pretty enough to make a decent income as a harlot in a fancy bawdy house, certainly. I thought of Lucy, who flattered and simpered better than any of us at Berwick Street and who wore the finest silks as a result.

Molly shrugged. 'She wants a husband. Or a man to keep her as his mistress, at least. A gentleman, a nobleman even, who might fall in love and set her up for life. It happens here.'

Sugden leaned over, his face near to Molly's. 'And I gather there's a grand person in the audience tonight, although she'll be fighting Mrs Hunter for this one.'

Molly pushed him away, but she was as keen for the gossip as I was.

'What have you heard, Joe?'

Ketch's monkey jumped onto the table and began scratching itself in a lewd manner.

'There was some talk among the spares that Mrs Hunter's particular patron, Mr Astley, is bringing an old friend with him tonight. This one's an earl.'

I had taken a duke to bed once but managed to look impressed with this news.

'You could put good money on Hunter pushing his wife in an earl's direction,' Ketch said, pulling the monkey's tail.

Molly said, for my benefit, 'Mr Hunter is keen that his wife engages all the right people. She's seeing Mr Astley at the moment, but if Astley's friend is an earl, then Hunter will steer little Lucy under his nose.'

I sat back to take in what Molly was telling me. Lucy Hunter, young, pretty and almost a decent speaker of verse, was being pimped by her own husband, even as she was trying to bring the lines of Shakespeare to life. I was as impressed by her versatility as I was appalled by her circumstances.

'Poor old Kitty,' Molly laughed. 'For all the flirting, she won't hold a candle to Lucy Hunter.'

'Poor old you, then,' said Sugden with a grimace. 'It'll be like a battleground in the dressing rooms and you and Lizzie will be caught in the crossfire. You remember what it was like when Kitty told everyone she'd set her sights on taking Astley from her?'

Molly groaned. 'Lizzie, it's going to be hell for us, sweetheart. The vicious cats will turn on us when they've scratched each other's eyes out. Nothing we do will be good enough. I've still got the bruises from their last spat.'

'I'll do my best not to irritate either of them, miss,' I said.

'Who's the earl, Joe? Did you hear?' Molly asked.

'Hawkridge, Hornridge, something like it,' said Sugden, the precise details of this juicy gossip escaping him.

'Hawbridge?' said Molly.

'That's it. Hawbridge. How do you know the name?'

'Oh, I know all the quality,' Molly said, smiling brightly. 'I've been about, remember?'

The name was familiar to me too, but I couldn't recall how.

Ketch scooped up his monkey and began to tickle its ears – which the monkey didn't like. It gave a funny little squeal and climbed back onto Ketch's head.

'Ho, here comes trouble,' said Sugden, nodding towards the door. 'It's the Hunters.'

I recognised Mrs Hunter immediately from her performance the other night. But, whereas on stage she had seemed fragile and even a little lost, here she was at ease, confidently bestowing her hand to all who wished to kiss it. She was small and neatly made, wearing a gown of lavender silk that was cut to perfection, displaying her shape. Her face was delicately composed and a gentle pout played across her lips. Her fair hair had been persuaded into a cascade of curls. Such effortless beauty must have taken her hours to achieve. Her blue eyes, though, were hard.

The man who had her arm was, I took it, her husband. He was older than she was by some years, but he seemed more so because he walked with a stick. He was a large man, dressed in a purple coat embroidered with so much gold that it spoke of money rather than taste. The sizeable ruby on his right hand told the same story. It was brash, ostentatious. He leaned heavily upon the stick, his face set in a frown, as though some part of his body was causing him pain. His skin bore the unmistakeable colour of a man who drank too much. He scanned the room, looking for someone. He gripped the top of his stick and scowled when he caught sight of Garrick.

'The poor thing.' The words left my mouth in a whisper. I meant Lucy Hunter. I could see what sort of a life she was leading with a man like that as her husband.

Molly snorted. 'She's as bad as he is. Just you wait and see. They deserve one another.'

The Hunters had separated. Mr Hunter was shuffling towards Garrick, collecting a glass of wine and knocking it back as he went. When Garrick hailed him, he responded with a beaming smile and open arms. Mrs Hunter made her way to a gathering of players, who parted gracefully to admit her. She greeted them as dear friends, and they returned with kisses and comments on her gown and necklace.

'That's Nan Collyer,' said Molly, pointing out another woman in the group. 'She's not so bad as the others. Quiet off stage, noisy on it. She's playing Regan, the other sister in *Lear*.'

She was older than Mrs Hunter and Kitty Suckley. She was shorter than them too. A little stout around the middle and with hair beginning to grey, I expected that she was nearing the end of her career in the greater roles. I recalled her performance. What she lacked in height, she had made up for in volume, her booming voice carrying well into the auditorium.

'What happened to Mr Hunter?' I asked Molly. 'Why is he carrying a stick?'

'Damaged his leg in a fight,' she said, pouring herself another glass of wine. 'It ended his acting career.'

'A fight?'

Sugden and Ketch took up the story from Molly. Once regarded as a talented actor from somewhere in the north, Hunter had come to London to seek his fortune and would have made it, had it not been for his temper. He had been part of John Rich's company at the theatre in Covent Garden, but had fought with another player. The men had been spoiling for a while, but a lost wig proved so incendiary that the pair tore into each other.

'Hunter plunged a sword into the other man's shoulder and very nearly killed him,' said Ketch. 'He himself was left with a broken hip that was poorly set and he was forced to walk with a stick.'

Rich had thrown the two of them out of his company. No one knew what had become of the other man.

Hunter was a quick-tempered man contained in a weakened frame. He was conversing amiably enough with Garrick, but it would not take much to turn him violent even now, I thought, if something as frivolous as a lost wig had caused him to attack a man. I could imagine him breaking up a chair with that stick or slashing at a costume, if his anger got the better of him. I watched him with interest.

'Where does his wife come into this?' I asked.

'She met him in the provinces, when he was the rising star and she was an unremarkable strolling actress. She hitched herself to him in a bid for associated fame and fortune and then found herself burdened with the responsibility of bringing in the money,' said Sugden.

'Hunter coached her in stagecraft until she was tolerable,' said Molly, 'and then guided her towards the wealthiest audience members, where she could exercise her real talent. He's schooled her in that, too. She loves the jewels even more than the applause.'

The women of Mrs Hunter's group laughed along readily enough at her witticisms, but their faces displayed little natural jollity. The men were more interested. I didn't need to hear the conversation to know that she was flirting. She kept tilting her head and laughing, touching the arm of whichever man had made a comment.

Her gaze lifted briefly from the small crowd of admirers and she caught sight of our table. Frowning a little, she made her excuses to them and swept her skirts over to us. Now that I was nearer to it, I rather admired the lavender silk covered with tiny cream and blue flowers. No one would have guessed, from the mud-coloured sack that I was wearing, but I would have looked ravishing in lavender silk.

'Molly Bray, why haven't you mended my gloves?' The voice snapped me out of my reverie.

'Sorry, Mrs Hunter, we've been clearing the green room for most of the day. Things were in a state after...'

'We?' Mrs Hunter's mouth pinched into a rosebud tighter than any of those on her lavender silk. She cast a swift glance in my direction and then swung back to Molly. 'If you had assistance with the cleaning, I fail to see why my gloves have been neglected. I expressly wanted them for tonight.' She picked up Molly's glass and poured the dregs of wine on the floor. 'All I can see is a girl idling about and drinking the day away with a grubby little trull.'

She thought me the lowest of the low, and she didn't even have the courtesy to make my acquaintance. What a charming woman.

'See to my gloves without delay, or I'll see you lose your place here.' She twirled away to greet another actress, but not before pinching the top of Molly's ear.

'Can she really have you put out for the sake of a glove?' I asked in a low voice.

Molly was unmoved by the insult she had received, although the tip of her ear was glowing red. 'Well, she's thick with Garrick, and her current lover would probably make it his business to throw me out if she wished it. So yes, she can. Still,' she sniffed, drawing herself up, 'she knows there's no one else who can dress her like I can.' She leaned across the table, picked up my glass, helped herself to the last mouthful of wine, and wiped her mouth with a smile. 'She's terrified, you know. Of being on stage. It's why she forgets her lines. I am the one who calms her down as I'm fastening her costume. She needs to be on the stage in order to attract the lovers, after all.' She shrugged her shoulders. 'So, she's probably conning, the stupid slut.'

Lucy Hunter, then, was vain, grasping, and rude to the one person who helped her walk onto the stage. And I would never forgive the woman for calling me grubby.

Chapter Ten

Molly sloped off to find and repair the gloves, leaving me alone with Sugden and Ketch. I stayed still, not wanting to leave the green room while it was filling with such interesting people. Even as I was trying to assess which of them might be scheming against Garrick, I might enjoy the show. At present, they all seemed to be trying to ingratiate themselves.

'Mr Garrick is like a king in his court,' I said to Ketch. 'It's wonderful to see how everyone flocks around him.'

'They're all hoping that some of his magic rubs off on them,' he said, like me, transfixed by it all.

'The actors are all hoping for another role,' said Sugden, who had the benefit of greater experience. 'The spares and the stage hands are hoping to be paid. Garrick is doing his best to reassure them all, with his most sincere looks and his handshakes.'

'But he is magnificent, sir, you must agree,' I said. 'He's so graceful as he walks.'

Sugden gave a small grunt. 'That's not grace, girly. He minces about in that dainty fashion, in case, by some lapse of concentration, he lets out a fart by accident. He's that tight, he wouldn't even grant his own wind willingly.'

Ketch sniggered, cracking a whisper of a smile at last.

'That's what we all say, when he's forgotten to pay us again,' Sugden said, as he took a mouthful of wine. 'Ah hell. Looks like I'm needed.'

Mr Dinsdale, watch clasped in a meaty hand, was looking over and Sugden, recognising that he was being summoned, put his drink down. 'Gather up some of the glasses for washing,' he said this to me, and not to Ketch. 'There are trays somewhere.' He waved a hand towards the large trestle bench at the side of the room. I knew the trays were there – I had tided them earlier. 'They go to the Shakespeare tavern – through the door over there.' He jerked his head to a side door – a fourth entrance to the theatre that I had not noticed. A servant's door.

'Yes, Mr Sugden.'

He went off in the direction of the stage. A group of actors was laughing at a joke – one man so heartily that tears were streaming down his face. He reached into his pocket and pulled out a handkerchief, scattering a couple of coins from the pocket as he did so. He didn't notice them falling because he was now wiping his face and being slapped on the back by his friends. As Sugden neared the door, he stooped down and picked up the coins. He slipped them into his pocket, unseen by the men, and carried on his way, his pace quickening a little.

I might have been irritated at being forced to clear tables like a tavern wench, but this was the perfect opportunity to pay closer attention to some of the conversations. Now I had the chance to do Davenport's work, as well as Sugden's. No one paid me heed, except to put a glass down on my tray, or to ask for fresh wine or beer and could I possibly bring some bread, or a plate of those little sweetmeats?

I threaded my way about the clusters of painted men and women until I reached the place in the corner where Dinsdale had been. His seat had been taken by a fair-headed young man with a bandaged leg. I took this to be Tom, whose fall from the ladder had ended the performance of *King Lear*. He was cupping a glass to his lips and watching the green room from his seat. He shifted slightly, and I saw him wince. The way in which he threw back the liquid suggested he was trying to dull the pain. I nodded to his leg.

'What you do to it?'

He squinted at me, a newcomer with a tray full of empty pots. I gave him a wide-eyed look; the picture of innocent inquiry.

'Your leg. What did you do?'

'Fell off a ladder,' was all he said, but he didn't turn away. I took this as an invitation to ask another question.

'Does it hurt?'

He shrugged. 'Not much,' he lied.

I smiled at him. Although slightly built, his arms were strong. By now, he would usually be carrying scenery or lighting candles or moving furniture in readiness for the performance. As an active man, forced to sit and watch the fashionably witty, he was bored. I decided to sit next to him – and not just to ease his boredom. I wanted to know what had happened.

'Are you the one Molly told me about? The one they thought was dead?'

He rolled his eyes. 'It was Peg's screaming that did it. Peg West, the girl laughing over there,' he nodded over to one of the girls still playing cards, a cheap-looking redhead in a gown that wasn't quite containing her breasts. 'She was shouting that I was dead.'

I giggled. 'You are not dead, then?'

A small smile crept over his face. My gentle flirting was beginning to have an effect.

'Nah, not dead. Tom Firmin, by the way. You're new here. Not seen you before.' He shook my hand as I gave him my name. 'A fall from a ladder don't kill you, Lizzie Blunt. I wasn't too high up... but...' His voice dwindled a little.

I raised an eyebrow to encourage him.

'But the ladder was broken. I should have checked, but we were in a rush as always.'

'Broken?'

'One of the rungs near the top. I'm usually sent up the ladder because I'm light and quick. I'm not too fond of heights though, so I take my time and take care. That night, I was being hurried by Mr Dinsdale and I didn't see that the rung was loose.' He shook his head. 'Should have checked. Stupid, really.'

'What were you doing up the ladder?'

He rubbed his forehead. 'Sorting the hangings out.' He saw my puzzlement. 'There's a big drape that covers the background scenery at the end of the play, to signify something or other. I have to throw it over the top from the back – Mr Garrick prefers us not to keep walking on and off the stage. Lots of theatres have stage hands walking on, but Garrick says it spoils the flow of the play. I have to climb the ladder instead.'

He had been behind the painted background, then, with a ladder leaning against the scenery, and carrying an armful of fabric. I risked the question that was burning.

'Why did you say you should have checked the ladder rungs? Are they often loose?'

'Sometimes. I expect it was rotten. Not that I was in any state to look at it afterwards, of course. I hit my head and knocked myself out. But I'd say it was rotten. Not repaired, probably, or bought too cheap and badly-fitted. Garrick won't spend money on anything that isn't seen on stage.'

He had not examined it, then.

'You don't think that someone could have broken it? Weakened it?'

'What? On purpose? Why would anyone do that?' He stared at me, confused. Then his face softened, comprehending. 'Oh, I see. Someone's been telling you stories, haven't they? Broken furniture, slashed costumes, props going off for a walk by themselves?'

I nodded.

'No. I don't think anyone's got it in for me. I'm too useful to damage.' He gestured to his leg and gave a wry smile. 'Well, when I'm on two feet I'm useful. No, this is all Garrick's doing,' he said, his face hardening. 'If he paid for proper ladders, not rotten ones, I'd be on stage with the lads, setting up for tonight. He's too tight. One day it's going to cause a real injury, I reckon.'

He wasn't the first person to complain about Garrick's reluctance to spend money. Joe Sugden had been similarly disgruntled.

'I've been told not to expect any wages.' I didn't ask him about the note that had been found near his fallen body. He didn't speak of it, or deem it worthy of mention, and I only knew of it from Davenport. It seemed wise to hold my peace, at least for now.

The sharp-nosed actress sitting with Peg West was tilting her glass at me, tapping it with her finger. She wanted wine.

'I'm being called over, Tom,' I said. 'But it was nice to meet you. I hope your leg mends soon.'

He favoured me with the sort of sunny smile that I see so rarely in my life. A smile uncomplicated by financial transaction.

I supplied the card-players with refreshment and carried the glasses and tankards over to a woman who had arrived from the Shakespeare tavern next door. The Shakespeare tavern on Russell Street was, I could tell from her manner and her dress, an establishment with a better reputation than its notorious namesake on the piazza. She loaded my tray with fresh supplies and sent me staggering back accompanied by a small lad, who carried a basket of food that was nearly as big as he was. I was embarrassed by my comparative weakness. The capable child directed me to unload the basket on the table at the side of the green room and set out the jugs of wine. He went off to collect the rest of the fare. He was remarkably unbothered by my ineptitude and informed me in the sort of fluty but serious tone that only a child can adopt, that Garrick laid a small dinner for the distinguished members of the audience, who were visiting the green room before the performance. The tavern made two deliveries in the day, an earlier supply of wine, beer and small bites to eat was supplemented later by more exotic fare – and a lot more wine – that would serve for the long interval and the party after the performance.

The green room had now emptied of stage hands who had wanted little beyond beer and bread. As Tom had said, they had gone to prepare the stage and were out of the way.

For now, with nearly two hours still to go before the play began, the company welcomed a few well-dressed gentlemen, who would be in the audience later. These were the men whose good opinion and support Garrick so assiduously sought. A word from one of them in the right ear would turn a play from being acknowledged as a shambles into the last word in dazzling drama – or vice-versa. Over wine and in affable company, Garrick and his players would make sure that these men understood the subtleties of their interpretation in a particular role, or the detail of a line they would later utter. They would flatter the men, intimating that only the cleverest or the most knowledgeable would understand why a phrase was declaimed in the manner they did it – thus ensuring that the information was passed to other discerning gentlemen as being of absolute importance. The fine gentleman, having dispensed his wisdom, would settle back in his chair, confident in his own reputation as a man of the arts, as a serious critic, and think fondly of Garrick and his theatre. He might even come to a play next week.

The actresses, meanwhile, were engaged in different manoeuvres. For a gentleman about town, an actress held a more elusive mystery than a plain and ordinary harlot – although she might perform much the same function as the night wore on. If she flirted with him before the performance began, then he would spend the entire performance in a state of delightful anticipation, knowing that this beauty, who so captivated the whole audience, was his alone once the curtain fell. And who knew what little scenes she might be encouraged to play out with him, once they were alone? He would be happy to pay well.

George Hunter was filling his glass again and laughing loudly at the conversation of his immaculately-attired companion. That gentleman, I gathered, was Mr Astley, his wife's current lover. Astley was a man in his fifties. His dark green coat was cut and trimmed to perfection, he wore a neat emerald pin at his neck, and he carried his tall frame with elegance. He was not handsome at all. His nose was large and shaped like a beak and it dominated a face that was lacking in animation or interest. He was looking down that nose at Mr Hunter with an expression that suggested that he looked down on everyone.

Regardless of his lack of physical appeal, Astley was a generous patron. Mrs Hunter had done well from his attentions, especially if that gown was anything to go by. Jewels sparkled in her ears and at her throat. But Mr Astley was not generous enough or well-connected enough for Mr Hunter. I could see what Mr Astley could not: Hunter was, all the while, watching his wife, and was only engaging himself so fulsomely with Astley so that she could work her charms on another man. She was sitting with the talked-of Earl of Hawbridge.

I positioned myself next to the door to watch, still holding the tray, lest anyone think that I was not busy. She was rather good: hanging on his words as though they were the wittiest thing she had ever heard, tilting her head in agreement, enabling him to see more of her pretty neck and making a little pout of her lips, so that he might imagine kissing them. All of these arts I have employed myself – although I am never in the position of begging a man to bed me.

But Hawbridge I knew.

I wasn't certain when Sugden said his name, but, seeing him, I knew him.

He had once, people said, been in possession of a handsome face, round and full of life, with soft cheeks and sparkling eyes. By now, a life committed to excess and dissipation was worn on his features as clearly as if his life's deeds had been painted on a canvas for all to see. I knew he was the same age as Mr Astley, but he might have been ten years older. His chief attraction lay in his lineage, and because of it, he was a man fully confident in himself and his importance. The Earl of Hawbridge did not need to court attention because attention came to him, courtesy of his title. But his face, with its lines and shadows, told everything. His eyes danced over Lucy's breasts and shoulders, enjoying what was being offered. Few would know, seeing him at ease in the green room, quite how cruel and violent he could be.

Lord Hawbridge would not remember me, not dressed as Lizzie Blunt. In fact, he didn't even know Lizzie Hard-wicke. Our paths had crossed some years before, when I was still living in my father's house. When I had been Elizabeth Vessey.

A shiver ran down my back as a memory from my old life returned to me. A man with a fearsome temper, beating his riding whip across the shoulders of our stable lad. A man whose brutality had only been halted by the sight of a girl standing at the stable door, open-mouthed at the fury of the blows and the screams of the boy.

Now he sat with Mrs Hunter, his brows lifting from time to time as he flicked his gaze from her to take in the rest of the room. He was perfectly charming, this old school friend of my father's, who had been such an amiable presence in our home for a week or two – when he wasn't trying to beat the life out of poor little Adam Bate.

They were no longer alone. Another man had joined them. He was dressed in the brightest green coat I had ever seen, richly embroidered with purple flowers and decorated with gold braiding. He was much younger than Hawbridge, wide-eyed at the flesh on display and far too ready to chatter and pull faces like a schoolboy. Two more actresses squeezed in to create a companionable circle. I had no doubt that Mrs Hunter thought them a nuisance, but they were unlikely to take away her shine.

Hawbridge pulled a snuff box from his pocket and held it for a moment as he leaned down to pick up his wine glass from the low table. Even from a distance I could see that it was an unusual design. It had the shape of a large scallop shell, but was decorated with white enamelled feathers, each feather delineated in gold, and topped with a greeny-blue eye. Taking a mouthful of wine, he flicked it open, one-handed, with a thumbnail. The effect was marvellous. As the lid sprang up, the feathers rose as a peacock's tail, displaying to the assembled company. The two actresses even clapped – which was surely what he expected. He glanced over the top of his glass and saw me watching. A slight frown, and then the smallest twitch of a smile crossed his face. I lowered my eyes quickly. I heard the snuff box click shut and glanced up again. His eyes were still on me, even as he engaged politely with his companions.

Chapter Eleven

Molly returned with Mrs Hunter's gloves, tapping me on the shoulder with them as she breezed into the room.

'Why are you standing here with a tray?' she asked. 'You're not here to wait on the tables.'

'Sorry miss,' I said. 'Mr Sugden asked me to clear a table, and then everyone seemed to want a drink, or some food, or something. And then the boy from the tavern came and brought a basket of things—'

'I'm teasing you,' she said. 'I know what it's like here. Just don't let that Joe Sugden have you doing every bloody job. You're working with me.' She surveyed the room. 'Where's Lucy Hunter?'

'Over there,' I said. 'She's sitting with the Earl of Hawbridge and a few others. I think he's already smitten with her. Poor Mr Astley.'

'Which one's Hawbridge?'

'The older one in the pale blue coat.'

Molly's eyes narrowed as she watched Mrs Hunter. 'He looks keen enough.'

She strode over to the small gathering and offered Mrs Hunter her gloves. Had she not told me of how much the actress needed her, I would have been shocked that Molly had interrupted the conversation. As it was, Mrs Hunter favoured Molly with a gracious smile before waving her away. One of the other actresses was trying to persuade

Lord Hawbridge to open the peacock snuff box again, and, briefly, his eye was on that saucy piece, but Lucy was quick to touch his arm and return his attention to herself. Molly stood, a step away, watching them with a scowl.

Joe Sugden was suddenly at her elbow. I saw him say something to her. She rolled her eyes and followed him out of the door. Mr Dinsdale had come in too, but he went to Garrick and exchanged some words. Garrick jumped up from his seat and, apologising to his companions, left through the same door.

I, curious as ever, exchanged my tray for a jug and wandered over to the actors he had just abandoned, proffering more wine in the hope of finding out what was going on. These were the same men who had been playing with the pistols earlier. The props had been abandoned, lying on the floor, where anyone might trip over them.

'It's a death trap, it is.'

'Good job no one was underneath it.'

My ears pricked. Slowly pouring the wine as they talked, I learned that there had been another incident. The large candle ring above the stage, the girandole, had suddenly dropped one of its candles. The candle had been unlit, and no player had been on the stage, but the sound of a heavy wax column hitting the stage with a bang had caused a furore among the stage hands. They were jumpy. And now the actors were anxious.

'It's such a useless piece. Poor workmanship, I say,' one of them said with a shudder. 'It's not the first time it's happened, Joe Sugden told me. The candle holders are all disintegrating.'

'Garrick should have a new one made – and soon. I had wax on my coat sleeve last week. It's not good enough,' the other agreed. 'What would have happened if it had fallen during a performance? Or if I'd been underneath it? I don't want to worry about a candle cracking my head open if I'm in the middle of a speech.'

'Someone should speak to him about it,' said the first. 'When we close after *Lear*, it really needs to be replaced. We can't be expected to work like this.' He took a sip from the wine I'd poured. 'I don't know what's going on here lately. Garrick needs to get his company in order. Damage to costumes and scenery is one thing, but injury to the players is quite another.'

His companion grunted agreement. 'He was far too casual when that boy fell off the ladder the other night. That letter they found next to him, telling him to leave the theatre: did you hear about it? Perhaps he'll be more concerned when one of the flats falls on his own head.'

I looked up and saw that Mr Astley had detached himself from George Hunter and gone to sit with Mrs Hunter and Lord Hawbridge. The circle around the earl expanded to accommodate the rejected lover. Lucy Hunter gave him a beautiful smile – the man currently paying for most of what she was wearing – but glanced at her husband. The earl, she would have been told, was the greater prize. I wondered whether she had any affection for Astley? As an actress, she would convince him of her genuine adoration. Gentlemen who keep mistresses like that sort of thing. I could never have a keeper: I could manage to take any man to bed, but his need for regular flattery would kill me.

Astley did not like Hawbridge. There was an awkwardness between them which was possibly due to Lucy Hunter's behaviour but which, knowing the gentlemen of quality as I do, probably stretched back some years. The young man in green eased himself into the role of amiable mediator, making a small comment to Astley, drawing him into the conversation in a way that Hawbridge was unwilling to do. For a moment, the actresses were minor characters in this play; the men commanding my attention by the energy that crackled between them. They operated by strict rules of conduct. No one would be publicly rude or offensive – on the contrary, they would be faultlessly polite. The actresses, even Mrs Hunter, might not catch the small slights they gave to one another, but from the vantage point of several feet away, I could see it all.

'Are you going to stand there all night, girl?'

My observations of these softly-spoken gentlemen were interrupted by someone addressing me in harsher tones. It was Mr Dinsdale. Whatever had been going on with the candles, everything was now under control on the stage and he had returned in search of refreshment.

'I'm sorry, sir. Would you like some wine?'

He didn't respond but held out his glass. Mr Hunter, standing with him, also held out a glass. He didn't speak to me either. I was invisible.

'The girandole?' Hunter asked Dinsdale, an eyebrow raised.

Dinsdale nodded as he took a gulp of his wine. 'Same trouble as before. I keep telling him, of course.'

'Well, if he won't listen to his stage manager, there may yet be consequences,' Hunter puffed out his red cheeks. 'He can't say he hasn't been warned.'

Dinsdale said nothing, but his face showed that he agreed.

'What's been done?' Hunter asked, his speech a little slurred.

'Usual,' said Dinsdale, with a shrug. 'We've lowered the whole thing and tried to make good the particular candle holder, but it's fallen apart, just like the rest of them.'

'These accidents keep happening, don't they?' said Hunter, tutting. 'Perhaps he should leave the theatre before something serious happens. I mean, it's not a long drop, but if a candle fell on someone's head, say, it would give them a nasty crack. Knock 'em out, even.' He sighed. 'Or there could be a greater tragedy...'

'Let's hope that lovely wife of yours is out of the way if any more candles fall,' said Dinsdale, in a sneering voice. 'Wouldn't want to damage that pretty head.'

'She's too busy playing to the audience at the side of the stage to stand underneath the light,' said Hunter. He looked over at his wife. She was fixing Hawbridge's cravat, whispering something into his ear and giggling like a little girl over whatever it was he was saying to her in return, while Astley looked on with his mouth fixed in a hard line. Then she turned to her lover and stroked his face with such sweetness that the line disappeared. Astley took her hand and kissed the palm slowly, so that her attention was again with him completely.

'Isn't she glorious?' Hunter breathed.

Dinsdale said nothing. Perhaps, like me, he was wondering how a man could stand and watch his own wife flirt with two other men, both of whom, despite their age, were more attractive in every way than he was. There was something in the way that George Hunter watched her, sighed his admiration, that made me think that he really did care for her. He was working her, certainly, and she was the key to the wealth he craved, but they were, I thought, a team.

Garrick returned. Hunter regarded the manager with disdain. He nudged Dinsdale and they parted, Hunter to the younger actors and Dinsdale in the general direction of the stage. Neither appeared concerned enough to speak with Garrick. It was nearly time for the performance to begin and criticism of the lighting was not wanted now.

Chapter Twelve

Molly was at my elbow. 'All hands are needed in the dressing rooms,' she said. 'They'll be coming down to dress soon and I want you to help. I'll take Nan Collyer, who's like a lamb, and Lucy Hunter, as she can be tricky. You can have Kitty Suckley, if you like.' She looked around the room. 'Where is she?'

Miss Suckley had moved to sit next to Mr Astley. Astley, aware that his mistress had been flirting with Lord Hawbridge, decided to turn the tables and was now giving Kitty Suckley his undivided attention.

'Shit,' Molly muttered. 'There'll be trouble. We'd better keep her away from Mrs Hunter.'

'Come on,' she said, 'we need to be moving. Mr Garrick will be sending them down in a minute.' She pushed me out of the door, not too gently.

In the mending room she gave me my orders. My place was in here, or the dressing rooms when the play was on, I was not to linger in the green room. I was to be ready with my needle to stitch, and stitch quickly, any hem, fringe or cuff that was damaged during the performance. I showed her that my needle box was in my pocket and assured her that I understood the instructions.

The dressing rooms ran along the passageways in two directions from Molly's room in the corner, the men dressing in one corridor and the women in the other.

Separating the men and women had less to do with decency, and more to do with the practicality of sorting their costumes. All of them wandered about half-naked. It was like being at home.

If Lucy Hunter had been bothered by Miss Suckley's play for Mr Astley, there was no mention of it when she arrived in her room. Instead, everything was about Lord Hawbridge and how he had entertained her so splendidly along with his friend, Mr Callow, who, although not much more than a boy, had been very sweet in his pretty green coat. Mrs Hunter had been delighted by his lordship's snuff box and gave Molly a spirited account of how it worked.

I left her prattling away while Molly made suitably interested enquiries about his lordship and went next door to fit Kitty Suckley into her gown. The spares shared a larger room and dressed themselves. Kitty, by this time, had arrived in her dressing room and was waiting for me with a mean look in her eye.

After half an hour of attempting to dress Miss Suckley to her exacting standard, I limped back to Molly, to find her on her knees, surrounded by a pile of clothes. In all my days, I have never known a woman so spiteful as Kitty Suckley. And I live with Emily Greville and Lucy Allingham.

'How many times did she hit you?' Molly didn't even look up as she folded a petticoat into a trunk.

'I lost count after ten,' I said. 'The slaps I can manage; it was the pinching I didn't care for. She said I had stuck a pin in her. I wish that I had.'

She stood up and looked at me, hands on hips. 'I don't know why they have to pinch. They all do it. Even Nan, sometimes. Lucy pulled my hair tonight as well – even after I had calmed her stage fright.'

We stood looking at one another, silently noting our battle scars.

'I left a piece of apple pie here,' I said, gesturing to the table. 'Would you share it with me? I didn't pinch it, miss, honest,' I said, seeing her eyes narrow, 'Mr Fielding's housekeeper gave it to me.'

She gave me a wry smile, as if she almost believed me.

'In that case, I would be honoured, you little scrap. The gowns can wait.'

Unless a garment was torn on the stage, and we were called up, we were safely out of the reach of vicious actresses while the play ran on. Molly regaled me with scandalous tales and a few stories that I already knew, about how scenery had been falling over and how her costumes had been savaged.

She had no idea who was behind the accidents but was happy to speculate after a glass or two of wine.

'It's got to be someone who knows the theatre,' she said. 'Someone who knows where to find flats, or costumes in the first place.'

'You think it's one of the players? Or a stage hand?'

'Not the stage hands,' she said with some conviction. 'Joe would know if it was. Everything has to be in good order as far as he's concerned.'

'Mr Sugden isn't troubled by such things?' I asked. 'I think I'd get jumpy if furniture and scenery kept breaking. Like there was a ghost, or something.'

She laughed. 'He gets agitated. He says it looks bad for him if things are broken or stolen, like the discipline among the stage hands is breaking down.'

'Isn't Mr Dinsdale in charge?'

'Overall, yes. But Joe looks after the men and makes sure the orders are carried out. He's protective of them, thinks they don't get a fair deal from Garrick when they work just as hard as the players. But if he thinks any of them is damaging the stage... well, I wouldn't want to be in that man's shoes if Joe Sugden's in a fury.'

I went outside to relieve myself, wishing that I hadn't drunk so much wine with Molly. Members of the audience find relief in the tavern yards during the intervals, but the area around Drury Lane is adequately supplied with dark passages, if you're not fussy. I do not like pissing in a busy street, but I wasn't dressed to be fussy and I didn't have time to dodge the cat-calls and groping hands of a tavern. I found a cart at the side of the street, pulled up hard against a lodging house, and ducked behind it for privacy, finding nothing in the small gap between the cart and the wall but a skinny dog. He soon moved.

The rooms in the lodging houses above were bright enough, and showed signs of life and activity, but the passageways below, although full of people, were not well-lit, so I hurried back as quickly as I could, past the hard-faced, half-dressed whores, and the pimps and bawds lurking in doorways. I was grateful to see the theatre ahead of me, a welcoming brazier burning by the back door, grateful too that no one had bothered me out in the squalid and noisy streets.

The dressing room passage was better lit with candles now that the play was underway, but it was empty. Any actors not on stage were probably in the green room. A man emerged from a doorway, bumping my shoulder and causing me to stagger. He did not apologise; indeed, he turned to scowl with indignation at the girl his way, the light from a wall sconce making his face glow.

It was Lord Hawbridge. Presumably he had come down to find Mrs Hunter.

The scowl faded; there was recognition in his eyes.

'You were in the green room earlier,' he said. The voice drawled, thick with wine.

I nodded. It had not been a question.

'Are you lost, my Lord?' I asked, rubbing my arm. 'Are you looking for someone?'

'Perhaps I came to find you.' There was a hint of mockery. 'I know you.'

Did he know me? Had he recognised me as Edward Vessey's daughter? I shrank into the shadow, unwilling to let any light fall on my face, just in case.

'I don't think so, my Lord. I don't think you know me.'

He touched my cheek and I flinched.

'The innocent act doesn't fool me, y'know,' he said. 'You're surrounded by players here – better ones than you. But I can see what you are.' He stepped closer, so that I could now smell the wine on his breath. 'You were flirting with me, little cat, flashing your eyes at me. Don't deny it.'

I did deny it. I denied it most sincerely, but he didn't seem concerned by my response. Instead I found myself shoved up against the wall as he began to kiss me, laughing into my mouth when I tried to move away.

Eventually, he pulled his mouth off mine. I wiped his saliva from my lips, aware that he still had his hands on me.

'I need to be back at work,' I said, breathing hard and hoping that the kiss was enough for him.

It wasn't.

I was dragged through the door from which he had just emerged. It was the mending room. Molly was nowhere to be seen. She had probably gone in search of more food or wine. He kicked the door shut behind him and backed me to the edge of the table; the little plate that had lately held my apple pie shunted along with a clatter. He was blocking my escape.

'You know what I want?'

It wasn't difficult to guess.

The circle of his fingers tightened on my wrist and I heard him grunt as he unbuttoned his breeches with his free hand.

'Lift your skirts.' The order was abrupt.

I was about to obey and get it over with quickly. But I did not want to. I did not want this. No one would hear me if I screamed. I could not fight him off – he was strong, and I was pressed against a table – but I still had my wits. I could take a gamble.

I hesitated.

'What are you waiting for?' Annoyed by my reluctance, and ready to take what he wanted, he began to pull up my skirts himself. I pushed his hands away and took a breath.

'I'm sorry, my Lord, it's… I don't think I'm clean.'

'What?' He continued to press against me, even with this interruption, his breath hot against my neck.

'I'm not clean, sir.'

Now he stopped.

Holding my skirts in one hand he grabbed my chin with the other, forcing me to look him in the eye. 'Not clean? What? Are you telling me you've got the clap?'

I nodded. 'Yes, sir. And I wouldn't want to curse you with it.' I said in a whine. 'Or your lady. It itches and stings so badly.'

At the mention of his wife, he bristled. Whatever ardour had been driving him a moment ago, the thought of a nasty disease deflated him. I imagined he'd experienced it before.

I might have been lying. I was lying. But he didn't want to risk it.

Thwarted, exposed and breeches still undone, his expression turned to anger. I was not quick enough. He grabbed the hair at the back of my head, pulled me away from the table and threw me hard at the wall, banging my shoulder. My forehead cracked against a shelf, and I yelped at the pain as I crashed to the ground.

'Wasp!' He spat the word. 'You're a fucking wasp.'

A whore with a sting in her tail.

I was dangerously close to his feet. He was furious, and I had seen him enraged once before. I remembered what had happened to our stable boy and drew myself into a ball, arms around my head, bracing myself for when he kicked me, knowing it was inevitable, trying not to cry out, and now cursing my utter stupidity.

I saw him take aim and squealed in fright despite my intentions.

The door was flung open.

'Lizzie, you're needed in the green room. There's an emergency. Mr Garrick has torn a cuff.' It was Tom Firmin, crutch tucked under his arm.

He checked his step as he caught sight of Lord Hawbridge. The two men froze, neither fully knowing how to address the situation he encountered.

'I'm sorry, my Lord,' Tom began. 'I didn't realise you were in here...' his voice fell away as he saw me on the floor. I prayed that he would not back out of the door.

I scrambled to my feet as fast as the pain and terror would allow. 'Does he want Molly?' The words came out in an undignified half-shriek. 'If it's Mr Garrick, I mean? I don't know where she is, if it's Molly he needs.'

He shook his head, eyeing Hawbridge who was calmly rebuttoning himself. 'No, no, you'll do. It's just a cuff. Molly's up on the girandole, helping Joe. She told me to find you.'

I tugged the needle box from my pocket, hands trembling, and brandished it like a trophy. 'I'm ready to come now. Look, I'm ready.'

Hawbridge had enough grace to know he had been beaten. He pulled a face and stood aside to let me pass. As I moved to the door, though, he grabbed my arm, yanking me towards him, and put his mouth to my ear.

'We'll forget this misunderstanding, won't we, *Lizzie*.'

'Yes, my Lord.'

His hand tightened, hurting me.

'Any word from you, and I'll have you whipped, as well as thrown on to the street – where you so obviously belong.'

He dropped me. I gave a small curtsey, then lurched towards Tom.

'Let's go, Tom,' I said, pushing past him and nearly falling into the corridor.

I ran as fast as my shaking legs would carry me, Tom limping on his crutch behind me.

'You all right, Lizzie? Did he hurt you?' he panted, struggling to keep up.

I shook my head, anxious to get away from Hawbridge and into the safety of the green room. He had hurt me, in truth. My shoulder was throbbing, as was my head.

'No, but I'm very glad you came in when you did.' I cleared my throat, trying not to cry, keen to change the subject. 'What's Molly doing?'

'Not sure', he said. 'I think she's replacing the candles on the main lights.'

I thought about the conversations I'd overheard; about the candles falling out of the disintegrating holders. It was a delicate and important task, making sure that candles were secure. I slowed my pace and let him catch up.

'That's Molly's job?'

'It is when I'm injured. The big girandole over the stage can be lowered by a rope, of course, but Garrick doesn't like it done during a performance. He's not prepared to shell out for better candles, so some of them burn down too quickly and need to be replaced.'

I still couldn't see it. 'So what does Molly do? Or what do you do?'

'The thing hangs on a ring fixed to a beam. There are several beams across the stage, some of the scenery, or the effects, are hung on hooks or rings in the beams. The girandole is raised, rather than lowered, then she climbs across a beam, leans out and changes the candles, before it's lowered again.'

'That sounds dangerous.'

He laughed. 'For most of us. I hate it. But Molly was a rope-walker. She has no fear of heights. She says that walking the beam is child's play compared with a rope. And she gets a few coins from the gentlemen sitting on the stage who watch her – not that the players appreciate that.'

'Ha! I can imagine.' No wonder Lucy Hunter was so spiteful. Molly was causing heads to turn and collecting up coins for her fairground trick, even as she struggled with her soliloquies.

Tom caught my arm as we reached the green room door.

'Are you sure he didn't hurt you, Lizzie?'

I gave him a practised smile, ignoring the pain in my face and shoulder.

'I'm not hurt, Tom. There's no harm done.'

Chapter Thirteen

'It's come off at the underside of the cuff. Again.' Mr David Garrick, the finest actor of our generation and manager of, arguably, the finest theatre in the world, was waving an arm at my face, a lace flounce flapping and dangling from the end of his shirt sleeve.

'It might help me, sir, if you could keep still, so I can see it,' I said, becoming dizzy as I tried to focus, pain still coursing through my shoulder.

'Yes, yes, yes. Look at it.' He shook it at my nose again.

I grabbed his wrist – which he was not expecting – and gave him a severe stare. He, surprised by this, gave in and stood still.

'Thank you, sir.'

The lace had been stitched several times over. The stitching was not poor, but the edge of the lawn shirt that held it was fraying.

'I can tack it on for now, if you wish, but the whole sleeve needs to be repaired. See how the cuff has become worn.'

He peered down at his wrist, still firmly locked in my hand.

He gave a very loud sigh, as if this were the most tiresome experience of his life. 'Oh, do what you can, please. And be quick about it. I have people to see.'

He condescended to sit, and even to pull his arm out of the sleeve, allowing me to sew as swiftly as I could. All the time, he held court with gentlemen who sought his advice, his opinion, even his blessing on matters of the day. I wondered how he managed to compose his wits to return to the play in character, he was so busy being himself.

The long interval had just begun, and the green room, filling with players and gentlemen from the audience, was already foggy with tobacco smoke. Even so, through the haze, I could see Peg West sitting on someone's knee, encouraging him to kiss her neck and fondle her splendid bosom which had released itself from her gown. Another of the spares sat idly stroking a man's thigh as he chatted to her friend. The lower orders of actors and audience members mingled comfortably with the noble and important; anyone who was a friend of Garrick, or a friend to the theatre was welcome. If they brought patronage, publicity or even notoriety, so much the better.

'My Lord!' Garrick jerked his arm away from my needle, leaving a thread dangling. He stood to greet Lord Hawbridge, who had, by now, made his way back to the green room. 'How delightful to see you. Are you enjoying our little play? How is Lady Hawbridge?' This volley of questions was accompanied by much hand shaking. Lord Hawbridge, I surmised, would be a very useful friend to Garrick's theatre, and Garrick was far more concerned to engage him in conversation than to have his cuff repaired. He was, even now, pushing his arm back through his sleeve. I put my needle away and shrank into my seat, avoiding Hawbridge's eye.

'Garrick, come and join us.' Hawbridge's voice was smooth. 'You know my dear friend Astley, of course. He's always here mooning after Mrs Hunter. Do you know Mr Callow? A family friend of my wife's...' He steered Garrick away.

Ketch took Garrick's place as I was rolling up my thread and nodded towards the earl.

'Magnificent fellow, isn't he? Garrick loves it when the quality arrives.'

I said nothing. Magnificent wasn't the word I would use for the Earl of Hawbridge.

'Lucy Hunter has her work cut out if she wants to claim that prize,' he chuckled.

Lucy Hunter would need a suit of armour to survive.

I watched Garrick play the generous host to Lord Hawbridge and his guests, calling for more wine, and hurrying one of the spare horses to find some. All the time, he was mirroring the gestures of these fine men. This was subtle. They wouldn't have noticed, but he was, even amid the laughter and fuss, calmly and deliberately making them feel comfortable without fawning over them.

I can spot a whore at fifty paces. He was after money.

There was a commotion near the door. Someone was shouting and pushing his way in. A man, waving a handful of papers, red in the face.

'Simmot,' said Ketch. 'Now there'll be trouble.'

He was short, pudgy-faced and dressed in an over-decorated rose-coloured coat that was too gorgeous for him. His cherubic face suggested youth, so that he looked like a school boy who had dressed up in his father's best clothes. A boy without manners or finesse.

The people in the green room largely ignored him. Molly, fresh from her climb over the stage beams, eased past him, rolling down her sleeves. Joe Sugden was with her. I waved to Molly.

'William Simmot,' said Sugden with a grimace as he sat down. 'That's all we need.'

'Who is he?' I asked Molly.

'A writer. He keeps calling with his plays. He's here most nights, asking Mr Garrick to look at them, but Mr Garrick doesn't want to be bothered.'

Sugden snorted. 'That's what Simmot says, when he's shouting like this. Garrick has read his plays, Mr Dinsdale says so. Garrick calls him a talentless hack.'

'Mr Garrick is overlooking his undoubted talent,' said Ketch. 'It's what he tells everyone. Anyone who'll listen.'

'Aye,' said Sugden. He pulled a face. 'I'm no expert in plays, but I've been in this theatre long enough to know that Garrick understands what the public wants to see.'

'And what he thinks they ought to see,' said Molly, making a grab for a pot of beer. 'He's not fond of the dancers and tumblers, and the people want to see those – along with their Shakespeare and farces.' She put a hand out to the monkey, who climbed down from Ketch's head and on to her forearm.

'What sort of plays does Mr Simmot write?' I asked.

Sugden shook his head. 'No idea. But Garrick can't have anything political, so maybe he writes those sorts.'

Satire was frowned upon, I knew that. Anything too critical of the government could lose a theatre its precious licence. From where I sat, Mr Simmot did not look like a man sharp-witted enough to write anything too dangerous.

'Or perhaps the plays are just not very good?' I said.

Ketch laughed. 'He thinks they are.'

Mr Simmot was fizzing with anger. He strode to where Garrick was making polite conversation with his high-born guests and stood, feet apart, brandishing the papers. The noise of the green room dropped to a low murmur. Even the fog of tobacco smoke seemed to part a little, allowing everyone to watch the confrontation between the overgrown child in pink and the king of the green room.

Garrick introduced Mr Simmot to his guests, fault-less in his conduct, confident in his position. Simmot, confused for a moment by such impeccable decency, shook hands with Lord Hawbridge and the others. He was, it seemed, a gentleman of sorts; his manners briefly returning. Garrick gestured that he should sit with them and Simmot, the wind well and truly taken from his sails, was forced to behave with stiff propriety when he had been spoiling for a row.

The green room once more began to hum into conver-sation, at first low, and then gradually back to raucous. Somewhere, a woman was shrieking with laughter. Glasses clinked. I wanted to hear about Molly's climb over the beams and leaned close to ask.

Simmot's voice rose, high and explosive, above it all, before I had the chance.

'Damn you. I'll see you ruined, Garrick, don't you believe it. This theatre will be nothing. You'll be nothing very soon. And you'll be damned to hell for your arrog-ance.'

With everyone else, I watched him throw his papers in Garrick's face and stamp out of the room, still shouting angrily, nearly falling over the abandoned pistols. Lord Hawbridge opened up his snuff box. This was not his fight and he sat back, content to watch. Mr Astley was more agitated and looked as if he was about to go after the man until Garrick stayed his arm. Mr Callow, the third of the group, looked uncomfortable.

Garrick stood up, made an open-handed gesture to the company and walked towards the door. 'Gentlemen, the interval is over,' was all he said, in the resonant tone he reserved for the stage.

Chapter Fourteen

I did not get the chance to ask Molly about her climb over the beams, or to ask about the damaged girandole, nor even to discover more about Simmot. Once the play ended and the after-piece was done, and the crowds spilled out into the green room, I found that I had plenty of work to do. Molly and I gathered up costumes, or parts of costumes that had been abandoned on or near to the stage. I was genuinely surprised to discover kerchiefs, ribbons and even a necklace when we moved the chairs. A length of lace was snagged under a piece of scenery: Garrick's cuff. I wished he had let me stitch it properly and grumbled about it to Molly. She simply shrugged and said that wandering on to the stage and losing his cuff was the sort of thing that Garrick would do.

'When he's lost in a part, Lizzie, especially something like Lear, he won't even notice what he's wearing. He could be out here in just his shirt.'

I could hear the sounds of drunken laughter echoing from the green room but, for the moment, I was unable to spy on the company. The players, their favourite audience members and patrons were there. The stage hands and theatre servants – of whom I was one – were setting things back to rights. Men and women straightened chairs, shifted the benches in the pit, cleared the floors of the boxes and some poor devils swept out the galleries. Having cleaned the green room earlier, I was glad to be spared that task. Molly and I sorted the clothes in the dressing rooms, trying to assess, by the light of a few candles, which needed to be mended or brushed out.

'It's late,' she said, as we laid the mending pile on the table of her own room. 'We'll deal with these in the morning.' She picked up a shawl and wrapped it around her shoulders.

'Where are we going?' I asked.

'*We* aren't going anywhere,' she said. '*I* am going out for a drink with Joe Sugden.'

I was at a loss to know what to do.

'Get some sleep, Lizzie.' She gestured to the floor. 'You can make yourself comfortable here, if you like, or you can go to one of the dressing rooms. You'll find a couch in Lucy Hunter's room, and she won't be back for the night. But don't crease any of the clothes or there'll be trouble.'

I wasn't ready for sleep but was reluctant to go out alone in this part of town. I had already experienced the reality of how a badly-dressed servant in a theatre was treated by a man of breeding; how she would fare on the street with the drunken culls falling out of taverns made me long for the security of Berwick Street.

Besides, I had work to do. The theatre had fallen quiet. I could no longer hear the sound of feet running up and down the corridors; no one called out for players to remove to the stage. The low noise of the orchestra had disappeared. The musicians had long since sloped off to find ale and alternative entertainment. Now, at last, I might have the opportunity to look around. I would begin with the area at the back of the stage. That was where most of the accidents had happened.

The corridor outside the dressing room was dark again. A few candles burned in the sconces, but some had burned out and not been replaced. I took a candlestick and went back to the green room. The players and their guests had all disappeared. If they had not gone home or to lodging houses, then they would be at a club, or in one of the many taverns or gaming hells nearby, frittering the night away, along with their fortunes. The only people left were a couple of stage hands, men who I had seen carrying furniture, lighting candles, climbing ladders and shifting the great pieces of painted scenery for most of the night. They were sitting amid the mess, playing dice and smoking at one of the tables in the corner. The man with the ginger hair and bad breath was among them. I screwed up my courage and walked in the direction of the stage as boldly as I could – as if I had every right to walk wherever I chose.

'Where are you off to, sweetheart?' asked one of the men.

I cleared my throat and stood a little taller. 'Mrs Hunter's hat is missing a feather. Need to see if it's on the stage.'

He shook his head. 'Can't do that. Mr Dinsdale's closed the stage area for the night.'

'I only want to look for the feather. I won't be long…'

Still he shook his head. 'You're new here, girl. No one goes on the stage once it's cleared.'

The ginger-haired man caught my wrist and tugged me towards him. 'Come and play with us, little wagtail,' he cackled, the other hand smacking his thigh. 'Come and sit on my lap and look for your feather. You might find something harder down here—'

I pulled my hand free and stepped away quickly as he made another grab for me.

'Goodnight, sir. I thank you, but I'll not stay.'

'Just one kiss, then.' He leered at me, eyes wide and mocking. 'To bring me luck.'

'Leave her alone, Sam,' said one of the others, laughing. 'Even her kisses won't turn your luck tonight.'

I gave the man a grateful smile and fled from the room. Now, I reflected, was not the best time to search the theatre after all. Drunken men and dark passageways were not helpful to my investigations. Perhaps early morning might be better. I made my way back to Lucy Hunter's room, annoyed at my lack of progress. I could do nothing now but turn over the events of the evening in my mind.

It was William Simmot's outburst that had intrigued me the most. A man so full of his own importance, and so full of anger that he felt able to walk into a room and give vent to his fury, regardless of who was present. Was he malicious, though? He was certainly angry, but was Simmot the man who had caused so many unsettling things to happen in the theatre? Would Simmot break a ladder rung, or misplace a candle on the girandole, so that it fell? Would he slash a costume, or ruin a panel of scenery? He had seemed too full of bluster.

Players and stage hands were anxious. Even a falling candle had been enough to concern them – because it was one incident among a growing number. As Davenport had said, to an outsider such matters looked like nothing, but put together, they suggested a plot to unsettle and spoil. But Garrick was not paying their wages properly; if he lost members of his company because they were also unhappy and jumpy, then his theatre would fail.

And Mr Hunter was certainly no friend of Mr Garrick's, even if his wife was one of the stars of the company. The look that he had given Garrick had been more than disdainful; it had been contemptuous.

I took care to lift a pile of clothes from the couch in Lucy's dressing room. It wasn't particularly soft, but I removed my shoes, pulled a shawl over me and lay down, thankful as always, even in my bad dress, for a place to sleep.

–

I woke early; my shoulder and face still sore after my encounter with Lord Hawbridge. The couch had given me very little cushioning, so I now also had a pain in my neck. A small amount of pale daylight was beginning to light the room, giving it a tinge of pink. It was not the light that had woken me, but the throb in my shoulder and the sound of carts clattering over cobbles right next to where I was lying so uncomfortably. Through the narrow window, set high in the wall, I could see wheels and feet hurrying past. It was barely dawn, but the traders were on their way to the Garden to set up their stalls. Above my makeshift bed chamber, market folk were beginning the business of the day. A cabbage fell from a handcart and I saw a man in a brown wool coat stoop to pick it up, unwilling to lose even one precious vegetable from his pitifully small load.

I yawned. I would never sleep for the racket outside, even if my bed had been comfortable. And now, surely, I might have opportunity to poke about.

I had no idea what I was looking for.

I glanced at my reflection in the long glass that stood in the corner of Lucy's room, smoothed my gown and ran her hairbrush through my straggled curls. I found the tattered ribbon in my pocket and tied up my hair. The mud-coloured gown was crumpled. The bruise on my face was beginning to bloom, making my skin look dirty. I was nineteen years old but looked a lot younger without my finery. I rubbed my stiff neck. A few more nights like that and my face would begin to carry the care-worn expression of a servant. I found a candle and a flint box. I knew that the corridors would still be dark.

I started with Molly's room. Molly had not returned, so I felt free to look about. Cupboards and drawers were full of clothes and small stage props. A brace of pistols, similar to those being paraded in the green room last night, lay in a box at the bottom of a wardrobe. Five long swords made of painted wood were resting in the corner. A short knife lay with them. This looked real, but when I pressed the tip of the blade, it gave way, retracting itself into the handle: a stage knife that would give a good impression of brutal murder, should the company be performing *Macbeth*.

Nothing here told me who was threatening Garrick. Papers I found in the drawers were also for show; empty scrolls rolled up with false seals, love letters with nonsense written in them, kisses drawn in a large hand at the bottom. I found a few receipts for items bought, but nothing of consequence: tailors' and milliners' bills, mostly. The room was stuffed with all sorts of things. I could have spent the whole day turning it upside down.

The doors to the dressing rooms on this passage were all ajar and I peeped into each of them. I learned little, beyond the personal habits of the company's players. More than one room contained a stinking chamber pot that no one had emptied. I grimaced, knowing that this foul duty would, undoubtedly, be mine. Kitty Suckley had three vases of fresh flowers on her table from her admirers. Nan Collyer had a teapot. Lucy Hunter had left a pair of earrings on her table, as I had already noticed, in among the make-up. A gift from Astley, perhaps. There was no one about. Members of the company did not sleep in their dressing rooms. They left with lovers and slept in vast beds until midday, or else rolled into the lodging houses located a few convenient steps outside. None of the players would be awake at this hour, having been only recently asleep. I couldn't see any of the stage hands now either and assumed that established theatre servants had lodgings too.

The green room was empty and in a state of chaos. The dice players had gone; discarded pots and old pipes littered their table. I tried not to notice the mice that skittered about the plates of food, oblivious to my presence. The theatre needed a cat or two. I might even suggest it.

From the green room, I made my way into the tunnel that ran along the back of the stage. I was not supposed to be here, so would need to work quickly to avoid being caught. It was, as all passageways in the theatre seemed to be, as black as night. I lit my candle and walked carefully, hunting for damaged scenery, or something left behind by whoever was breaking ladder rungs. The darkness wrapped itself around me and my heart began to beat faster.

When better lit, this was the place where the actors gathered their thoughts, rehearsed their lines, recalled their cues, before emerging from the wings. What was it like to step out on to the stage? How did it feel to emerge into the light with the audience whistling and cheering? I had had a small glimpse of that the other night, when the whole theatre had cheered my part in the downfall of a murderer. Had I enjoyed it, all that adulation? The truth was, I didn't really know. To be admired, noticed and even feted was, of course, the height of success for any lady of the town, but I was happier to be hidden away at Berwick Street, adored in my own home, and on my own terms, not prey to the fickleness of crowds.

The curtains of the wings were light to the touch, which was no surprise, as actors need to slip like wraiths in and out of the action on stage. I nursed the light at my breast, gently pushing away the fabric so that I did not set it alight. I felt the smooth boards beneath my feet and looked down. I was on the stage.

I passed the chairs where the rich and well-connected men like Lord Hawbridge had sat. They had been so close to the raw emotion of *King Lear* and I envied them for it. To be so close as to see and even smell the sweat and blood must be a wonderful experience.

My feet, tapping the edge of the stage, stopped of their own accord. I looked out into the cave of blackness that would be the auditorium. It was hard, without the lights, to imagine them there, all those people. But I felt as though I could smell their presence.

I sniffed the air. I could certainly smell something.

A cold and dreadful sensation began to run up from my feet and along the backs of my legs, making me tremble. I did not like the smell. I knew what it was. This was not the scent of an audience, or the smell of a vibrant performance.

I could smell death.

As I stepped further onto the stage, it grew steadily stronger and more hideous. I should have turned and returned through the wings to the safety of the green room, but I was drawn towards the smell like a dog to a leg of ham.

There was something sticky underfoot. I was stepping in a pool of something. The pulsing of my heartbeat began to bang in my ears and I knew, I knew that I was walking in blood. Lots of blood. I could smell blood and piss.

Something grazed my wounded shoulder and I swung around in panic. It was hanging above me like a carcass in a butcher's shop. My hand shook as I raised the candle to look. Immediately I wished that I hadn't.

The sight of him made me scream, before I could stop myself. I screamed out of sheer fright and terror, realising that no one would hear me because no one was here, and I was alone on stage with a dead man. A murdered man. I screamed again.

He was hanging upside down from the central girandole, a rope around his ankles. His throat had been cut so brutally that his head was half severed from his neck. The blood had gushed from his body and over his face so mightily that I could only truly recognise him from his clothing, from the pale blue silk he had been wearing last night. That too was destroyed by his blood.

I was standing in his blood.

Lord Hawbridge.

I felt myself gagging. I had little in my stomach to vomit but retched emptily until the taste of bile filled my mouth and nose.

'Oh God. Oh God. Oh God,' was all I could say over and over as my body bent, noxious liquid slipping from my mouth. Whether the words were a prayer for him or for me, I couldn't tell.

There were lights, suddenly, in the wings. Two figures with candelabra appeared. I had not been alone in the theatre – and someone had heard my screams after all.

'Stay back,' I shouted in warning, wiping my face on a sleeve, coughing at the acid in my throat. 'There's been a murder, a horrible murder.'

The lights did not pause. Instead, Sugden and Molly emerged through the chairs and held the lights up high, to see what I had wanted to protect them from. The stage was transformed by the increased lighting, and we could see even more of the appalling horror in front of us.

Molly shrieked – as I had done. One short, sharp shriek and she was done. Flinging out a hand to grab a chair, she sat down before she collapsed, showing remarkable foresight.

Sugden marched over to me, halting as he trod into the blood and then stepping back, making the sign of the cross over himself. 'Jesus Christ and Bloody Mary.' His face was a mix of revulsion and awe at the spectacle.

I wondered where they had come from. Somewhere close, if they had rushed so soon – and with candles – to the stage.

Sugden walked back to Molly and told her to compose herself, taking the candle stick from her.

'This,' he said, solemnly, walking back towards the corpse, holding the candles before him, as if in some sort of religious ceremony, 'this is the devil's work and no mistake.'

'It looks pretty human work to me, sir,' I said, gazing up at the body.

We looked down at the lake of blood under our shoes. I could feel warm liquid at my toes when I moved them. My stomach lurched again.

'Mr Garrick won't be pleased,' said Sugden, who was moving away from his demonic theory and on to more practical matters. 'The stage is going to have to be scrubbed.'

'Never mind the stage,' I said. 'This is the Earl of Hawbridge. There's going to be one hell of a fuss.'

Molly was watching us with wide eyes.

'Is there anyone else in the theatre?' I asked. 'Someone needs to fetch a constable.'

'I'll go,' she said. 'I don't want to keep looking at it. Makes me feel ill.'

'Go to Bow Street and fetch the magistrate,' said Sugden. 'It'll be all right, Moll. Don't fret yourself.' He gave her a single candle and she went swiftly through the wings. Sugden and I stood looking up at Lord Hawbridge's inverted body. I saw that he touched the little crucifix that hung around his neck; mouthed noiseless words as he breathed.

Chapter Fifteen

'Should we get some more light in here, Mr Sugden, do you think? Can we light the candles in the footlights, or some of the sconces? I expect the law men will want to see this properly.'

'I'll open the pit door,' he said, 'let some daylight in.'

'I don't think Mr Garrick will want the whole of London peering in to see *this* show,' I said, somewhat ruefully. Mr Garrick would be devastated. A wealthy patron butchered on his precious stage – the emotions would defy the pen of Shakespeare. 'Perhaps we should make do with candles?'

He grunted in assent and padded around softly at the edge of the stage, gradually lighting the oil lamps as if he were preparing for the evening performance – the one that would not be happening tonight. While he was engaged, I took the opportunity to have a good look at Lord Hawbridge, knowing that I would not have a chance once the stage filled with people.

The earl had been tied at the ankles and the wrists before being hoisted up from the stage. I wondered how he had allowed this to happen. He must have been stunned in some way, hit on the head or knocked out. He would need to be taken down and examined properly, but I expected that the constables would find a wound on the back of his head. His wig had fallen off, probably when he had been raised up. It had been kicked or thrown away and was now curled up like a small cat downstage. His throat had been cut in a gash from ear to ear. He had been sliced, rather than hacked, I thought. I wondered what had happened to the blade. It would have dripped blood enough to leave a tell-tale trail. And was the murderer also covered in blood? I was standing in a small pond of it; when his neck was sliced it would have spurted out, covering whoever was in front of him. Unless they cut from behind. Opened his throat and held his head from the back. That had to be it.

This was not a killing done in a temper or in a passion. It was planned, and it was calculating. The man had been lifted high in a grotesque spectacle. I shuddered.

On the floor, directly under Hawbridge's head, was his peacock feather snuff box. It was not covered in blood but shone in the candle light, the lid raised in display.

'What's that?' Sugden, having dealt with the footlights, stood at the edge of the blood lake and pointed to the snuff box.

'Don't touch it,' I said, 'I think we should leave everything exactly as we found it.'

He raised his eyebrows. 'Who are you to give the orders?' He stepped into the bloody pool, picked up the snuff box and turned it over in his hands.

'Must have fallen from his coat pocket,' he said. 'Worth a lot; more than a man's wages for a year.'

There was a noise from the passageway. Sugden's consideration of the box's value was brought to a halt by the arrival of the law. He shoved it into his coat.

'The magistrate will come down later, but he hasn't risen from his bed yet,' I heard a familiar voice.

Mr Davenport was striding through the wings carrying a lantern. Behind him came the tall figure of Mr Snow – known to the men of Bow Street as Snowy – and Molly, scurrying to keep up.

Davenport stopped as soon as he saw what was on the stage ahead of him. The inverted corpse, and his own spy, now fully illuminated by candles. I imagine it was an impressive sight. Dramatic, certainly. That, I realised, was the intention.

There was a moment of stunned silence, followed by a few muttered words.

'You there,' he addressed Sugden, and ignored me, 'have you touched anything?'

'No sir,' said Sugden, lying, 'we've touched nothing. Just lit the candles so's you could see him better. We thought you'd want to see.'

He nodded. 'Thank you. That was a good idea. Who found the body?' He looked between me, Sugden and Molly.

'It was me, sir,' I said in a small voice. 'I found him.'

He walked over to me, stepping carefully around the blood. 'You found him?' There was the smallest glimmer of concern in his eyes. 'You were sent here by the magistrate, were you not? Caught thieving. Remind me of your name.'

'Lizzie Blunt, sir,' I ducked my head down. 'I'm second seamstress here now.'

I expected a word of sympathy for the shock of my discovery, but Davenport was not given to niceties. Even so, his next question shook me.

'What were you doing wandering about the stage in the early hours, Lizzie Blunt?'

Sugden stiffened, as if he had not thought of this, as if he had not imagined I might be a killer. I avoided Davenport's eye.

'My room has no curtain, sir. I was woken by the sun, and the market traders. I got up and began to tidy.'

'On the stage?'

It annoyed me that he was pressing me like this, but I gave him an honest answer in my meekest voice.

'I'm new here, sir. I just wanted to see the stage.'

'And when you came here, you found it all, just like this?'

'Yes sir. I've touched nothing. Mr Sugden lit the candles and Miss Bray ran to Bow Street.'

Sugden shifted uneasily at the mention of his name.

'If you'll excuse me, sir, I think someone should go to Mr Garrick. He lodges near to the theatre when we're in season. He'll need to know... come and see...' his voice trailed off as he anticipated the response from the manager.

Davenport considered this. 'I agree,' he said. 'Take this young woman with you, Miss Bray, is it? I'll want to speak to you both later, but Mr Garrick may be less... immediately anxious... if there are two of you. Please tell him that William Davenport advises him to hurry here.'

Molly looked glad to be leaving the stage but nodded to me. 'What about Lizzie?'

'She can stay where she is for now. She's quite safe.'

Molly threw me a look of sympathy before the two of them hurried away. Snowy saw them out through the wings and then stood, at a distance, with his arms folded, watching. He was a man of few words, although he had once marched me to the magistrate's, thinking I was a thief and a murderer. I didn't think anyone suspected me of murder this time – but I was still relieved when Davenport's expression quickly changed.

'Garrick's worst imaginings have come to this, then?' he said.

Before I could stop myself, I let out a long gasping sigh of relief. His face twisted into concern.

'Are you all right?'

'My legs,' I said, my voice a strangled whine. 'I can't move my legs. I've been stuck here since I found him. I don't think I can move. It's the blood… all of this blood… it's in my shoes, Mr Davenport. I can feel it in my shoes.'

He frowned at me, whether out of concern or frustration, I couldn't tell.

'Stay where you are for now. I'll get you out of there in a moment. Can you bear it?'

I nodded. 'I'll do my best. I'm not good with blood. Sorry.'

He looked up at the corpse.

'Any idea who he is?'

'He's the Earl of Hawbridge. He was in the audience last night with some friends. Mr Garrick was entertaining him in the interval.'

He groaned. 'Shit.'

Snowy muttered darkly from the wings. 'That's all we need. As if we haven't got enough to do.'

'The Earl of Hawbridge, hanging upside down like a carcass in a butcher's shop on the stage of Drury Lane theatre. It's going to keep the newspapers busy for weeks,' said Davenport, rubbing at his forehead. 'And if Mr Fielding can't find out who killed him, and bring the killer to justice, then his lordship's friends will ask serious questions in the House about our funding. We'll be under significant scrutiny. As you say, Snowy, this is all we need.'

The whole country would be watching the men of Bow Street.

'Well, what do you think?' He gestured to the corpse with a sigh. 'You've been standing looking at him for long enough.'

I rehearsed my earlier thoughts. He listened, head on one side.

'An execution?'

'Look at what's been done to him,' I said. 'He's been strung up, put on display like the worst sort of criminal. He's been sliced from behind, but I think that must have happened only once he was hanging.'

'Why do you say that?'

'Well, if they killed him on the floor and then lifted him up there would be signs of him being dragged through the blood. I can't see from here – you might be able to if you walk around the back of him – but I would imagine he was knocked on the head and hoisted on the girandole when he was out cold. Otherwise, even if there had been two men, he would have struggled while they tied him, but you can see that his coat is perfectly intact. His cuffs are still in one piece.'

'Snowy, can you open the door on to the street? It would help to have more light. But stand at the door, for God's sake, and deter any onlookers.'

Snowy did as he was bid, and the stage filled with natural light.

Davenport walked around, keeping to the edge of the pool of blood and peered at the back of Hawbridge's wig-less head. His hair was cropped short, meaning that Davenport had good sight of the skin.

'You're right. He's been cracked over the head. There's a bruise and some blood here. Looks bad, but possibly not enough to kill him. I can't be sure without a closer look in better light.'

A dark thought arose in my mind.

'Mr Davenport, do you think he was out cold when they cut his throat, or was he alive?'

'I don't know. Why were you up here so early, on the stage? Really?'

'I was woken by the sounds of the market, as I said. I thought I could poke around, like you asked, see if there were any indications of a campaign against Garrick. There's definitely something going on. I picked that up last night.'

'Did you see anything? Or anyone about, while you were "poking"?'

'Not a soul. I thought I was the only one here. Everyone else must have lodgings of some sort or another – or had gone drinking. I didn't hear anything.'

'You don't sound sure.'

'I'm sure I didn't hear anything, but when I found him, when I screamed...' I tried not to sound embarrassed by my reaction '...Joe Sugden and Molly Bray arrived very quickly.'

'Do you think they were in the building last night?'

I thought for a moment.

'I don't know. Molly would begin early with the mending and stitching, but she wasn't in the room with me last night. Joe Sugden is a stage hand. They are together, I think. Possibly they went to a tavern, and hired a room for some privacy? Molly said that they were going out for a drink. They could have come here just after dawn, to begin work, wherever they went last night.'

'It might be worth checking that,' said Davenport, nodding to Snowy.

'Oh, and Mr Sugden picked up Lord Hawbridge's snuff box from the stage floor. You might want to ask him for it.'

'His snuff box?'

'Yes, it had fallen from a pocket. It was standing in the blood when we arrived. Mr Sugden has it.' I pointed to where the box had stood. It seemed rich to me that Sugden had taken it, having been so quick to mark me as a thief.

We stood, gazing up at the body, taking in the horror of it. He had not simply been killed, stabbed and left for dead, he had been lifted up for us all to see. The killer, or killers, wanted us to see how he had been butchered. There was something vindictive about it – although whether it was the hanged man who was being taunted, or those of us who looked on him, I could not tell.

A large group of people suddenly appeared in the wings, one man pushing through in a state of alarm. It was Mr Garrick.

'No!' His shout might have been thought theatrical, were it not for the fact that his face was genuinely horror-struck.

'My stage!' He threw himself on the boards, gasping with shock, more concerned about the stain on the wood than the body that had caused it, as Sugden had predicted. Other men came in and there were shouts of anger, fear and outrage at the sight. A woman shrieked, and several men began to shoo people back. The magistrate, Mr John Fielding, now up from his bed, was with them. He was an impressive-looking gentleman in an old-fashioned wig and a dark coat. He wasn't old, but he had an air of authority that made him appear so. Blind from his youth, he was supported on an arm by one of his men, Mr Carter.

Under the other arm, he carried his long white cane, which he tapped as he walked.

Leaving Garrick to be supported by friends, Davenport went over to speak with Mr Fielding while I stood, alone, in the blood, listening to them all shouting, crying and wailing at what they saw. The two men spoke quietly: a contrast to the chaos around them. Davenport would be describing in detail what the magistrate was unable to see for himself. When he had finished, the magistrate took charge and began issuing instructions. It appeared that the girandole was going to be lowered at last. In the bustle, Davenport came over to the edge of the blood pond.

'I'm going to help you out of there now, before they lower the body. Are you ready?'

He took a carefully-aimed step into the blood, caught me around the waist and picked me up. I heard the girandole being cranked down, and the shouts as Lord Hawbridge's body thudded softly on the floor into his own blood. I closed my eyes and clung to Davenport, trying not to think of it; the warm scent of his coat was the last thing I was aware of before I passed out.

Chapter Sixteen

'I'm sorry, sorry, so sorry, I'm sorry.' The words tumbled out, a series of conflicting memories and images rattled in my head. Pain and blood. Humiliation and rising panic. My uncle's face. My hand throbbing. Every part of me sore.

I had been set down in a chair in the costume room. The room began to arrange itself slowly into focus. I could see my needle box on the table, the crumbs of an apple pie on a cracked plate. The man standing in front of me, above me, arms folded, frowning a little, was not my uncle.

'What are you sorry for?' said Davenport. 'You fainted. It's nothing to be ashamed of, you've had a shock and, as you said yourself, you're not good with blood.'

I didn't know whether it was the finding of the corpse, the recollection of blood seeping into my shoes, or the terror of a memory that had suddenly come unbidden to my mind that caused me to weep. My right hand was clasped over my left wrist. I could feel the knife scars ridged and hard under my hand, and I knew. Tears began to fall.

Davenport dropped to his knees, putting a hand over mine.

'Bad memory,' I said with a sniff, seeing his concern. 'Sorry.'

He felt in his coat and pulled out a handkerchief.

'It's me that should be apologising. I'm sorry you had to see that,' he said.

I blew my nose. I had not been talking about the hanging.

Before I came to London, before my father threw me out of his house, before I took the squire's son to bed in the vain hope that he would marry me, I had committed a far greater sin. Restless and full of lust I had caught the attention of my uncle, Sir Francis Vessey, a man who was always open to the possibilities of vice. I had thought myself a woman of the world at eighteen but had found my uncle to be vastly superior when it came to playing bedroom games. Terrified by what I had done, I had sought to extract myself, but he had no intention of letting me go, binding me with threats of violence and reminding me of my shame. And then, one day, I summoned the courage to refuse him. He had held me and calmly cut my arm with a knife, slowly and deliberately, until I passed out. He had told the servants that I had been careless with a glass.

The sight of blood now makes me feel faint. Even when it's not mine.

I blew my nose again, in defiance of him and tucked the handkerchief into my sleeve.

'Sorry.'

'You'll want to see to your shoes,' said Davenport. 'They're ruined, of course.'

'I'm sure that there will be spare shoes here. Molly will know where I can find a pair. And stockings,' I said, feeling the dried blood on the soles of my feet. 'What I really need is some water so I can wash, if you don't mind.'

He stood up. 'I'll see what I can do.'

Molly came into the room and, as if she had heard my words, she was carrying a bowl, a jug, a lump of soap and a towel. She grimaced when she saw my shoes, the full horror of their condition illuminated by the morning light streaming in through the window.

Davenport left the room as Molly and I tugged off my shoes and peeled away the stockings, the blood now black and cracking. I soaked and scrubbed at my feet, grateful to find the water was warm, while she rummaged in drawers and cupboards to find shoes that would fit and pulled a pair of stockings from the pile I had darned only yesterday. The bowl of water turned dark red. The activity, unpleasant though it was, stopped me thinking about my uncle.

'What's happened to the corpse, miss?' I asked Molly. 'Is it still on the stage?'

She nodded, wiping a smear of blood from my calf with an old piece of rag. 'Laid out. There's one of the magistrate's men guarding him.'

'That'll be Mr Carter,' said Davenport, returning through the door behind her. 'I've examined the body now, so he's waiting for someone to come and remove it.'

'The magistrate wants anyone who's in the theatre to go to the green room,' she said, looking up at Davenport.

He nodded. 'Then you'd better go. I'll bring the girl up with me when she's put her shoes on.'

Once she'd gone, he took a seat and I gave him a swift account of what I'd seen and heard last night, of Simmot's threats to Garrick, Tom Firmin's fall from the ladder, the candle holders in the girandole, and what I'd seen of the Hunters.

'You've picked up a lot in one day.'

'It's not difficult. This place has more gossip than a bawdy house. Tell me about Lord Hawbridge's injuries.'

He grimaced. 'It's unpleasant. Are you sure you're ready to hear?'

'I'm not going to faint again, I promise.'

Even so, he hesitated. 'He wasn't dead when his throat was cut. The bruises, the location of the wound – they were enough to knock him out, or stun him, but not to kill him outright.'

I had promised not to faint, but the news made me feel mildly dizzy.

'Would he have been conscious when he was cut?' I struggled to get the words out. 'Might he have woken to find himself upside down?'

I saw him swallow. 'I don't know.'

We sat in silence.

'Come on,' he said, standing up and straightening his neck cloth in the mirror, 'we'd better go upstairs. Mr Fielding will want to question you, of course, along with everyone else, but try to stay in the green room and watch how people behave. Listen to what they're whispering, but don't speak of what I've told you. If the person who did this is in the theatre, they will surely give themselves away.'

I wasn't so certain. The death was brutal, but it had a careful and considered aspect to it. Whoever killed him was cold-blooded and devoid of mercy.

–

The green room was quiet and sombre. It was still early – for theatre folk at least – and, apart from Garrick and the servant who had accompanied him, the rest of the gathering was made up of stage hands, Molly, the little girl who lit the fires, and me. The men stood clutching beakers of small beer and muttering under their breath. Molly sat, gazing into thin air, her hands clasped in her lap, saying nothing to Sugden, who was next to her at the table, or to Ketch who was hovering behind her with his monkey asleep in his arms. There were no raised voices, no one was laughing, and the rowdy behaviour of the previous evening was like a dream. Daylight lit the company, and the fire burned merrily in the grate, but the room was dull, cold and still a mess. No one had cleared up.

The magistrate sat at one table, flanked by two of his men, as if he were about to hold a court session. Except that he needed something to eat first. It was impossible, he was declaring loudly, to ask questions on an empty stomach. I stole over to Molly's table, while Davenport went to Mr Fielding. He put a hand on the magistrate's shoulder and mouthed a few quiet words into his ear. Mr Fielding would know that I was present, I was sure of it.

A round-faced and round-bellied man in an apron pushed through the door carrying a tray. The landlord of the Shakespeare tavern next door, I supposed, given that he was accompanied by the small but capable scrap that I had encountered last night. The boy trotted in with three baskets of warm bread rolls, piled one on top of the other, and set one of them down on Mr Fielding's table and the other two on the side table. The landlord had brought a pot of coffee, along with more beer, and bowed a lot to the magistrate. I expected they were familiar with one another. Fielding knew everyone in the area.

Mr Fielding suggested that everyone found themselves some breakfast, while he readied himself to speak with them. Davenport pushed the bread nearer to him and filled up his coffee cup as the hum of conversation began, slowly, to increase. Fielding's other foot soldiers wandered towards the side table for beer. Mr Snow ignored me. The other man was Jack Grimshaw, a mountain of a man, and little more than a thug. I did not like Mr Grimshaw. His size, and the mean look in his eye, had always bothered me. Our paths had crossed before, and I did not wish to build on our acquaintance, even though he, like Snowy and the others, would know that I was acting for Mr Fielding in the theatre. I ducked my head as he passed, suddenly interested in the state of my fingernails. He paused as he reached my chair. It was only the slightest check in his step on the way to the beer jugs, and no one would have noticed it but me, but he wanted me to know that he had marked my presence.

Mr Garrick was attended by his own man and sat apart from the rest of the company. He looked spent. The man who, hours ago, had enthralled a theatre packed to the rafters and who, in this very room, had exuded such charisma that everyone had wanted to be near him, had no life in him now. He looked for all the world like a man who had just lost his entire fortune on a throw of the dice. If ever an actor wished to study how to portray dejection, then he would only need to look at Garrick. His shoulders sagged, his face was ashen and there was no spark in his eyes. His life's work lay in tatters.

Except, of course, the English public being what it is, the murder would draw almost as many people to the theatre as Shakespeare. As a rule, the English public loves scandal, especially when it concerns the nobility. Once the stage had been cleaned and freshly painted and the theatre re-opened, the crowds would flock to point at the girandole. Ladies in the boxes would pretend to swoon and declare to their companions that they saw the shadow of the hanging man cast upon the boards. Lively-minded young gentlemen would leave the theatre discussing not the finer details of the play, nor even the charms of the actresses, but the best method of stringing up a man by his ankles. Garrick, so skilful at satisfying the dramatic tastes of the theatre-going public, could not yet see the potential of this death. He would.

He rubbed his cheeks and pushed his knuckles into his eye sockets. For now, he was concerned, as we all were, only with the horror of what had taken place on his stage in the small hours.

Finally, when the magistrate had eaten and drunk enough, we began another drama as, one by one, we were called to his table.

Garrick's face twitched into life again. He moved to sit with Mr Fielding, as if he too were examining the witnesses. It would, of course, have been thought extraordinary for Garrick to be questioned in front of his stage hands, although I imagined that the magistrate would engage him in private conversation later, when he had composed his wits. For now, Fielding seemed happy enough to have his company. Davenport sat the other side of Fielding taking notes of what was said. Mr Fielding's memory was notoriously good, but he would expect a record to be made. The magistrate's other men seated themselves nearer to the side table, where they could make sure that every person was questioned. They would also be better able to refresh themselves when necessary.

Chapter Seventeen

Mr Dinsdale, as befitted his status as the stage manager, went first. His easy walk to Fielding's table gave no hint of concern. Indeed, the slight swagger suggested that he had no qualms about being questioned.

Dinsdale painted a picture of a well-ordered stage. He had a team of men who were committed – loyal to Garrick and loyal to him. He boasted of this rather loudly, so that every man listening was sure of the line that he should follow when his own time for questioning arrived. It annoyed me that the magistrate was conducting his questions in this way. Far better, surely, to have his men speak with every person privately and then compare the answers? By establishing himself in grand style in the green room, Mr Fielding was imposing – which he liked to be in his own courthouse – but he was also an intimidating person, and this style was unlikely to be conducive to getting at the truth.

I could see that Davenport thought so. He was chewing his lip. His head was down as he wrote out Dinsdale's words, as if it wasn't worth him paying close attention to the man's face or manner. Like me, he would be longing to observe the stage manager when he was not performing to his own audience. He was relying on me, as he said, to notice what was going on away from this ridiculous charade.

'The stage was left clear, as it always is, after the performance,' Dinsdale told the magistrate, nodding to Garrick as he said it. 'I checked it myself once the men had finished.'

'And what does leaving it clear entail?' Mr Fielding asked.

Dinsdale seemed perplexed by the question, as if the answer were obvious.

'Any props left out are removed or replaced ready for the next evening's performance. The audience chairs are tidied and straightened, and the stage is swept. The last thing I do is lower the girandole...' he paused, probably reflecting on how it had been used in the night, '...and extinguish the candles. I carry a small lamp to see myself off the stage.'

Mr Fielding leaned forward a little. 'Do you do this alone? Isn't it heavy? Can the girandole be lowered by one person?'

Dinsdale shrugged. 'It's heavy, but any of my men can raise or lower it.'

Davenport looked up sharply at this.

'Not that any of them would have done such a terrible thing, of course,' Dinsdale added swiftly.

Mr Fielding betrayed nothing of his thoughts. Instead he asked, 'And what about the rest of the theatre? Who clears the audience?'

'We do,' said Dinsdale. 'While the players are in here, enjoying the good company like they do, my men are dealing with the mess that's left behind.' I was certain that neither Dinsdale nor any of his men would want to mingle with gentlemen of quality, but he wanted to make a point to Garrick.

'They're good men,' he said, building on his theme. 'They work hard for little pay and there's not a rogue among them.'

Garrick nodded graciously to Dinsdale and to Mr Fielding. 'And I am always grateful to them all,' he said, unaware of the ripple of irritation that ran around the room near where I was sitting. Gratitude did not satisfy in the way that coin did.

The magistrate, if he picked up the mood, did not show it. Instead he mused, mostly to himself.

'Would it have been possible for someone to have hidden on the stage in the darkness, I wonder? Or in the auditorium? A man might hide on the stage.'

Dinsdale considered this, trying to work out whether his attention to his job was being called into question.

'It's possible,' he said, with some deliberation. 'Yes, it is possible, but I would say it's unlikely. I'm thorough in what I do, sir, very thorough, and none of the company is allowed on the stage once it's cleared, without my permission.' He lifted his chin a fraction. 'But there is no door between the stage and the back corridors,' he went on, as though suddenly struck by a new thought. 'The doors to the street are locked when we close for the night, but anyone could come to the stage from the green room, or the dressing rooms or anywhere else inside the theatre.'

There was no collective intake of breath, but everyone in the room sat up at this insinuation. It was an unwitting comment. Dinsdale looked dismayed as soon as he realised what he had said.

'No,' said Garrick, quietly but firmly. 'No, I cannot believe that this was done by anyone of my company.'

'I didn't mean that, sir,' said Dinsdale, quickly. 'Not one of our own, certainly. But anyone from outside might have come into the green room last night. There's a door to the Shakespeare, for a start.'

'Of course,' Garrick said, clapping a hand to his brow. 'Anyone with access here. Anyone…'

The magistrate straightened his back against the chair and felt for his coffee. Davenport refreshed his cup with a weary expression. He could see, as I could, that Dinsdale's elaboration made, potentially, the whole of London suspect. If a man could wander in from the street to the green room, then he didn't need to be hiding behind the wings. All he need do was mingle in the uproar of the party that took place, drink a pint of ale even, and then make his way to the stage when he saw fit and hide there in the dark until later.

How and why Lord Hawbridge might have gone there to join him, we had no clue.

'Simmot.' Garrick smacked a hand on the table.

'Eh?' Mr Fielding paused with the coffee cup at his lips.

'William Simmot,' said Garrick. 'Of course. It must have been him. He was in last night, as usual.'

Dinsdale grunted, as if in agreement. 'He's a hot-head, that one.'

'Who is William Simmot?' Mr Fielding appealed to his friend, even as Garrick was still striking the table, repeating his name.

'William Simmot is, or at least he likes to think he is, a writer of plays. He writes scandal pieces for newspapers and has all of the literary finesse of the lowest hack.'

Mr Fielding frowned. 'He has reason to butcher the Earl of Hawbridge?'

'No, no. At least, I don't think he has a grudge against Hawbridge. He does though, bear a grudge against me and against this theatre.' Garrick was coming alive again. He was playing to the room as he expanded his theory.

'Simmot threatened me in this very room last night. Indeed, Hawbridge was with me, with two of his friends. We sat *there*,' he pointed to a couch, 'when he insulted me and threatened to ruin this theatre. You'll find many people who will bear witness to that.'

There was a murmur of assent. We had all heard Simmot threaten Garrick and say that he would ruin the theatre. He had thrown his papers at Garrick in full view of everyone.

'Why was he threatening you?' Mr Fielding asked.

Garrick waved a hand in the air. 'It was his plays, Fielding, his terrible plays. They were so ridiculous. I could not accept them.'

'He was threatening you because you disliked his plays?' Davenport laid down his pen, incredulous.

'He was. I refused to buy them. They were dreadful nonsense. He disagreed.'

Davenport shook his head, unable to understand how a disagreement about the worthiness of a play might lead to murder. To Garrick it was clear enough: Simmot had threatened to ruin him and he had murdered a member of the nobility to do it.

Garrick stood, looked out across the company and addressed them. 'You heard him, didn't you? Those of you who were in here during the interval last night?'

'Aye,' voices responded, some quiet, some more certain.

Garrick made an open-handed gesture to Mr Fielding – one that was entirely lost on him. 'There you are, sir. It was Simmot.'

The magistrate was not so sure and began to demur.

Garrick was about to sit again, when he sprang back up in agitation.

'Fielding! It was Simmot, I tell you. His play, the last one he sent.' Now he was shaking. This, I thought, was real emotion, rather than the studied display we had just witnessed.

'What about it?'

'It had a hanging. It was ghoulish, I told him so. Utterly ghoulish. But there was a hanging in it – and the man was hanged *upside down*.'

Dinsdale thumped the table. 'That settles it for me, sir,' he said. 'A play with a man hanged upside down. That's what he did to Lord Hawbridge.'

Molly, at our table, was convinced too. 'It's got to be him,' she said, leaning close to me. 'Why write such a thing in the first place? And then to do it – it's dreadful.'

Sugden agreed. 'It must be Simmot. Anyone can see that.'

But the one man who couldn't see, didn't quite see it. Mr Fielding appealed for calm in the room.

'Garrick, I will need you to find this play of Simmot's. And I will speak with Mr Simmot as soon as he can be found, but we must do this in order.' He took control once more as his theatrical friend sank back into his chair, exhausted by his performance. 'Mr Snow, would you be kind enough to find this William Simmot? I think we should hear what he has to say for himself.' Snowy drained his pot and stood to leave. 'In the meantime,' said Mr Fielding, 'we will continue with questions to the company.'

Garrick begged to be excused. He needed to make arrangements, write to patrons, tell them what had happened.

Mr Fielding turned to his friend, gave him a kind smile, patted his hand and sent him away to be alone with his thoughts and his pen. The rest of us were afforded no such luxury.

Chapter Eighteen

The theatre's most charismatic member had left the room, but we were still gripped by the drama. Everyone was talking about Simmot. Everyone, it seemed, had known all along how it must be him. He was a disappointed man, a failure, casting around for someone to blame when his work was not well received. Spurned by the most influential man in theatre, he had wreaked a dreadful revenge, based on a scene from his own lamentable play. Even as Mr Fielding called each member forward in order of seniority and rank, and exchanged words with them, they muttered and chattered. Sugden, I noted, at a word from Davenport, drew the snuff box from his pocket and presented it to Mr Fielding. He had wanted to keep it clean for the magistrate, he said, rather than see it kicked over the stage, or lost, when everyone turned up.

Molly was certain it had to be Simmot so Ketch naturally agreed, as did Sugden. Each of them said so to the magistrate, even as they answered his questions about where they had been and what they had seen when Hawbridge was killed.

I said nothing, but nodded every now and then as if in agreement. It was convenient that a man they all disliked had written about a macabre hanging in his play. No one imagined that this was anything but a slight against Garrick.

'Lizzie Blunt.' Davenport eventually called my name. I was nearly the last, being almost the lowliest of the theatre's servants. I saw him touch Mr Fielding lightly on the wrist – a silent reminder that he was interviewing his own spy.

There was enough noise in the green room for us to speak seriously, and no one would pay attention to my account, but Mr Fielding knew, as did I, that a lengthy conversation with the second seamstress would excite attention. We had to maintain our roles for now.

'The girl's been here for only a day, sir,' Davenport reminded him of the story as I sat down. 'She's here thanks to your leniency and generosity. You'll recall she was last before you for stealing bread.' He was enjoying this play-acting more than I cared for.

A hint of a smile crossed Mr Fielding's lips. 'Ah yes, I remember. How are you finding the work, Lizzie?'

'The sewing is not difficult, sir,' I lowered my voice a little. 'The green room is much like a brothel, so I'm right at home, but I find that I do not enjoy discovering dead bodies or standing in pools of blood.'

'Ah. You found Lord Hawbridge. Mr Davenport told me. I am sorry for that.'

I shrugged. 'It was better me than one of the young maids, sir. Although I did cry out when I saw it.'

'I don't doubt it. Tell me,' he leaned forward a little, 'what do you make of this business with Simmot? Did you see him threaten Garrick last night?'

'I did, sir. He was very loud about it. But,' I kept my voice soft, 'it seems to me that everyone here has got it all wrong.'

'Meaning?'

'Well, they're all convinced Simmot is guilty, but no one has asked about Lord Hawbridge at all and why it was him that was murdered.'

He smiled. 'Not yet, I haven't.'

'I didn't mean you, Mr Fielding. I know you'll be asking about him. I mean everyone here. They're so concerned about the theatre, and how this murder is an affront to Garrick, they've lost sight of the dead man.'

'You, on the other hand, Miss Blunt, have no loyalty to Garrick as yet, having been here for only a day. So, what do you recall of Lord Hawbridge, if you saw him at all?'

'Oh, I knew Lord Hawbridge.'

Davenport dropped his pen. I tried not to smirk.

'Knew him? From Mrs Farley's establishment, I presume,' said Mr Fielding.

'No sir. He was a friend of my father's.'

Davenport picked up his pen but decided not to write notes.

'He visited my father some years ago. They had been at school together, and he was passing through the area. He stayed for a week or two.'

'But you remembered him when you saw him at the theatre?'

'I once watched him nearly beat a boy to death. That sort of thing sticks in the memory.' I told him what I had seen from behind the stable door, and how the brutality of if had horrified me.

'Did he see you in the theatre? Recognise you?'

'He would have no reason to expect Edward Vessey's daughter in a London theatre,' I said carefully.

'And I suppose your paths were unlikely to cross here, an earl and a girl from the dressing rooms.'

'No sir.'

I decided not to tell him what had happened when they had crossed, in case he thought it gave me a motive for murder.

'But I watched him. I was carrying a wine jug about and saw him with his friends, Mr Astley and Mr Callow, and the actresses that they were sitting with.'

'How did he appear to you, when he was in the green room?'

'A man who knew his own status and who expected attention. A man of wealth, given the styling of his coat and the jewels he wore.'

'We have his snuff box,' Davenport said. He looked down at his notes. 'Joseph Sugden, the assistant stage manager, handed it to us when he came to be questioned. He says it was on the stage under the body; that it had fallen from Lord Hawbridge's pocket.' He pulled it from his own pocket and laid it on the table. 'It's a very fine piece.'

'I'm glad you asked him for it. I thought he might pawn it.'

'Why would he pawn it?'

'He's spent the last day grumbling about how Garrick doesn't always pay the staff. You'll have caught that from Mr Dinsdale's comments – and from several of the others.' I gestured to the little box in front of me. 'But that is, as you say, a very fine snuff box. Lord Hawbridge made use of it last night. Open it.'

He flicked the catch and the lid popped up, the peacock tail displaying itself.

He gave a short laugh and then described the movement to Mr Fielding.

'So, not only a man given to outbursts of violence, but also one who liked to display his wealth and status,' said the magistrate. 'Who was with him did you say?'

'Two friends. A Mr Astley, who is a man of similar age, and a younger man, Mr Callow. They spoke with others, of course, and Garrick was with them when Mr Simmot made his threats, but they were, I think, a group of three.'

Mr Fielding looked thoughtful. 'I suppose I'd better let you go. But… is there anything else you can tell me?'

'Mr Davenport will share what I told him earlier about the breakages and accidents,' I said. 'And there's a lot of gossip about Lord Hawbridge, Mr Astley and one of the actresses here.'

He cocked his head. 'Really? Which one?'

Old goat. Everyone loves a bit of scandal, even him.

'Lucy Hunter. She's very pretty – in an affected sort of way. Her husband has thrown her in the direction of Mr Astley. I understand that this is how they work together. She's not much of an actress, but she's attracting wealthy patrons. Last night she was flirting with Lord Hawbridge. Molly says George Hunter put her up to it.'

'Molly? That's the head seamstress?'

'Yes sir. She thinks Hunter has set his sights on a bigger prize than Mr Astley.'

'Interesting. I wonder whether there was bad blood between Astley and Hawbridge as a result. Keep watching. Come to us at Bow Street if you discover anything more.' He rubbed his nose and then spoke a little louder. 'Very well. Thank you, Lizzie. You'd better return to your mending now. I am grateful for your cooperation.'

I stood up, dropped him a curtsey and skipped back to Molly, as Davenport called the little maid forward. She, the last and the lowliest of all of us, looked as though she'd been summoned to the gallows.

'How was he?' Molly asked as I sank into a chair.

'He's mighty terrifying,' I said. 'I was almost as frightened of him as I was in the courthouse. But he was kind to me when I told him about finding the...'

She patted my hand. 'Don't think about it.'

'I try not, miss.'

Joe Sugden narrowed his eyes. 'You were with him a long time. What was he asking you?'

I was tempted to invite him to mind his own business. 'He asked me how I was getting on here, and how I was liking the work. It was, after all, due to his mercy that I came here. Then he asked about the body. I told him all about that. The man with him, Mr Davenport, he showed me the snuff box – the one you picked up off the floor.'

Molly stared at him. 'You didn't tell me you found a snuff box.'

Sugden threw me a mean look.

'It was on the boards, Moll, underneath the corpse. Fell out his pocket, I'd say. I picked it up and handed it to the magistrate when he was asking questions.'

'What sort of box?' Ketch leaned across the table to hear better. 'A snuff box?'

'Aye,' Sugden said. 'A fancy piece with pearl and gold peacock feathers all over it. Must be worth a fortune.'

'Peacock feathers, you say?' Ketch's eyebrows raised at this. 'That is fancy. One of a kind, even.'

'You did the right thing, Joe Sugden,' said Molly, cutting across Ketch. 'Even if it was worth a fortune, you were right to hand it over.'

'I would always do the right thing, you know that, Molly. Stealing's a sin against God.' His lip curled. 'And they knew I had it.'

Molly stood up. 'Do you think we can go if we've been seen? We might not be opening tonight, but there's still work to be done.'

'You're right about that,' said Sugden. 'Dinsdale will want us back in the hell soon.'

'Hell?' They all looked at me. Then, realising that I had no idea what they meant, they began to laugh. It was a relief of sorts, to hear laughter, even if it was at my expense.

'Hell, when it's not the home of tormented souls, is what we call the trap room,' Molly said.

I was still confused.

She went on. 'The trap room? It's under the stage. Under the stage,' she said patiently, 'there's a space where actors wait to be sprung up on the boards. Sometimes a play calls for a character to appear all of a sudden. Rather than fly on through the wings, they pop up from under the stage, by a trap door. There are a number of trap doors over the boards, if you know where to look. And under the stage there are pulleys and hoists and springs that help them emerge like magic.'

I was impressed by this. It had not occurred to me that such mechanics might exist. Or that there was a room under the stage at all. I wondered why Dinsdale had not thought to mention it to Mr Fielding.

'But why is it called hell?'

She shrugged. 'I would have thought it was obvious. It's under the stage, under the earth.'

'It's where we store some of the scenery flats,' said Sugden, dismissive, and still scowling at me. 'It's just a room.'

'I'm sorry, sir,' I said. 'It's just with the dead body and all that blood, it made me all shaky again to think of hell.'

'Come on, Lizzie,' said Molly wrapping an arm around me. 'The best cure for a shock is hard work. I can offer you plenty downstairs.'

But even better than hard work, of course, is entertainment. And, just as we were about to leave the green room, the entertainment arrived in the form of the players.

Now, the real fun was about to begin.

Chapter Nineteen

In so far as any man with a walking stick could make a dramatic entrance, George Hunter was that man. His wife trailed in his wake, carrying, of all things, a small, floppy-eared spaniel. Behind her came Kitty Suckley, with Peg West, Nan Collyer, and a handful of men and women whom Molly helpfully pointed out by name – as we sat back down to watch the show.

Dinsdale sent a lad scurrying to find the manager – although whether Garrick's presence would calm things down or enhance the inevitable drama was uncertain. The players had been appraised of the murder. Someone had been sent to give word and the news had travelled among them. It was still far too early, as Molly said, for them to be arriving for rehearsals. But they had been given enough time to compose themselves and decide how they would respond to the death. Whereas the stage hands, called upon to lower the dead man to the ground and mop up his blood, had reacted spontaneously – with unmitigated horror and, in the case of one poor lad, a lot of vomit – these people had enjoyed an hour or two to dress, converse and prepare themselves while Mr Fielding had eaten breakfast and questioned the rest of us. The players had chosen to arrive together.

George Hunter was their leader, and he carried himself like a man who had been born to the stage. He had an air of one who still needed – craved – an audience. The stick had become a theatrical prop, but his heavy frame contained a violent energy that simmered under the guise of flamboyance.

'Garrick!' he roared his entrance to the theatre manager, now returned to the green room. 'What's all this, dear man? Who's dead? What's happened?'

Garrick, still with a pen in his hand, ran to his friend and nearly fell on him.

'George, George, it's such a dreadful thing. I'm ruined, I'm damn near certain of it.'

Now Lucy Hunter came upon the touching scene. She meant to lay her hand gently on Garrick's arm, creating a charming tableau with her husband to be seen by the company, but she had forgotten about the dog in her arms. The creature, which fell to the floor, howled at the indignity, shook itself, cocked a leg in defiance of the world and watered a table leg.

Mrs Hunter began to scold the dog – for doing what had come naturally – and then to fuss him and fondle his ears. She picked him up so that Garrick, who hadn't noticed the pool of piss getting closer to his feet, could inspect him. The dog, Garrick was informed, was a gift from an admirer. She told him this in quiet tones that were just loud enough for us all to hear, although the intended audience was undoubtedly Kitty Suckley. Miss Suckley smiled so benignly that it was certain she was furious. Mr Astley had sent the dog to Lucy.

George Hunter, like his wife, knew very well who had died – and how. He asked for information, all the same. Garrick was about to give him a full, and probably very lurid account of the morning's discovery, when he was interrupted by the magistrate.

'My dear Garrick, please be so good as to calm down. Ladies, gentlemen, kindly seat yourselves and find some refreshment while I continue to ask my questions. A man, a nobleman, is dead, and it is my intention to discover who killed him.'

The sound of shock, distress, annoyance filled the green room as the players did as they were bidden. Most of them ambled to the side table and helped themselves to drink. Lucy Hunter's dog, set on the floor again, began to snuffle at the floor, looking for crumbs. I saw Kitty jolt Lucy's arm and then apologise profusely when the wine slopped over her glass. The two women smiled graciously at one another, but the air between them was poisonous.

Davenport moved about them, adding names to his list, before taking his place next to Mr Fielding and calling them forward – as he had with the stage hands and servants. Molly, I was glad to see, was as keen to watch the performance as I was, rather than hide away in the dressing room darning more stockings. She sent Sugden over to the table to find more food for us. The landlord of the Shakespeare, alert to the news from the theatre, had replenished the table with heartier fare. Sugden returned with a large plate piled with bread rolls, still warm, as well as slices of ham and beef and a mound of cheese. Molly sent him back to the table for a thick wedge of pie, and when he returned a third time at her bidding for a jug of beer and four pots, I knew that we were settling down to watch the drama unfold.

The players were, sadly, disappointing. Most of them had spent the hours after the performance firstly in the green room and then in the Shakespeare tavern next door, or else the Rose, or other places further afield. Not all of them could recall who it was they spent the rest of the night in bed with – some even claimed they had gone to bed alone. Most of them had lodgings in the Drury Lane area. Most of them could account for the movements, or likely movements, of everyone else in the company. Most of them, as with the stage hands, laid the blame at the door of William Simmot, whom they had all heard berating and threatening Mr Garrick.

Kitty Suckley was wearing the same yellow gown as the previous evening – and even the same jewels. I knew, because I had dressed her after the performance. This could only mean that she had spent the night somewhere other than her own lodgings. I could not judge her for that.

I watched Lucy Hunter's performance with more interest. It was she, after all, who had kept Lord Hawbridge company on the couch and she who, according to Molly, was intending to become his mistress. At the same time, I kept an eye on her husband, who was affecting nonchalance, glass in hand, to hide his agitation as his wife answered Fielding's questions. She was calm, offering gentle smiles to Fielding and to Davenport and speaking in a pleasant, unhurried tone. Yes, she had been devastated to hear that it was Lord Hawbridge who was dead. She had made his acquaintance only last night when they had been introduced by Mr Astley. She had enjoyed a short time in his company and found him charming and engaging.

I had found him rude, violent and presumptuous, but then, I was not the star of the theatre.

Mr Fielding, who had learned from me that her husband was pushing her in Hawbridge's direction, was delicate, almost deferential in his questions. It was not as if she were of noble birth, nor even a decent gentlewoman, so this surprised me. He was usually more direct. He enquired how she had spent the evening after the play, and she said that she and her husband had gone directly to their lodgings.

'I was tired, you know,' she said with a little sigh. 'Cordelia always takes it out of me. It's an exhausting part to play, such a drain on the gentler feelings.' She gave Davenport another smile. He returned it and, ridiculously, this appeared to be a genuine response. Another man captivated by her beauty and soft voice.

He took her hand and helped her up from her seat – he had afforded the second seamstress no such courtesy – and led her back to her husband. Again, I watched Hunter and noticed how he reacted. The arm around her shoulders was genuine enough, but his manner towards her suggested that he was applauding a performance, rather than comforting her distress.

Mr Hunter's own account of the previous evening chimed, unsurprisingly, with his wife's. He added very little of note, except that he was aware of the on-going disagreement with Simmot and had witnessed the playwright's explosion of fury. He had not, himself, read any of Simmot's plays, but trusted the good judgement of his dear friend, Mr Garrick. If Garrick thought they were unworkable, then they could not be produced.

Davenport asked him how he had known Lord Hawbridge. Hunter said, as his wife had done, that he had briefly made his acquaintance last night.

Davenport, cutting across Mr Fielding a second time, asked about his acquaintance with Mr Astley.

There was a ripple of sound around the green room as we all leaned forward to catch his reply.

'Mr Astley is an acknowledged man of good taste and discernment,' Hunter said, with a casual air. 'He is a friend to my wife and to me. I think that I can call such a gentleman a friend, when he has done so much to support us – my wife in her career and me…' he gestured to his leg '…in my enforced retirement.'

Davenport explained Mr Hunter's situation to Mr Fielding.

'How did you come about your injury, Mr Hunter?' the magistrate asked.

Hunter cleared his throat. 'An accident, sir. A foolish quarrel and my temper got the better of me. I was lucky only to lose my livelihood and not my life as a result.'

He was not going to say any more. He twisted the ruby on his finger.

Fielding nodded thoughtfully. 'And you left Mr Rich's company and moved here with your wife.'

Hunter, who hadn't mentioned John Rich, gave a little start. Fielding had known of the story already. For some reason he had decided to rattle the husband rather than the wife. Perhaps, like some of us, he found the misuse of Mrs Hunter objectionable. Perhaps he detected a tone in Hunter's voice of a man who thought that he was above the law. I knew that the magistrate had little time for men such as that.

Hunter's response, though, was lost to us.

A tall footman in bright blue livery strode up to Mr Fielding, bowed to him and to Garrick and quietly informed them that Mr Astley and Mr Callow had arrived. They had come, it seemed, to remove their friend's body. They had brought undertakers with them. As if this were not enough, the footman also informed the magistrate's table that the Countess of Hawbridge was outside, in her coach. He tried hard not to say it, but it appeared that the widow had insisted on visiting the theatre. An excited whisper ran around the room.

Mr Fielding was not happy to learn of her presence, judging by the look on his face.

Davenport moved to greet Mr Astley and Mr Callow, and then drew the two gentlemen to Mr Fielding's table. He explained in a low voice that the earl's body was still on the stage and guarded by one of the magistrate's men. In the meantime, he hoped that they would assist with Mr Fielding's questions, so that Lord Hawbridge's movements that night could be understood.

They readily consented.

Fielding began comfortably enough, by asking about the play, how they had come to see it, and how they had found it.

Astley, the older of the two, took the lead in answering.

'I'm often here,' he said. 'To my mind, there are few events finer than a Shakespeare play as performed by Mr Garrick and his company.'

Garrick inclined his head in acknowledgement at this.

'It was my idea to invite Lord Hawbridge,' Astley went on. 'Thought he might enjoy the evening…' his voice drifted a little as if he only now realised how Hawbridge's evening had ended.

'Was he enjoying it, sir?' Mr Fielding asked. 'How did he appear to you?'

Astley shrugged. 'He was exactly as he usually is: good and affable company and, by and large, the centre of attention. Except,' he added, with a look at Garrick, 'when we were in the audience, of course. There, even greater lights shine.'

'Had you known one another for a long time?' Davenport asked.

Astley sat a little taller in his seat. 'I've known him since boyhood. We were at school together, and then Oxford.'

'You would count yourself as a friend, then?'

'Of course I was a friend,' Astley said, testily, looking down his large beak of a nose at Davenport. 'Else why would I still be in his company after these years?'

Davenport said nothing more but wrote something on his paper. He might have been reflecting, as I was, that people may keep company with one another for years, without any bond of true friendship. And here was another man who my own father would know. It was a pity that he was no longer speaking to me. If I had been able to call on him, he might have made a useful witness to the relationship between Astley and Hawbridge.

'And you, sir,' Fielding directed his unseeing eyes in Mr Callow's direction, 'were you so long acquainted with Lord Hawbridge?'

Callow gave a wan little smile. What Mr Fielding could not see was the evident youth of his witness.

'No sir, I am only lately in his lordship's circle. I am a family friend of the Countess of Hawbridge, being distantly related to her.'

Mr Fielding, hearing the younger, chattering tone in Callow's voice, nodded, now comprehending.

'But you were invited to the theatre by Lord Hawbridge? Or did you happen to be here last night by yourself?'

'Lord Hawbridge asked for my company. Astley had invited him, and I joined the party.'

'And would you agree with Mr Astley, that Lord Hawbridge was in his usual mood?'

Callow cocked his head to one side. 'He was as he always is: charming to the ladies, and at ease with the gentlemen.'

Neither of them liked Hawbridge. The answers were too polite and bland. Perhaps they had been on the receiving end of his temper at some point.

The magistrate was keen to press on. He turned back to Astley.

'Mr Astley, can you tell me what happened at the end of the performance? Where did Lord Hawbridge go, and with whom?'

There was a pause. Around the room, there was a sense of expectation. Was this the moment when we discovered that the earl had spent the night with Mrs Hunter, or had she returned home with her husband, as she had already said?

Astley cleared his throat. 'I am of little use to you, I'm afraid, Mr Fielding. I decided to return home before the after-piece began.'

'You went home before the second play?'

'Yes. I came to see *King Lear* and I did not care for *Love's Expense*. I left Hawbridge and Callow here at the theatre. My servants will tell you what time I arrived home, but it wasn't late.'

Fielding nodded to Callow. 'You remained here with Lord Hawbridge for the after-piece?'

'I did. I didn't care for it either, but Hawbridge wanted to see it. The galleries loved it, of course. That sort of thing appeals to the late-comers.'

'And after *Love's Expense*?'

'We parted. I went to the Rose with him, at first, but the food is unpleasant there, so I took a chair to the Bedford Head on Southampton Street.'

Fielding smiled. 'It is still the better place to eat, then? You were alone?'

There was a brief hesitation. Fielding caught the whiff of discomfort and guessed at its probable cause. He decided not to press the point. Callow had picked up a girl somewhere near to the Bedford Head tavern, if he had taken a chair alone. I imagined that the girls at the Bedford were of better quality than the girls at the Rose – just like the food.

'Do you know what happened to Lord Hawbridge when you parted?'

There was another hesitation. 'We were certainly at the Rose together, as I say. That's where Hawbridge wanted to go. But he found different company. I decided to leave, giving word to one of the tavern girls to tell him I'd gone.'

'You left him at the Rose?'

'Yes. He was alive and in good spirits the last time I saw him.'

Davenport cut across again. 'Did he tell you of his intentions for the remainder of the evening?'

Callow fidgeted. 'I had the impression he was planning to meet someone, but he didn't say whom.'

'A woman?'

'He didn't say. And it really was just an impression.'

We didn't hear any more about Lord Hawbridge's intentions.

His wife had arrived.

The Countess of Hawbridge was veiled and in black and accompanied by her maid as well as a male servant. As she came through the door, all eyes turned to her. I saw her brace herself slightly, readying her spirit for the inevitable scrutiny of dozens of eyes.

Garrick and Davenport leaped to their feet. Garrick flew to her and there was a great deal of fussing – from him, but not from her. Once the magistrate knew what was happening, he too sought out the widow. The three men gathered around her, like a trinity of protective fathers.

She had come to claim her husband from the rabble of players and whores with whom he had chosen to spend his final hours. This was brave. No one expected a noble widow to venture out in public so soon. She would usually mourn in private while others dealt with matters on her behalf. It would have been her decision to come. Watching Callow and Astley, I thought that she was acting against their advice. That, in itself, was remarkable.

As if suddenly seeing us for the first time, the dissolute and vice-ridden lot we surely were, she raised a small white handkerchief to her lips, her courage failing for a second. I felt a pang of sympathy for her; now confronting, in public, an aspect of her husband's life that she might have ignored.

Discreetly, the undertakers slipped into the room behind her, and made their way to where the dead man lay, accompanied by Dinsdale, Sugden and another of the stage hands. Mr Astley, now also at her side, guided the Countess of Hawbridge as she stepped unsteadily towards the chair that had been pulled for her and sat down. A glass of wine was brought, but she waved it away.

'Don't fuss. Please don't fuss. I am quite in possession of my senses,' she said to her protectors. 'I needed to come. To be here. To see where it was that he…' her voice drifted a little, but only because she was considering how best to phrase her intention. 'I wished to see where my husband died.'

She lifted the veil and looked again around the room at us. We, in our turn, looked at her. I had expected her to be a mouse. Old, perhaps, or at least beyond her glorious years. I imagined that the Earl of Hawbridge, who dangled after actresses – and tried to screw second seamstresses against tables – would have been married to a plain but dutiful wife. Lady Hawbridge was anything but plain. She was dazzling; and all the more so for her grief.

The heavy black lace veil had hidden a lovely face. She was younger than the earl. If he was as old as my father, then his wife was easily thirty years his junior. A second marriage, then, for I knew he had grown up sons. Her face was unlined, the little flush of colour on her cheeks brought about from being gazed upon added a delicate pink to the creamy skin. A halo of blonde curls made her look like a heavenly being. She was, in everyone's estimation, a beauty.

Ketch, still between me and Molly, gave a soft sigh. Davenport, I noticed with irritation, was smiling at her. I imagined that he was sighing too.

She put a small white hand out towards Mr Fielding, touching him on the wrist. 'Thank you, sir, for all that you are doing to bring his murderer to justice.' Her voice was clipped, crisp. 'I am truly grateful to you.'

Mr Fielding cocked his head. He could not see her face, but I knew that he would be taking in her voice, her scent and the reaction of the room. He would know that she was beautiful. He would also know that even though she was young, she was a lady of rank and confidence. She had strength, too, to come here.

'Lady Hawbridge, your courage at coming here is exemplary,' he said, echoing my thought. 'Your presence has, I know, touched us all. Please accept not only my condolences, but my firm pledge to find your husband's murderer as soon as I can.'

Garrick murmured something to the same effect and she nodded stiffly to him, as well as to the magistrate.

The footman drew close and spoke to Mr Astley. He, in turn, bent to Lady Hawbridge and said something to her that we were not privy to hear. She nodded and gave him her hand as she stood.

'Mr Fielding, my dear friend advises me that my husband has been carried from the stage.' She raised the lace handkerchief to her nose again, as if fending off the stench of death. 'We shall take him home and make arrangements for the burial.'

'Of course, my lady.'

Mr Fielding would not ask her whether she had known of her husband's plans for the previous evening – not in public, certainly. If Lord Hawbridge had told her that he was visiting the theatre, I doubted that he would have shared his intentions for the remainder of the night – gaming house, brothel, mistress. It was hardly the sort of thing one discussed over the breakfast table. Even so, she might have guessed.

She pulled down the veil once more as Mr Astley offered her his arm. Nothing more was said as the party left the building, the countess leaning on Mr Astley as she went. Mr Callow, blushing and boyish, fell in behind them.

We had learned little from her about her husband, or what she felt for him. Lady Hawbridge would have been bred to contain her emotions. I doubted, having encountered him, that she could have held much fondness for him, but his death was a shocking one. There would be a scandal, shouted of in the press, and – worse – talked of behind hands and fans in drawing rooms and ballrooms up and down the country. The beautiful Lady Hawbridge was calm enough, but she would forever be marked as the woman whose husband was butchered in a theatre.

My memories of the noble families I had encountered in my childhood told me just how vicious people of quality could be to one another. She was arming herself with the story she would tell to counter her critics. I was truly sorry for her, not for what was past, but for what was yet to come.

Mr Fielding's work appeared to be complete for the day. Davenport, looking weary, began to fold his papers and pack away his ink pot and quills. The conversation began to swell once more in the room until Garrick banged on the table and called for attention.

'Friends, Mr Fielding thanks you for your time and your willingness to give your account of the dreadful events of last night. I too am grateful. Mr Fielding's men are, even now, searching for William Simmot, whom we know has threatened this theatre with violence. I will not rest until they find him. We will close the theatre this evening – I know, I know, but the stage is in need of repainting,' this to cries of 'no' from the players. 'Tomorrow is Sunday, so we have two days for repairs. We will open as usual on Monday evening. I will not be cowed or beaten.'

At this the company, stage hands as well, gave a cheer.

'The season is coming to a close. A few more weeks and we will break for the summer. We will not allow Simmot to threaten us. We will act, and act in defiance.'

Another cheer. Like Henry V rousing his troops, Garrick was stirring his company out of their fear and into bravery – even if they were not quite storming the walls of Harfleur.

Fielding clapped him on the back, to quieten him rather than to encourage him.

'Garrick, my friend, I shall hear Mr Simmot's account when he's found. I promise to keep you informed.'

Davenport gave the magistrate an arm to help him find his way around the tables, until he could walk aided only by his long cane.

It was still not yet noon, according to the clock on the wall, but we were all exhausted by the events of the morning. Dinsdale and Sugden, who had accompanied the undertakers, were talking to the stage hands, no doubt sharing their observations.

'What did you make of all that, miss?' I asked Molly.

'Well, I agree with everyone here, I expect,' she said. 'It must be something to do with Simmot. That thing about his play having a hanging…'

'What about that Mr Callow?' I asked. 'Mr Fielding should have pressed him further, I think. He wouldn't say who he was with in the Bedford Head. It might have been him who killed the earl.'

She laughed. 'Mr Fielding didn't press him because he's a gentleman, Lizzie, and his friend's death has nothing to do with him. It was clear enough that he was with a harlot, and he would rather not admit it in public.'

'But will the girl say that he was in the Bedford Head?'

She snorted. 'You think Mr Callow needs to account for his whereabouts? Girls like that will say anything if you pay them. Besides,' she leaned in, 'I might tell the magistrate myself, but I saw Mr Callow in Southampton Street, I'm almost sure of it.'

I stared at her. 'Really?'

She nodded, squinting as she remembered. 'Joe and I went out that way. Mr Callow's not the only one who finds the Rose too noisy. I wanted something a bit more refined as well.'

I hardly thought Southampton Street refined, but then, I live in Soho. I said nothing.

'He was wearing a bright green coat last night, wasn't he? Lighter than Mr Astley's. I liked the look of it and, when we were near to the Bedford, I swear I saw him in there.'

'And was he with a girl?'

She pulled a face. 'I can't say. I didn't notice. I just saw the coat.' She shrugged. 'Comes of seeing clothes and costumes all day, I expect. I recognise what people are wearing more than I see what they're doing.' She laughed at this, then she put a hand to my shoulder.

'Speaking of clothes, there's work to do, Lizzie.'

I tried not to sigh too heavily. There was nothing I wanted less than to mend clothes. 'I'm tired, miss.' I wasn't tired at all; I was frustrated.

She gave a half-smile. 'We're all tired. But you have, I suppose, had the worst shock of all of us. I'll tell you what,' she stood up to leave, 'we'll work until the middle of the afternoon and then we can rest. Lie down in the costume room and have a sleep – it'll be quiet enough. As Mr Garrick says, we've two days before we open again.'

I gave her the most grateful smile I could.

I wanted to be out of the theatre. If Mr Fielding was content simply to wait for William Simmot to tell his story, then I was not. I wanted to know more about Mr Astley and Mr Callow, and what they had been doing while their friend was being hung upside down. I was not going to find out by stitching. I could not, of course, wander over to visit Lady Hawbridge in whichever charming street or square was her London home. I could no more visit the gentlemen themselves, certainly not when I was dressed as a second seamstress in a gown that looked like mud.

I would go to the one place where I could be sure of information about gentlemen of fashion and consequence.

I would go home to Berwick Street.

Chapter Twenty

I slipped out of the theatre unseen. Molly had left me dozing in the costume room, so she thought, but I had sneaked out of the back door as soon as she had gone to find Sugden and Ketch. None of them could know where I was going.

The tall, dark-skinned doorman at Mrs Farley's decided not to recognise me. Foolishly, I had gone to the main entrance rather than to the kitchen at the back of the house. Habit took me up the four steps, to the large black door. I smiled, as I always did, at the sign proclaiming that we were milliners – a nod to a respectable life that fooled no one. Anyone who came to this door knew what we were selling – and bonnets played a very small part in our trade. But usually I skipped up the steps in a fine gown and an elegant cloak, with my copper curls piled high and a hat threaded with silk ribbon. Today, I looked like a street walker down on her luck.

'Sydney, don't be foolish. It's me, Lizzie.'

Sydney peered at me in the condescending way that only he can manage. Sydney came to London from France with Ma. Having worked with her in the finest brothels of Paris, he is always immaculately dressed, and strongly disapproves of anyone who does not meet his standards. He has been known to send me back inside if a cuff or a ruffle is in need of mending.

'Miss Hardwicke?'

'Exactly. Let me in.'

His mouth began to form a thousand questions. He had not been party to dressing me as a seamstress – it would have distressed this elegant creature to let me out of the house in such a state.

I pushed past him before he could stop me and made my way to the back parlour.

It was not a busy hour of the day, and even before I opened the door, I could hear Lucy and Emily having an argument. Ah, the sweet sound of home.

My entrance settled whatever the dispute was about. However much they rubbed each other the wrong way, they were united in their delight at seeing me looking so dreadful.

'Lizzie! How well you look,' Lucy cooed. 'That colour really suits you.'

'Shut up, Lucy, and pour me some tea.' I sat down, not before smacking her gently across the back of her head. 'I'm worn out.'

'You've been working the Strand?' Emily asked, a nasty sneer on her lips.

I threw her my most evil look.

'There was a murder. At the theatre.'

That quietened them.

'Death tends to follow you around, darling,' said Lucy, pausing with the teapot. 'I'm beginning to think Ma should throw you out as bad luck.'

Emily sniggered. 'Did you tup this one as well?' A previous customer of mine had been murdered. It was a heartless comment and typical of Emily to ask it. Especially as, after a fashion, I had only just avoided it.

'I found the body.'

'You found the body?' Lucy repeated.

'Hanging from that large chandelier over the stage. Upside down, with his throat cut. There was a lot of blood.'

They said nothing. There was nothing to say. Lucy poured my tea in silence. Both of them looked appalled.

'I'm not surprised you've come home,' said Lucy in a quiet voice. 'You should never have let Mr Davenport persuade you to go. Your face looks battered and you're covered in dirt. You belong here.'

I beamed at her, ignoring the pain this caused to my cheek. 'Right where the two of you can make my life hell. It's the place I choose to call home.' I took a large mouthful of tea. It was good to be drinking something that had a taste to it. Ma always has the best that money can buy. Emily pushed a plate of sweetmeats towards me, in a fit of uncharacteristic generosity. I didn't hesitate and helped myself to the largest confection.

'I came home,' I said, mouth full of sugar, 'to seek your advice, as it happens.'

'Mine?' Lucy sat back. 'Or Emily's?'

'Both. I want some information and I know the two of you have all the best gossip.'

Both girls prided themselves of being bearers of news.

'Two very high-born gentlemen. One is Mr Astley and the other a Mr Callow. Astley's older, a man in his fifties. Callow is, I think, nearer twenty-five or thirty.'

Emily shook her head. 'Neither of them has been to me. Not using those names, at least. They don't always, of course. What are they to the dead man?'

'They were with him at the theatre last night,' I said, reaching for another candied fruit. 'The dead man was the Earl of Hawbridge. He was the same age as Astley, in his fifties. They were sitting together for the performance and drinking with Mr Garrick in the interval.'

Lucy was looking thoughtful.

'Mr Astley? The one who's taken up with one of the actresses at Drury Lane? What's her name? Lydia? No, Lucy Hunter.'

'That's the one.'

'I've not seen him here, but he was at a party in Grosvenor Square a month ago. That was a very lovely party.' By which, she meant that the men were wealthy, and they paid her a lot of attention.

'What do you know of him, Lucy?'

She shrugged. 'I know that he has known Lord Hawbridge since school.'

'I know that already.'

Lucy was rubbing her temples, trying to remember something. 'I don't think he was a friend, though, Lizzie.'

'Well, he was sitting drinking with him last night...' I said.

'Oh, people can drink together without being close friends. Look at us.'

It confirmed what I had thought.

'True. Go on.'

'The story's coming back to me now. Rumour has it that Mr Astley had been on the point of asking a woman to marry him, when Lord Hawbridge stepped in and proposed to her himself. The present Lady Hawbridge, I mean.'

This was interesting. I thought of how Astley had taken the countess on his arm and led her away from the green room. The care, the tenderness. Had he held her in such high esteem that he had wanted to marry her?

'So, Astley wanted to marry Lady Hawbridge, but Lord Hawbridge got there first?'

'Stole her from under his nose, someone said. And it was a very big nose. She's younger than he is, you know.'

'Yes, I've seen her. Extremely beautiful.'

'And extremely wealthy, more to the point. She has an impressive fortune, so the story goes.' Lucy was warming up. She loved gossip, loved sharing her privileged inform- ation, gleaned from the most fashionable parties – and the most noble beds. 'Hawbridge had been widowed for a while. His first wife gave him two sons, and he had no need to marry, but he does like to live well. A fondness for gambling and expensive women.'

'Lived,' I corrected her. 'He lived well. He's very dead now.'

Emily snorted.

'Oh yes. So he is,' said Lucy, thrown off her stride. 'But when he was alive, he racked up enormous debts. He married... oh what was her name before...? Harriet Elsom. He married Harriet Elsom, whose father has an extraordinary amount of money and pretentions to great- ness. And, as you say, she is exquisite. And probably docile,' she added as an afterthought.

Was she docile? I had thought her controlled, contained.

'So this other one, Astley, he wanted to marry her?' Emily, stirring sugar into her tea, was interested now. She and Lucy could tear each other's hair out like wild cats, but both enjoyed the intrigues of society. 'Is he impoverished too?'

'No, not at all,' said Lucy. 'I think he genuinely wanted to marry Harriet Elsom. But, Lord Hawbridge... he has a title, you see. However well-born Astley is – and I think he is – he's not an earl.'

This put a new complexion on Hawbridge's death. I had wondered whether George Hunter had been jealous of the earl, even as he intended to make his own wife Hawbridge's mistress, but now there was, potentially, another jealous lover in the wings.

'You know, Hawbridge was beginning to make eyes at Astley's mistress,' I said, my thoughts emerging out loud. 'Mrs Hunter spent most of last night wrapped around Hawbridge, when she wasn't on the stage as Cordelia.'

'Poor Mr Astley,' said Lucy. 'He loses the woman he loves to the earl, and then his mistress is taken from him too.'

A silence fell as we contemplated the implication of what Lucy had said. The first situation was tragic, the second was an affront. It would make anyone nurse a grudge.

'Is Astley really that ugly?'

'Emily!'

'What? I'm only asking. He can't have much to commend him if two women abandon him for this Hawbridge.'

I laughed. It was good to laugh again.

'He's not that bad. A pompous old prick with an enormous nose – you've entertained far worse, Emily. But he's not got a title.'

'Well, if he feels like paying, I'll be happy to make his acquaintance. I'm not fussy about their titles or looks as long as they pay handsomely enough.'

That was true for all of us.

Chapter Twenty-one

Conversation with Lucy and Emily had given me food for thought. I climbed the stairs to my own room and sank down on the bed. The pain in my shoulder was easing, but it still throbbed, and it was good to lie flat in comfort and think.

There was enmity between Hawbridge and Astley, then. I could see no way of discovering more about it by myself, but I was convinced that such a ghastly murder would have more to do with Hawbridge's relationships than it did with Garrick's theatre. The death had been made to look dramatic, but it was, at heart, a nasty thing. It spoke of a deep hatred rather than a fit of pique. Had Astley nursed his resentment over the years? One might assume that he had, if he had indeed loved Harriet Elsom. But to be bested twice by Lord Hawbridge? To find his own actress falling for Hawbridge's noble charms? Had that angered him enough to kill the man he had known since childhood?

William Simmot bore a grudge against Garrick, and Garrick was convinced of his involvement in the murder. But from the brief glimpse I'd had of him, Simmot appeared to me as someone who would shout a lot, and make threats, but shy away from physical violence. I recalled the small red-faced man, inflated with his own importance in his ridiculous pink coat. He might, for dramatic effect, throw papers at Garrick, or write a critical piece for a scandal rag, but I couldn't see him hanging a man by his ankles, still less cutting his throat.

And then there was George Hunter, whose dissembling bothered me. He was hiding his contempt for Garrick behind wide smiles and false laughter. He was forced to contain his talent and temper in a weak frame, while, at the same time, he watched his wife taking roles on stage that were, in truth, beyond her capabilities. They could not make money from her acting alone – she was not that good – so he threw her in the way of rich men, knowing where her real ability lay. He wasn't the only man in London to pimp his wife, and it was easier for her to take Astley to bed than to memorise lines of Shakespeare. Had Hunter overreached himself with Lord Hawbridge? Had there been a quarrel, a misunderstanding? Had his wife tied the rope?

I couldn't see any of them killing Lord Hawbridge. Something nagged me, though. Something I had seen or heard. I couldn't recall what it was.

I washed my face and brushed my hair. I was desperate to bathe and change my clothes but knew that Davenport would be annoyed if I did. If I was going back to the theatre, I had to return as Lizzie Blunt.

The bruise on my cheek bone had spread to cover my right eyebrow. I pressed it gently, wincing a little at the pain. If it grew any larger, my eye would start to close. From the drawer of my table I pulled a glass jar of ointment – a comfrey leaf salve that Emily made for us, for when, inevitably in a brothel, we found ourselves bruised or sore. I dabbed a small amount on my face and sighed. Lord Hawbridge had showed me no kindness; quite the reverse. His death was but the end of a violent and badly-lived life.

I had no reason to seek out his killer. But I had stood in the man's blood and seen his body swaying above me and thought that we were, strangely, connected. I had to know what had happened.

I had to speak with Davenport.

I made my way downstairs again, meeting Polly and Ma in the hall. They had been shopping and had returned ready for the evening's work. Polly squeaked with delight at seeing me. Ma was not at all delighted.

'I thought you were supposed to be in Drury Lane. I don't want you in my house dressed in such a pitiful state. You'll drive the gentlemen away.'

I glanced down at my gown as if it had not occurred to me that I looked like I'd been rolling in dirt and blood.

'This old thing? And Lucy told me that brown suited my complexion, the spiteful cat.'

'Get out of my house or change into something decent,' she raised her voice. 'I am not running a bawdy house for sailors.'

I might have thrown back another quip, but at that moment there was a knock on the front door. The gentlemen, who were not sailors, were arriving already. I knew better than to banter with Mrs Farley where her business was concerned, so I scrambled for the kitchen – and left by the back door.

—

It was not yet dark, but the streets between Soho and Covent Garden were beginning to shed their small claims to respectability and take on their customary night-time appearance. I hurried to the theatre. A well-dressed harlot might wander these streets in the dusk, assured of comments, calls and offers of business, but she could also command the help of passers-by if she felt alarmed or unsafe. A small, badly-dressed girl could be pulled into a dark passageway and attract no concern at all, even if she screamed murder. Around me, the sort of women I never usually had cause to notice were walking quickly to get home, to be safe. The poorer sort, the sort that no one really missed if they never made it to their destination. I was one of them, for now. I pulled the shawl across my shoulders, ducked my head and matched their speed.

I had turned from Bow Street into Russell Street when I saw them; two burly men I recognised were in conversation by a cart. I checked my pace. Dinsdale and Hunter. They did not see me, not only because I was beneath notice, but because their heads were close, and the street was busy. Dinsdale looked up and glanced around, scratched his cheek and turned his scowling face back to Hunter, shrugged his shoulders and said something. They looked like two halves of the same coin.

I walked past them, almost touching them, but I was unable to hear even a snatch of the conversation, it was conducted so furtively.

Ahead of me now there was a scuffle. Several men were jostling together. Someone was shouting; more than one person was shouting. These men were also known to me. Snowy, Grimshaw and Carter – Fielding's men – were dragging a gentleman towards a neighbouring tavern. The portly young man was protesting noisily. It was William Simmot.

I looked back. Dinsdale and Hunter had vanished.

The shouting men bundled Mr Simmot through the door of the Rose tavern.

The Rose has a certain notoriety. It is loud, brash and usually full of young men drinking strong punch. In the Rose, on a wild night – which is most nights – clothes are optional. Women dance naked on the tables, men lose their dignity, along with their money, their silk handkerchiefs, and their pocket watches, courtesy of wily, quick-fingered harlots. A gentleman who walks through the doors of the Rose is assured of a night he will never forget – because he is unlikely to remember it in the first place.

It was, though, still early in the evening. There was a buzz of conversation, and the sound of laughter, but the serious debauchery of a night at the Rose had yet to begin.

I grinned as soon as I saw Davenport, sitting at a table, waiting calmly for Mr Simmot to cease his raging. I slipped in behind the men of Bow Street and found an empty alcove from which to watch what was going on. Unhindered by the formality of Mr Fielding, Davenport would question Simmot in his own way: patiently, thoroughly, unsparing of the man's sensibilities. I had seen him do this before and settled back.

The young man raged and protested; Grimshaw's meaty hand planted on his shoulder, the pistols tucked in Snowy's breeches barely inches from his face. Davenport glanced in my direction as if he knew I was there. I offered only the smallest inclination of my head, and received nothing in response, but he had seen me. Of that I was certain.

Chapter Twenty-two

'Do you know who we are?' The voice was civil, but sharp as a razor.

Simmot stared at Davenport across the table.

'Thieves, rogues, murderers?' His response grew louder with every guess.

'We work for the magistrate, Mr Fielding,' said Davenport. 'My name is William Davenport. You've already become acquainted with my colleagues. We'd like to ask you some questions about a murder. I see you know the murder of which I am speaking.'

Simmot was beginning to squirm under Grimshaw's hand. Grimshaw was not letting go. He enjoyed making people squirm.

'I had nothing to do with it. Terrible business.'

'Terrible indeed,' Davenport agreed. 'A man found hanging from a chandelier is very bad. A man found hanging upside down is even worse.'

'What?'

Simmot appeared not to know the details. Or he was a better actor than he was a playwright.

'What?' he repeated faintly.

'The Earl of Hawbridge was suspended from the girandole over the stage. He was tied up by his ankles and someone opened his throat with a knife. Almost took his head off.'

I felt the bile rise in my own throat at the memory.

'No.' Simmot's voice was barely a whisper. He slumped under Grimshaw's hand. The fight had gone from him. He went white.

'Now, I understand, Mr Simmot, that you were in the theatre last night. In the green room,' Davenport spoke in that easy tone he used when he already knew the answers to his questions. I began to feel sorry for Mr Simmot. 'You were in the green room during the long interval and you were overheard making threats against the theatre manager, Mr Garrick.'

Simmot could hardly deny it. Instead he went for the obvious riposte, offered in the offhand manner of a man who has no idea how much trouble he is in. 'I fail to see what my argument with Garrick has to do with anything. Or even if it is your business.'

'Oh, it's my business, sir, when you make threats against him in his own theatre, when he is seated next to a man who is murdered later that night and when the play that you throw in his face contains a hanging.' Davenport favoured him with a cold smile. 'That's what makes it my business.'

Simmot ran a finger under his cravat. His chubby hand was shaking slightly, as if he knew what was coming next. Davenport did not disappoint him.

'Indeed, I understand that the character in your play is suspended upside down and left to die? An unpleasant way to go in a piece of make believe; far worse in real life.'

Simmot made a choking sound.

'So, perhaps you'd like to tell me where you were last night?' Davenport said. 'And whether anyone can vouch for you.'

The choking sound continued and became a wheeze and then a cough. Davenport, irritated, called for the tavern boy to bring a pot of beer and waited for Simmot to compose himself. His eyes never left his face.

Another man, young, red-cheeked and with his wig slightly askew, tried to sit next to me – or on my lap. He was drunk. Experience tells me that it's better to be polite to drunken men than to push them rudely away, so I told him, very cheerfully, that I was waiting for a prize fighter from St Giles who was twice his size and prone to be quick-tempered. He gave me a lop-sided grin and stumbled away. Davenport's lips twitched.

Simmot took a gulp of his beer and wiped his mouth. 'I was writing. In my lodgings. It's what I do. I write.'

'Anyone with you?'

He shook his head.

'Anyone see you come in?'

'I don't know.'

'How very unfortunate for you.'

Davenport sat back, regarding him. Grimshaw had, by now, decided that Simmot was unlikely to make a run for it and had wandered away to find a drink. I could see him talking with one of the regular Rose whores, a rat-faced girl with buck teeth and a large black spot under her jaw. Snowy had stopped swaggering with the pistols and was seated on a chair next to Simmot, idly flicking a crumb of bread along the table. Carter, the oldest of the men, was watching Simmot with Davenport, but the expression on his face suggested he thought he had better things to do with his time. There were real rogues about, cut-purses and thieves to be caught. This man Simmot was ridiculous; his eyes spoke it.

'What manner of man are you, Simmot?' asked Davenport. 'What sort of person writes stories about hangings? You don't look like one of those ghouls who sits at Tyburn scribbling the last words of murderers. You don't look like the usual scrawny hack. Where are you from? What's your family?'

It was what I appreciated about Davenport: his curiosity almost matched my own. Simmot intrigued him. He did not, it was true, conform to the picture of a writer. The scandal merchants of Grub Street had hard faces, hollow cheeks, inky fingers and mean eyes. Simmot looked like an over-indulged child, playing at making a living. It was the question I would have asked, had I been in Davenport's shoes, rather than tucked into a corner trying not to be noticed.

Simmot sat up straight, puffing out his chest.

'I come from Lichfield, sir. The same as Dr Johnson. It's a fair city and has an uncommon number of great men.' He saw himself in that category. He cut a similar figure to the good doctor, it was true. I knew that Davenport would be struggling not to smirk.

'If Dr Johnson can come to London and make a name for himself, then so can I,' Simmot said, sounding petulant.

'And your family? What do they think of your hopes of literary success?'

'I am a gentleman, Mr Davenport. I have land, or I will have when my father leaves it to me. I have an education. It is my intention to use it and write plays fit for today's audiences, rather than squander my life in brothels and taverns, as many men do.'

Davenport nodded gravely. 'A noble sentiment, Mr Simmot, but does your family share your aspiration?'

He was getting to the nub of the matter, and he knew it.

'Regretfully, my father is not a man who understands literature. His idea of a night at the theatre,' he winced a little, 'is more about being seen by people of consequence, rather than understanding the play.'

'Ah.'

'I have tried to persuade him that the life of a writer brings fortune of its own, but he holds more traditional opinions about the life his son should lead.'

Poor Mr Simmot. I could see it now. His father – a fat landowner from the provinces if his son's form was anything to go by – had sent his son to university and thence to London for a little 'polish' and was expecting him to return and take up the reins at home. His son, having had his head turned by the theatre, was writing dreadful plays in the hope of making the same name for himself as Dr Johnson. He had none of that man's wit or character, although he was doing his best to emulate the great man's pomposity. There is little to be done for one who has such illusions about his own worth.

He was an unlikely murderer. Davenport knew it, but nevertheless wanted to establish his relationship with Garrick.

'Mr Garrick doesn't think much of your plays, sir. Perhaps you should return to your father after all? Live the life for which you are intended?'

This caused something of an explosion from Simmot. Even Snowy looked up from his crumb-rolling.

'Garrick? Gah. The man has no imagination! He is content only to strut about playing the best parts in Shakespeare, or to offer the most wearisome plays from the last century. Nothing new is commissioned unless it appears like something already known, or else is so light that it is of no consequence.'

It was all perfectly true: Garrick was known to be wary of performing untried writers, for fear of incurring the wrath of the Lord Chamberlain and losing his licence. It was a common complaint, but it was delivered with such anger that Simmot's face turned dark red. Davenport noticed his temper.

'Mr Simmot, many people in the theatre have named you as the person most likely to have killed Lord Hawbridge. Many people saw you lose your temper in the green room and threaten Mr Garrick. I would have a care about what you say.'

Simmot shrank back into his chair, but he was not going to be cowed. 'Why would I want to kill Lord Hawbridge? I don't know the man – except that he was with Garrick last night. I was introduced to him. I had never met him before in my life. And yet, almost immediately, he was forced to witness Garrick making a spectacle of me, as he likes to do. Garrick is an ignorant bastard, but I have nothing against Lord Hawbridge at all.'

Even in the bluster, it was clear that Simmot's argument was with Garrick, not Hawbridge. If Simmot had wished to harm Garrick, he would have harmed Garrick. The best he had done so far was to cause a scene and throw papers at him. He was a silly young man with a vivid imagination but he possessed very little boldness to act on his threats.

'Oh, go away, you foolish boy,' said Davenport, laughing and picking up his cup to drain his beer. 'Go and write whatever nonsense you like. You're free to walk the street, Mr Simmot, but if anything occurs to you about why Lord Hawbridge was suspended over Mr Garrick's stage last night, please do come and find us at Bow Street.'

Simmot, now that he was released, stood up and scowled at Davenport. It was not murder in his eyes, but it was certainly malice. He gave a stiff, if slightly wobbly bow, before running through the door.

Chapter Twenty-three

Fielding's men melted away into the tavern and Davenport was left sitting alone. One of the serving girls went to his table to collect the pots. She put an arm across his shoulder, and I saw them exchange a few quiet words before she went on her way. He looked over to where I sat and jerked his chin, indicating that I might join him.

I clapped my hands in applause as I sat down.

'Bravo, Mr Davenport. I enjoyed that.'

He grunted. 'I might have enjoyed it more if he had confessed to killing Lord Hawbridge, but as soon as I saw him, I thought it unlikely.'

'He's not a man who would willingly soil his hands with someone else's blood,' I agreed. 'It would be far too much effort. But you were quite rude to the poor creature.'

'Affected little puppy.'

I giggled. 'Oh, I don't know. Garrick won't perform his plays, so we'll never know how brilliant he really is, will we?'

'The world may have lost a true genius,' he agreed with a laugh.

'I began to feel rather sorry for him when you reminded him of the hanging part in his play. But then he became so full of his own importance that I lost my sympathy.'

The serving girl brought over two fresh pots of beer. 'He would be better served by a few months rolling around the taverns and brothels he despises,' I said, savouring a mouthful, still chuckling. 'I know of one or two places.'

Davenport's face lost its laughter. 'I wouldn't have thought him your sort,' he said in a tight voice.

'He's not. I'd send him to Emily.'

He stared at his beer in silence.

'I have news about Lord Hawbridge,' I said. 'Do you wish to hear it, sir?'

He lifted his eyes. 'Yes.'

'Mr Astley was once set to marry the woman who is now Lady Hawbridge.'

He was interested. 'How did you come by such information?'

'I went home. Lucy always has the best gossip and I was annoyed that Mr Fielding chose not to ask too many questions of Mr Astley and Mr Callow.'

He gave a short laugh. 'That irked me too.'

'People of quality do not commit murders, he thinks?'

He pulled a face. 'He is readier to believe that it could be an actor or a stage hand with a grudge against Garrick than a man of wealth and consequence.'

Mr Fielding's men had raided brothels and gaming houses in the poorer parts of town and were stringent about upholding the law when it came to the common people. Rich men were allowed to indulge their habits. It was one of the reasons why Mrs Farley was so keen to style our house as respectable: fit for gentlemen of breeding who were able to do as they wished without fear of redress. It lent security to her business.

'Tell me about Astley.' Davenport was less careful about upsetting people. I liked that about him.

'As he told you, he's known Hawbridge since childhood. I don't know that they were friends, but they knew one another well enough. Hawbridge married, had two sons and then his wife died.'

'The present Lady Hawbridge is his second wife?'

'She is. Pretty thing, isn't she?' I said.

The colour rose in his cheeks. 'I didn't pay much attention. And she had a veil.'

'Liar. You were hanging on her every word. As I say, she's very pretty. But she brought other advantages to the marriage.'

'I'm not a liar. Don't provoke me. Go on.'

'The Earl of Hawbridge didn't need another wife, having bred his heirs, but apparently he does have something of an addiction to gambling and women. He needed money. His title carries weight with creditors, of course, but it doesn't pay the bills.'

'And now you're going to tell me that Lady Hawbridge had an impressive fortune.'

'You are so very clever, Mr Davenport. Always one step ahead of me.'

'I told you not to provoke me. Where does Astley come into it?'

I repeated what Lucy had said. He was thoughtful.

'You think Astley bore a grievance against Hawbridge and killed him for it? Why wait so long? Why such a public death, such a spectacle?'

'I don't know, but I'll wager this has more to do with the lovely Lady Hawbridge than the weeping widow act suggests.'

'She wasn't weeping. She behaved with great dignity.'

'She was bred for dignity. You may depend upon it.'

He gave a short sigh. 'Well, I'll discuss it with Mr Fielding, see if I can go and speak with Astley. He was, after all, at the theatre last night, whether he was an admirer of Lady Hawbridge or not.'

'He was also Lucy Hunter's patron,' I said. 'And Lucy Hunter was all over Lord Hawbridge last night.'

'Aha. Another woman leaving him for Hawbridge, you mean? You think his jealousy got the better of him?'

I bit my lip. 'I don't know, Mr Davenport. I don't know.'

Across the tavern, the company was becoming lively. A gathering of men had ordered a large bowl of punch to share. I had no desire to linger in the Rose tonight. I would hardly have my pick of the customers dressed like this and sporting a black eye.

'I have news of Mr Callow too,' I said, moving my chair nearer to the table. 'Molly saw him.'

'In here?'

'No. She and Mr Sugden came here after the performance, and after we'd all cleared up, but, like Mr Callow, she didn't care to stay long. She says that they walked together down Southampton Street and she saw him in the Bedford Head.'

'Was he alone? Did she see anyone else?'

I shook my head. 'Molly Bray spends her days with clothes and costumes. She recognised Mr Callow by his bright green coat but paid no attention to whether he was alone or with a companion.'

He rolled his eyes. 'Ah well, at least we may be sure that his coat was in the Bedford. I'd prefer to speak to whichever girl he picked up, but I expect she would be impossible to locate. He probably won't remember her name, or even what she looked like.'

'Or I could find you half a dozen within spitting distance who would swear they spent the night with him – if you gave them a small payment,' I said. 'You're right. But Molly has a clear eye for coats and trimmings. If she says it was his coat, then it was Mr Callow.'

He folded his arms and frowned. 'So we have Astley going home, but possibly nursing a grudge against Lord Hawbridge, Callow spends the night with a whore from the Bedford, and William Simmot is alone in his room writing bad plays. What am I missing?'

'There's something going on in the theatre – beyond the murder, I mean. Garrick has cause to be alarmed.'

'I know. That's why you're in there.'

'Mr Dinsdale is up to something, I think. And George Hunter too.'

'You think this is about Lucy Hunter?'

'No. I don't think so. I think something else is going on. I saw Dinsdale with Hunter out in the street just now. They were discussing something and looked very thick together.'

'They're involved in Lord Hawbridge's murder?'

'I've no idea. They're up to something, though.'

He smiled. 'You'd better go back to the theatre and find out what it is, then, Miss Blunt, hadn't you?'

I gave him my nastiest scowl.

His expression suddenly changed. He caught my chin in his hand, turning my head to the light of the candles.

'You've a bruise on your forehead. And on your cheek.'

'It's nothing,' I said. 'Don't worry about it.'

He didn't let go of my face but leaned across the table to get a better look. He touched it and I pulled away.

'Ow. Don't prod it.'

'It doesn't look like nothing,' he said. 'Did you bump into the scenery, or do I need to break someone's arm?'

I stood up to leave, unwilling to tell him anything more.

'I can take care of myself, Mr Davenport.'

—

It was dark now. Posters along the theatre's walls announced that the evening's performance was cancelled. There were no crowds queuing for seats, no young men hoping to catch the hand of actresses, no families laughing and joking on a night out. Without the audience, the theatre was just a building like any other, gloomy in its darkness. The back door was unlocked, so I let myself in.

I was hungry. I made my way to the green room, in the hope that there would be some bread at least. All that I had eaten since this morning were candied fruits. A few candles flickered in the passageway to light my way. The green room was brighter and the fire was burning, but it was deserted. Garrick, I assumed, had given the stage hands a night off. If there was no performance, then, as long as they had completed their tasks – including repainting the stage – there was nothing to do. No lights to be lit, no scenery to be moved, no chairs or benches to set straight.

The side table had been cleared of food, which was a great pity. My stomach gurgled loudly.

'Where in God's name have you been?'

I jumped at the voice and turned to find Joe Sugden standing in the doorway, sour faced, a candlestick in one hand and a large lump hammer in the other.

'Mr Sugden?'

'I said, where have you been? Who gave you permission to leave the theatre?'

I hesitated. I had slipped out in order to avoid explaining where I was going.

'I'm sorry, Mr Sugden, I thought that we were allowed to leave once we'd completed our work. Miss Bray and I finished with the linens and folded the clothes and she said I could rest, but I went out for a walk.' I gave him a little curtsey. 'I hope that I did no wrong, sir.'

He glared at me. 'You should have asked Mr Dinsdale before leaving. Or me.'

I ducked my head. 'I think Mr Dinsdale was out, sir.' I knew he had been out. I had seen him.

He frowned. 'Molly said you were asleep. Then she couldn't find you and began worrying, and some of us have been looking for you.'

I said nothing, judging it best to keep silent. He tucked the hammer under one arm, lifted the candlestick and looked me up and down. I turned away, not wanting him to see the bruise on my face.

'I don't want to ask again. Where have you been?'

'I don't really know, sir,' I said, uneasy at his tone of voice. 'I'm not so familiar with London. I looked around the market and I walked to the river to watch the traffic.'

It sounded far-fetched, even as I said it. Who walks to the river to look at boats?

His eyes narrowed. 'That's a fine tale,' he said. 'I don't like little liars, any more than I like little thieves. You'd better get down to the dressing room before I take you to Mr Dinsdale and let him deal with you. Move!'

I moved, skirting past him out into the corridor and down to where Molly would be waiting. I had no idea what being dealt with by Dinsdale would involve, but I didn't want to find out.

Chapter Twenty-four

Molly was sitting in near darkness. A single candle lit her face making her cheeks glow. They were red from wine already. She was just sitting, staring into space when I entered.

'Oh, there you are, Lizzie,' was all she said.

'I'm sorry, miss, I went for a walk when we finished and lost track of the time. Mr Sugden's already given me a right scolding.'

'Joe?' She looked lost. I had interrupted deep thoughts.

'He said you were worried about me. That people were looking for me. He told me that I should not have wandered away without asking permission.'

Her eyes were hazy, bloodshot as well. 'You shouldn't. I don't know what you've been used to, Lizzie, but around here you ask first. Here now,' she said, as I dropped my head, 'don't worry about Joe Sugden. He's very particular about people doing as they're told, that's all. His bark is worse than his bite.'

'His bark scared me. He threatened to take me to Mr Dinsdale.'

She snorted at that, got up and lit another candle. 'That jumped up little prick? Thinks he runs the place, but he's nothing. Just another traveller like the rest of us. Garrick treats him like a dog, so he kicks the rest of us now and then, just to make sure we know that he's the top dog.

If his wits matched his own opinion of himself he'd be dangerous.' She gestured to the plate on the table. 'There's bread and cheese, if you're hungry.'

'Very hungry. Thank you.'

She poured out a cup of wine and we sat and ate silently by the candlelight. The room was chilly, but the little lights gave the sense of warmth and the food was very welcome. I tried not to bolt it down too quickly.

'Joe's always worrying about something,' she said. 'He was worrying about money the other day, about when the men would be paid. He's been fretting about the accidents and the damage, wondering if it's one of his men. He's taken to sleeping in the trap room, instead of his lodging house, so that he can be up and about early, to check what's going on, make sure everything's in order. I stay with him there sometimes.'

The trap room: that was what had nagged my thoughts earlier. If it were possible for an actor to be sprung on to the stage through a secret door, surprising the audience, then it might also be possible for a man to hide there when the stage had been cleared for the night. Dinsdale hadn't mentioned the trap room to Mr Fielding. Joe Sugden might have been in the trap room when Lord Hawbridge was killed. He had been quick enough to appear when I screamed. Molly had arrived on the stage with him.

'Are you and he...?'

She shrugged. 'I tell him I won't marry him, but he keeps trying. He's a good man, you know, just a bit pious sometimes, he likes to follow the rules. His mother was a Catholic.'

'What about Ketch?'

She laughed. 'Ketch is an old friend. And I mean old. He knew my mother, years ago, before she died.'

'Is that who you were remembering?'

She gave me a strange look.

'You looked like you were sitting here with ghosts when I walked in,' I said. 'Were you thinking of your mother?'

'You're right. I was thinking of her – and my brother. When he died, the grief killed her.' She gave a little sigh. 'Ketch swore to her that he'd protect me, so he's here with that dreadful monkey. He managed to persuade Garrick to let him have a turn on the stage the other night – it was a disaster. He's better off at the fairs, but he hangs around, helping out here and there, just to keep an eye on me.'

'I thought he was sweet on you.'

'He's not interested. Not in that way.'

She reached over for the wine jug. I realised, from the way she lurched, that she had drunk more than one cup. The jug was empty.

'Shit. I'm out of wine.' She was bent on drinking, I could tell.

'Lizzie, would you be a good girl and go and fetch us some more?' She rummaged in her pocket for a coin. 'Go out to the tavern next door, no, not the Rose, go to the Shakespeare. Ask for John and get us another jug.'

It had been a long and difficult day. I was happy to end it drinking. An excess of wine would make the couch in Mrs Hunter's room more comfortable. I took the jug and made my way out of the theatre.

I returned, nursing the wine as carefully as I could in the dark passageway. Before I reached our room, I heard voices and, by instinct, slowed to listen. This was Lucy Hunter's dressing room, and someone was inside. It was not Lucy.

'I'm not sure. This death is unfortunate, like I said earlier.'

It sounded like Dinsdale's voice, surly and low.

Someone else responded, but I couldn't hear. I held my breath and leaned a little closer to the doorway, hugging the wine to my chest. The voice spoke again. George Hunter.

'And I told you I had nothing to do with it. Hawbridge was going to be my new source of income, why should I want him dead?'

'I thought you was fretting over Lucy again.'

There was a snort. 'She's learned to keep her mouth shut and do what I tell her.'

'What are we doing, then?' Dinsdale asked. 'I don't like this waiting.'

'I don't fucking like it either,' Hunter's tone was sharp. 'It wasn't what we needed.'

A chair scraped the floor. Someone was standing up, about to leave the room. I was torn between wanting to hear more and not wanting to be caught listening.

'We'll talk about it tomorrow,' Hunter was coming towards the door.

Ahead of me another door opened, and light spilled into the passageway. It was Molly's room. Joe Sugden stepped out. I gave a start when I saw him. It was only because the jug was clamped tightly to my chest that I didn't drop it.

Mrs Hunter's door then opened behind me and George Hunter limped out. He stared at me briefly, and then at Sugden, but said nothing as he walked back towards the green room, stick thudding heavily on the floor.

Sugden stood watching me, arms folded, as I hurried to take Molly her wine. I avoided his eyes as I passed him.

Molly was sitting where I had left her, at the little table under the window, but she had lit more candles, and the room was much brighter now.

'You took your time,' she said with a scowl. 'I'm dying of thirst here.'

'Sorry, miss.' I put the wine down on the table and she refilled her cup.

'You want some, Joe?' She lifted the jug, anticipating his response.

'In a minute, Moll,' he was still at the door, staring at me. 'Once I've dealt with her.'

'With Lizzie?'

In two strides he reached me and, before I had chance to breathe, let alone move, he had grabbed me by the hair, lifting my head until I was standing on tiptoe.

I shrieked.

'Joe! What are you doing? What's got into you?' Molly leaped to her feet and slapped at his shoulder. He shook her off and twisted his fist in my scalp. I yelped at the pain.

'Let me go! Let me go!'

He dropped me and I fell to the floor. For the second time in as many days, I was far too close to a man's boots.

'Get up,' he barked. I scrambled to my feet but edged as close as I could to Molly, who stood amazed by his attack.

'Right. What are you about?'

'I don't know what you mean, sir.'

'Sneaking about, listening at doorways.'

'I wasn't.'

'Don't you lie to me, girl, or I'll make you very sorry.' He raised a hand to strike me and I shrank behind Molly. 'I told you I don't like liars.'

He didn't like it that I had told Davenport about the snuff box – that was the heart of it. It takes a thief to call

179

a thief. I'd seen him pocket someone else's coins from the green room floor. He had intended to keep the snuff box too, I was sure of it.

'Joe, stop being ridiculous. Leave the girl alone.' Molly put herself between us.

'She went out earlier,' he said. 'When I asked where she'd been she gave some story about wandering to the river.'

'What of it?' Molly asked.

'Ketch says he saw her in the Rose, drinking with one of the magistrate's men. That one who was taking notes this morning.'

Molly turned to look at me, pale-faced. 'Really? What you doing with the likes of him, Lizzie?'

I decided, faced with Sugden in such a temper and now Molly, my protector, gaping at me, to give them the truth. Well, some of it. I'm not that stupid. The words came out in a rush.

'Mr Fielding found me a position here, as I told you before, when I was sent to him for stealing bread. But he also told me that there were strange goings on in the theatre, scenery falling, and threats being made, and he wanted to know what was happening.'

'A spy?' Molly started to laugh. 'You've been spying on us, Lizzie?' I wasn't sure why this was amusing, but she laughed heartily. Sugden, on the other hand, remained silent.

'When he asked me questions this morning, he told me to meet with his man at the Rose later. That's why I was there. And he bought me a beer. Mr Davenport, that is, not the magistrate.'

'Well, there has been plenty going on, it's true,' said Molly.

'And what have you found out, Lizzie Blunt?' asked Sugden, his voice soft and threatening. 'What have you heard, when you're listening at keyholes?'

I tried to keep breathing, tried not to stammer. 'In truth, sir, not much. I did, as I think you guessed, go walking about early this morning. That's how I came to be on the stage with…' I paused '…with Lord Hawbridge. Apart from that, I haven't found anything. I'm not very good as a spy.'

He was watching me, trying to decide whether I was telling the truth. I thought I would offer just one more scrap of news while his fists were still clenched.

'I saw Fielding's men speak to William Simmot in the Rose.'

'Simmot?' Molly was interested. This would stop them from quizzing me.

'They were quite rough with him at first, but I don't think they see him as a murderer. I don't know if he's been causing scenery to fall over, though, to frighten Mr Garrick.'

Sugden nodded slowly. 'Aye, it's Simmot. That's what we all think, ain't it, Moll?'

'It was Simmot that killed Hawbridge. They'll see it eventually.'

I stepped out from behind Molly, but still held her arm for protection. 'I'm sorry for lying, sir. I don't like lying. I didn't know what else to say to you when you asked.'

'What did you hear at the dressing room door?' he asked. 'The one George Hunter came out of?'

'Nothing,' I said. 'I heard his voice, but not what he said. I just stopped to listen and then you opened the door and I was frightened.'

I shrugged at Molly. 'I'm not a good spy, am I, miss?'

She laughed again and handed me a glass of wine.

Sugden didn't say anything, but he didn't ask any more questions. He didn't believe me, I knew.

I had seen that he had sticky fingers as far as coins and trinkets were concerned. He might also be a killer. I recalled the hammer under his arm with a shudder. I would have to be careful, even as I watched him.

Chapter Twenty-five

For the second morning in a row, I woke early and with a sore neck. This time, I was on the floor of the costume room. It was deserted. Molly had been very drunk by the time we finished the jug of wine, and Sugden had almost carried her away. She had drunk fast, telling stories about the people she had known at the fairs, giving wild impressions of characters I didn't know, but whom I, being also merry with wine, had applauded. Then she became morose, as people do when they've had too much to drink and began to wail about her brother and her ma. She didn't mention her rope-walking father at all, so I guessed that they had not been close. That was when Sugden decided she needed to sleep. I had made a bed of some curtains and cushions.

The sun shone brightly, and shone early, as it had yesterday but there were no street traders because it was Sunday. Instead, the bells began to clang. I got up and tried to stretch my shoulders. The bruise on my face was, as I inspected it in the glass, now purple, yellow and brown. It matched my gown.

Mindful of Sugden's comments, when Molly returned, I asked if I could leave the theatre to get some air. Molly was nursing a headache and waved me out, telling me not to worry and that Joe Sugden wouldn't bother me as long as I was in her care, and that yes, she would be sure to tell him.

'You seeing that man from the magistrate's again?' She asked, as I was half-way out of the door.

'No,' I said. 'Not unless he sees me first.'

In truth I had no plan for the day, other than to find some breakfast and work out how I might discover more about Mr Astley. Of all the people who had a grievance against Lord Hawbridge, Astley must be the most significant. But I could hardly walk into his house and ask him questions. Certainly not dressed like this.

I looked down at the crumpled brown fabric, stained with blood, dust and now also wine. I looked, and I felt, like a girl from the streets.

Force of habit took me west and, ten minutes later, I stood at the doorway of a decent coffee house in Soho, one that ordinarily would have welcomed my custom – and the custom I would have lured in even on a Sunday morning. A man in an apron made it very clear, by the scowl on his face, that I was not welcome. He did not recognise me and, even if I had told him my name, he would not have believed this drab was the famous Lizzie Hardwicke of Berwick Street. I tried one or two other places before lowering my standards. The hovel that called itself a coffee house was not clean. I gave up Polly's lucky coin for a bowl of coffee that was almost undrinkable. The woman who brought it to my table had greasy black curls and several warts on her fat face, one of which was sprouting coarse hairs. I dodged three offers of business in the space of ten minutes, from the sort of men who liked their whores grimy and partly-battered and who don't like to pay more than a shilling. To one I said I was meeting someone, to another I said I was poxed, and the third man

I told to go and fuck himself, because I was heartily sick of being bothered.

I left half of the coffee and moved on, penniless and in a bad mood.

As I rounded the corner, someone grabbed my elbow.

'Come to church with me.'

'What?' If this was a proposition, it was certainly a new one.

'Come on, we'll be late.'

'Well, a very good morning to you too, Mr Davenport. Why am I going to church?' I hadn't been to church for many months, except when Ma dragged me to a service, in her bid to appear as an honourable and law-abiding woman of business. 'I'm not sure I attend church.'

'You'll attend today. Astley is going to be there. One of my men brought word.'

Davenport had spies all over London; men and women who gave him titbits of information in return for a small coin or two.

'Mr Astley? And is Lady Hawbridge going to be with him?'

'I don't know. Why don't we find out?'

My foul mood lifted almost immediately at the thought of the adventure, and the fact that he was sharing it with me. I looped my arm through his and grinned.

'Where are we going to church?'

'St James's.'

'Piccadilly? A very fashionable haunt,' I laughed. 'You won't want to sit too close to me. I fear I smell quite dreadful.'

'Miss Hardwicke, we are not sitting together. I am a gentleman, and one of the magistrate's men. You, however, are not a respectable woman, and I wouldn't sit

185

with you even if you were in your best gown and smelling deliciously of roses.'

I stumbled and very nearly fell, but he had my arm.

He had noticed my perfume.

But we would not be sitting together. He was right. I was not the sort of woman a gentleman would sit with in church. In a tavern, or a coffee house, yes. In the theatre, possibly, if he was happy to parade a lover. But church was for sitting with wives, sisters and mothers. Not with whores – however delicious they might smell.

'You're quiet,' he said, as we neared the entrance, passing a line of carriages drawn up along the street. Sir Christopher Wren's red-bricked building, its windows immaculately dressed in pale polished stone, loomed above as we walked up the path, as if to remind me of everything that I had lost. My past, my family, my respectability, and the possibility of sitting with decent people.

'Rough night?'

'Ah. I see.'

'Not that sort of rough,' I said, irritated. 'I slept on a hard floor and my shoulder aches.'

'I'm sorry. You're useful where you are. I hope you can bear it.'

There it was: I was useful. My mood did not get better when we parted at the door, pretending not to know one another. He went to sit with the gentlemen and their ladies; I sat with the servants, who were up and out of sight in the gallery, when they were not being useful.

Davenport faced resolutely forward. He did not have as good a view of Mr Astley as I did. Astley arrived with a woman who was not Lady Hawbridge. In fact, as far as I could tell, he was in church with his very elderly mother. Lady Hawbridge, heavily veiled, arrived with three others. The first was a young man of around twenty-five, who, from his manner, colouring and figure, could only be his father's eldest son. He was studiously practising seriousness. He was doing this by nodding gravely whenever someone spoke to him. This was the new Earl of Hawbridge, plucked from his life of undoubted leisure and ease to take over his father's estate many years before he imagined he would need to, and in a manner that would make even the merriest of hearts become quickly sober. The second man was Mr Callow, who looked as though he were already assuming the role of adviser to the young earl, even though he was barely older than him. The third was a stout woman who was covered in black and veiled like Lady Hawbridge. From the bustling and presumptuous manner of this person, I could only imagine an older relative, an aunt or cousin, had arrived to offer condolences and advice to the new widow.

Throughout my childhood, and until last year, I might have sat in the boxed pews occupied by the ladies below. In my father's church, I would have worn my best bonnet and tried to look interested in his sermon, even though he would have rehearsed its finer points over dinner for most of the previous week. I would have cast surreptitious glances across the rest of the congregation, keen to know who was sitting with whom from the village and alive to any gossip or scandal. All of this I had learned to do without attracting the notice of my father – who expected immaculate behaviour from his offspring, and particularly from his daughter. I was supposed to set an example to the girls of the village.

Now I was sitting with the servants in the gallery, I realised that no one was following the examples of their betters. Instead, we had a jolly time drawing pictures in the dust that covered the book ledge and sharing small items of food. They were a friendly lot, and they welcomed me in as one of their own. At least, dressed as I was, I looked more like a servant fallen on hard times than the sort of painted strumpet that even they would have declined to sit with.

The preacher was not bad. He knew his theology and his arguments were clever. The sermon dwindled at the end, though, and went on for far too long. I began to feel sorry for Davenport, seeing his shoulders slouch a little. Then I remembered his earlier comments and lost my sympathy. Instead, I gave my attention to the white barrel-like ceiling, studded with gold, and to the fruits and flowers of the carving under the east window – which bore the unmistakable style of Grinling Gibbons. It was a beautiful church. I could almost find peace here, except that phrases in the prayers, cadences from my childhood, made me think of home and I began to grow uncomfortable.

I had sat next to a girl who was keen more to talk than to listen, so I did not have to dwell on maudlin thoughts. The girl, whose name was Betsy, pointed out not only her own mistress and everyone else of consequence, but their servants too. She had bright blue eyes that sparkled as she chattered in a loud whisper. Her own lady, in the seats below, was almost as talkative, whispering to her companion behind her prayer book. Mistress and maid were well-suited. At the end of our bench, Betsy noted two servants from Hawbridge House. One of them sat with her hands neatly folded in her lap, a calm expression on her pale face. I recognised her as the girl who had accompanied Lady Hawbridge to the theatre. That, Betsy told me, was Hannah, Lady Hawbridge's maid. She had been many years in the lady's service, and was nice enough, although a bit aloof. Hannah heard her name and turned to glare, but her eyes softened when she recognised Betsy and the glare became more of a gentle warning to her friend to keep her voice down. The other Hawbridge girl was just a chamber maid. Betsy didn't know her name. Her face had not yet lost its childish pudginess. She was sullen and bored; dragged along to church for her moral and spiritual improvement, no doubt. I wondered whether Lord Hawbridge had ever sought her out and pressed her against a table.

I asked Betsy to introduce me to them both, seeing now how a fellow servant might gain access to the Hawbridge residence in a way that a theatre girl who was ordinarily a harlot would not.

As we left the church, Betsy was chattering excitedly to Hannah and (we discovered her name) Mary. None of us needed to say much as Betsy talked, because she could talk for all of us, but it transpired that we were all making our way down York Street in the direction of St James's Square and we could, as Betsy suggested, walk together. Hawbridge House, I learned, was in the square.

I caught Davenport's eye as I stood on the street with the girls. He wanted me to go with him. The small jerk of his chin was more like a command than an invitation and I resented it. I shook my head in response and linked my arm through Betsy's, turning around to see him with his hands on his hips, scowling after me.

Chapter Twenty-six

'Where's your house, Lizzie? Who's your lady? Is she here?' Hannah cast a look over my dishevelled gown and battered face. I did not look like a lady's maid, but she was kind enough to suggest that I might be. She herself was neatly dressed in light blue, with a very white kerchief and a plain straw bonnet. Even the sullen Mary was better turned out than me. Her bonnet had a ribbon. I didn't even have a bonnet.

I might have been poorly dressed, but I knew how to spin a yarn. One of the benefits of my usual profession is that I know enough about the social scene inhabited by worthy gentlemen to create stories convincing enough for servants.

'Ah, it's a sad tale,' I said, affecting some distress. 'I used to be in a lovely house with Mrs Woodmarsh. She was such a lady.'

There was a gentleman who had visited me only a week or two ago, who told me that his wife was lately dead. Mr Woodmarsh had spent nearly an hour lamenting her passing – such a fine creature, a saintly wife and loving mother to his children – and I had listened and made sympathetic sounds, pouring his wine and offering him food. He had dabbed at his eyes with a handkerchief and described, in nauseating detail, her many virtues to me, before pushing my face down into a pillow and doing what he had paid to do. I suffered no scruples about making good use of his recent loss.

I repeated her remarkable character to my audience, sniffing back tears. 'She was taken from us not twenty days ago.'

'Oh, that's sad,' said Hannah. 'When they're kind to you, you grieve them, don't you?'

'I'd hate to lose mine,' said Betsy. 'I love her more than I loved my own mother. She's never once raised her hand to me. Shares all of her secrets too – not that I'm telling.'

Betsy had proved to be a fabulous gossip in the short time I had been in her company, but I guessed that she would stay loyal to her own mistress. She was genuinely fond of her.

'What happened?' Hannah looked again at my clothes and my bruise, as if she were guessing at my current circumstances.

I put a little wobble in my voice and told them that Mr Woodmarsh, in his grief, had dismissed his wife's servants.

'The poor man,' said Betsy. 'It does take them like this, sometimes. I heard it even happen to a duke, once. His wife died, and he burned all of her clothes and sent everyone away. He must have loved her dearly.'

'Indeed, I don't know what he'll do without her.' I tried to shake the memory of Mr Woodmarsh grunting profanities into the back of my neck. 'But as for me, I am without a situation, without a home, and am very near to giving myself up on the street.'

This had a predictable effect on my companions. Even Mary looked horrified, although I wondered whether she quite understood.

'You must come to our house.'

'No, ours is bigger, we have opportunities, I'm sure.'

They fussed and suggested, pulling my arm. Eventually, with all the effort of one making a difficult decision, I plumped for the Hawbridge establishment.

'But you are only around the corner, isn't that so?' I said to Betsy. 'We might meet from time to time.' I squeezed her hand warmly. 'And if there is no position at Hawbridge House, perhaps I might come to you?'

'Depend upon it, Lizzie, you would be very welcome. But the best of luck to you. Lady Hawbridge is a proper lady, just like your Mrs Woodmarsh.'

She turned aside from Hannah, Mary and me, away to her own place of employment. We stood, for a moment, in the northern end of St James's Square, looking up at the impressive sight that was Hawbridge House, the Earl of Hawbridge's London residence.

It was not the largest house on the square, but the earls of Hawbridge could hold their heads high amongst the dukes and earls whose dwellings jostled for importance in this corner of London. It was certainly stylish, trumpeting the wealth and significance of the family with its widely-spaced windows and shining stonework. Even though the late earl had lost a fortune in gaming houses, his home stood among the best of those belonging to the English nobility. The family would, ordinarily, have been thinking about making its way back to the country estate for the summer. If I could recall correctly, the estate lay in Gloucestershire. They would be certain to travel from London after the earl's funeral. That meant I had only a few days in which to discover whether my information about Mr Astley and the Hawbridges was correct, and whether Mr Astley did, indeed, have reason to want Lord Hawbridge dead.

And I was still supposed to be in the theatre, sewing and mending, in Drury Lane, not in St James's.

This was going to be difficult to manage.

Hannah, who was not aloof, as Betsy had claimed, but rather charming once Betsy's incessant chatter had left our ears, decided that she had taken me under her wing. I still styled myself as Lizzie Blunt, but now I was a forlorn house maid, cast upon the wicked streets of London by a grieving master. I was, I admitted to myself, rather enjoying playing a variety of parts. If matters continued, I would be able to perform an entire play by myself.

'This way, Lizzie,' Hannah said, pulling me by the arm. 'Our door's the other side.'

Of course it was. I would never be invited through the front door of Hawbridge House, except on the arm of my father or one of my brothers. That was a shame: it was a splendid door in a very magnificent edifice. I would have enjoyed making an entrance.

The servants' door was not as gorgeous, but it was grand enough to remind Lord Hawbridge's servants that they worked for a nobleman of taste, means and influence. Or, they used to. They could only hope that the new earl would be as keen to make such an impression. Every servant, even as he or she grumbled against their master, liked to know that the master was significant in the world. I was ushered into the servants' hall; a large dining room with enough seats to tell me that this was a decent-sized household, even for a London house. The country estate would have more servants, especially if the earl kept a large stable and liked to entertain. Hannah left me with Mary, while she went to find the housekeeper.

The house was spacious, hushed and calm. A world away from Drury Lane.

'What's it like here?' I asked Mary, not having heard a word from her along the street. My voice seemed harsh and loud in these surroundings.

She shrugged. 'It's all right,' she said, staring at the floor. 'Mrs Kemp is vicious.'

I assumed that Mrs Kemp was the housekeeper I was about to meet. It's rare to find a chamber maid describe the housekeeper as anything other than vicious.

'You been here long?'

'Four months.'

She was not employed for her lively conversation or sunny countenance. I was grateful to see the vicious housekeeper appear in the doorway with Hannah, the tapping of their feet almost noiseless as they arrived.

'You're the girl who's looking for work?' Mrs Kemp was a large woman with a square jaw and beady eyes. Her greying curls had been strictly tamed under a white cap. She would not, in any situation, be described as a beauty, but her brisk and confident manner was that of a woman who was eminently capable of running a noble household. She ruled this house more surely than did Lady Hawbridge. I thought her wonderful, if a little terrifying.

'Yes please, mum,' I gave her a small curtsey. 'I was lately in Mrs Woodmarsh's employment, until she died. I have very little to live on at present.' I brushed at some dirt on my gown. I was aware that this was a futile action, but I hoped that it demonstrated that I was normally tidier in my appearance. I gave her what I hoped was an honest smile.

She shook her head. 'I'm sure you're a good worker, and Hannah has told me your sorry tale, but I haven't a position here. I'm sorry. The family has been bereaved and they'll be off to the country soon.'

This was not what I'd wanted to hear, although it was what I had expected. I hung my head.

Mrs Kemp might have been as frightening as an ogre to a mouse like Mary, but there was a kindness in her eyes. She took hold of one of my wrists and inspected the attached hand.

'You've very dainty fingers. I've got some mending that needs doing. The girl from the laundry normally mends, but according to the laundry man she's got the chicken pox. How are you with a needle?'

I almost laughed as I reached into my pocket to find my needle box. 'I am very good with a needle, Mrs Kemp,' I said. 'Why in my previous position, I was often asked to darn or mend because my stitching is so fine. As you say, my hands are small, and my mother was a seamstress, and she taught me well.'

She didn't want to know my history. Which was a good thing, when I was making it all up.

'I can't offer more than that, and I can pay you only a little, but if you're competent enough I can put in a good word for you hereabouts. I don't like to see a good girl fall on hard times.' She let go of my hand. 'Go with Hannah and you'll find what needs doing. Keep out of the way of the family, though. They are not to be disturbed.'

I thanked her profusely, like a girl who believed her luck was turning.

Chapter Twenty-seven

Hawbridge House was built so that the family never needed to see their servants, except when they summoned them. The gracious rooms, designed for entertaining, the copious bedrooms, ready to receive guests at any hour of day or night, were not to be used as thoroughfares for the staff.

In my father's house – comfortable, certainly, but not nearly as large as this – servants peeped into rooms before entering to clean and tidy. Then they would approach their task noiselessly, making themselves as invisible as possible, even when we could see and hear them quite easily. They would pad down corridors as if in soft slippers, not looking at us if we passed them, or unless we greeted them. But we mingled, we rubbed along together. We certainly knew they were about.

This residence had been set with corridors and passageways for the servants behind the walls of the main rooms. These were well-lit, even windowed in places, but hidden from view. In the drawing room, or the dining room, members of the family and their guests need never know, as they held a morsel of food to their lips, that a chamber maid was carrying her covered bucket of slops only a few steps away from them. Hannah moved swiftly and in silence, well-practised in staying out of sight. She kept turning her head to see that I was following, as if she were anxious that I would make a noise. She seemed on edge, as we scurried down the passageways, and only relaxed when we finally reached the linen room.

We found the basket of mending. It was the usual fare: cuffs on shirts and edges to handkerchiefs and neck cloths. It was not even full and could be dealt with very quickly. I wondered aloud why none of the maids in the house did this work.

'We could do. Well, I could do it,' said Hannah, 'but the laundry man's daughter has always done it. And I think Mrs Kemp took pity on you.'

'Betsy said your master died suddenly,' I said, as she was about to leave me. 'Is that what Mrs Kemp meant by the family bereavement?'

She nodded, glanced back down the corridor and pulled the door closed. She spoke in a low voice. 'I don't know much about it. Only that there was a lot of shouting yesterday morning, Lady Hawbridge was screaming and young Lord Shand – sorry, no, he's Lord Hawbridge now, the new earl, I mean – he had to be raised from his bed and was in a terrible state about it. They're all calm now, of course. I don't know how they can bear it.'

'Lord Shand was the young man with Lady Hawbridge at church? There was another man with her, I think, and an older lady?'

'Yes, that's Mr Callow. He's a friend of the family. He's known her ladyship since childhood. The other person is her ladyship's aunt, who happens to have a house nearby. They're close.' An aunt. She had looked like an aunt.

I wanted to ask about Mr Astley, but she hadn't mentioned him. I made use of the chattering Betsy again. 'There was another man at church, Mr Asprey, was it?

Betsy said he had been close to Lord Hawbridge – and Lady Hawbridge too.'

'Astley,' she corrected. 'He was a friend of the family, yes.'

'Betsy said your master was murdered,' I said, idly picking up the basket and fishing out a handkerchief.

Hannah jumped.

'I don't know how she knows that,' she said in a furious whisper. 'None of us knows how he died. The servants' hall was buzzing with stories about him having his throat cut. They said it happened in a theatre too.' She folded her arms and frowned. 'It seems that rumours are spreading quickly, if that little gossip Betsy told you.'

Betsy had said nothing, of course, but she was proving helpful. 'There'll be a scandal?' I asked.

'It's horrible,' she said, picking at her sleeve. 'You've no idea how awful it all is.'

I had an inkling.

Hannah opened the door again, her face still troubled. 'When you've finished, come straight back down to the servants' hall and help yourself to bread or cheese, but don't take anything else without permission. If anyone asks, tell them I sent you, but don't linger, and don't do anything to disturb the family. Don't forget to ask for Mrs Kemp; she'll pay you, like she said.'

There were a lot of prohibitions in this house.

She gave me a weak smile before returning silently to her own work. I sewed quickly and with determined concentration and it was not long before I had refilled the basket with mended items. I was rather proud of my efforts, but I did not have time to sit and admire them. I had other work to do.

Anyone unfamiliar with an earl's London home would be forgiven for getting lost in the back corridors, but I had enough experience to guess, roughly, how this house was laid out. The rooms for entertaining would overlook the square, so that guests might pass the time watching the comings and goings at the other fine houses. What could be more diverting than standing at the window, glass of wine in hand, noting the carriages arriving at the Duke of Norfolk's place, or the Duke of Cleveland's mansion, commenting to the assembled company on the style of the livery, the likely power of the horses, or the fashions of those who disembarked? The earl and countess would each have their private apartments at the back of the house, away from the noise of the square, and overlooking some sort of garden. The servants would be squashed into the rooms at the top of the house, even into the roof, enduring heat in the summer, and cold in the winter, running from the very top of the house to the very bottom of it via the hidden staircases and passageways.

I retraced the steps I had taken with Hannah and found the door I needed, slipping quietly through it, like any good servant, basket in my arms, but chose to follow the passageway towards the front of the house, rather than immediately heading downstairs. As I had trotted behind Hannah earlier, I had noticed one or two cracks and holes in the walls, where a person might peep at the family, or overhear conversations. I sought them out now, putting my eye to each and every gap that I found. I could see painted wallpaper, fine furniture, portraits on the walls, and even a gorgeous clock on the mantlepiece of one room, but not one living being. There was no sign of Mr Astley, let alone Lady Hawbridge.

The whole house was silent; holding its secrets to itself.

A small sigh of frustration escaped my lips. I had mended several of their cuffs and yet I was no nearer to any of them. I turned back towards the stairs, ready to claim my coin and hunk of bread.

A woman's voice drifted through the wall, not two steps from where I was. I stood rigid and listened.

'I can't. It's too soon.'

As softly as I could, and without daring to breathe, I searched for a spy hole.

Finding one, I pressed my eye to it and saw the back of a black gown. It was Lady Hawbridge. She was in conversation with someone, but I couldn't see who it was. She was standing in the way and right up against the wall. I willed her to move, but she did not.

There was a muffled response from a man. I couldn't hear what he said. I couldn't even hear who it was. The voice sounded low, serious. It must be Astley.

'No.' The woman's voice was clearer. 'It must wait. *We* must wait.' There was a hint of desperation, pleading even, in her voice. 'Nothing has changed. Nothing can change for now, you know that. Even his death makes it difficult, you must see that.'

There were further sounds from her companion. From the tone, he was ending their tête-à-tête.

'Very well. Tomorrow,' I heard her say. She began to step forward at last.

Behind me came the soft pad of footsteps. In a flash, I dropped to fiddle with my bootlace, setting the basket on the floor, as Mary came along the passageway carrying a bucket. She glared at me but said nothing. As soon as she was safely around the corner, I pressed my eye to the hole again.

Lady Hawbridge and her companion had gone.

I left the house with sixpence in my pocket. Mrs Kemp had been pleased with the sewing. Sixpence was far too generous for what I had completed, but I had the feeling that she was, as Hannah said, taking pity on me. Hannah had wrapped as much bread, cold meat and cheese as she could in a piece of cloth and sent me on my way with a warm embrace and the promise of her fervent prayers for my safety and good fortune. I was frustrated by my lack of progress – and hoped that Hannah's friendship might afford me another opportunity to discover what was going on in Hawbridge House.

Although I left the house, as I had entered it – from the back door – I took the opportunity to spend time walking the square. I wasn't dressed like a lady, but even in my dirty and dishevelled state, I could pretend to be one again. The houses, large and graceful, set around the pretty eight-sided garden in the middle of the square, were a world away from the cramped lodging houses of Drury Lane, packed into rancid courtyards, filthy inside as well as out. Even Berwick Street seemed grubby by comparison. My family was not noble, but it was significant and ancient enough to grant me admittance through any of these doors. The Vesseys had arrived in England with William the Conqueror; my great-grandfather had been made a baronet by Charles II. In another life, I might have come to this square for a ball or a party. I might have found a husband behind one of these windows; claimed this square as my abode.

I watched as a large carriage drove into the square, halting outside one of the more modest houses on the south side. A party of three young women emerged with an older woman following. They twittered and fluttered like exotic birds, full of life and promise, clad in soft silks of blue, pink and yellow. I could not take my eyes off them. They did not see me – just another drab on the streets and so far beneath their notice. The front door was opened for them, and then they disappeared from my sight.

I fingered the sixpence in my pocket. It was the first coin I had made by honest means since arriving in London. And the smallest by far.

I would not marry into a good family. My father had disowned me. I had to be back in Berwick Street soon, earning guineas not pennies, if I hoped to survive. I wanted a gown that did not stink.

I felt as disgusting as I'm sure I looked.

I had walked the whole square, and was considering walking around a second time, or circling the small lake in the centre of the garden, when I saw a man I knew.

He was standing, looking up at Hawbridge House with a keen expression.

It was William Simmot.

He did not take any notice of me. He would not have recognised me if he had.

He pulled some papers from the inside of his coat and read them over. Then he wandered towards the garden and sat down on the grass, cross-legged. He pulled from his pocket a tiny ink box and set it down in front of him, took out a pen, dipped it into the ink and began scribbling.

Garrick had said that he was nothing but a bad hack; a scandal-sheet writer. I watched him pause, mid-sentence, to find the right word or phrase and then scribble it down, looking over at the house. Was he, even now, getting ready to print salacious gossip about Lady Hawbridge or her late husband? I found it hard to believe that he had made his way to St James's for any other purpose. There was a secret in that house, I was certain of it. Had he discovered more than I had managed?

There was little I could do if that was his intention, beyond sending a warning to Davenport. I set off for Drury Lane.

Chapter Twenty-eight

I could hear a clock chiming five when I returned to the theatre. It was a way off dusk, and I was pleased to have made it back in good time. I might almost relish meeting Joe Sugden to show him that I had returned, were it not for the memory of him pulling my hair.

Sugden was not in the theatre. Neither was Molly. I assumed they were together. Ketch was in the green room with his monkey. I raised a hand in greeting, and he waved back. Even with his gloomy eyes, his was the friendliest face in the room, so I sat with him.

'How's your day going?' he asked, in his slow way.

'Lovely,' I said. 'I went to church, made some new friends and did some sewing.' All of that was true, of course. I did not say that I had also called at Bow Street magistrate's office on the way back and left a message for Mr Davenport – who had been out. 'You?'

'Aye, not bad. We went out for a walk.' He meant him and the monkey. 'Got frightened by horses in St James's Park but found a small place under the trees for a nap. It's been a fine day to be out.'

I nodded in agreement. I had not seen much of the day, but the walk from St James's Square to Drury Lane had been almost pleasant in the warm sun.

'I've not seen Molly,' I said. 'Is she about?'

His eyes took on a darker look. 'I've not seen her,' he said. 'I expect she's with Mr Sugden.'

'You don't like him much, do you?' It was an impertinent question, to which he gave a rueful smile.

'Don't matter what old Ketch thinks. I've known that girl for years, and she's always done whatever her heart tells her.' He scratched his chin thoughtfully. 'But I've nothing much against Joe Sugden, except that he's too easily led astray.'

I had no opportunity to press him on this comment, because the pair appeared in the doorway. Molly was flushed, her eyes bright and her face pink with the sun and fresh air. Sugden was as sullen as ever, scowling as he surveyed the room. They had been arguing. Molly's deliberately cheery approach told me that.

'Lizzie, did you have a good day?'

I repeated my story, watching Sugden out of the corner of my eye. He wasn't interested in where I'd been, this time. He seemed preoccupied. Molly asked about the new friends and I told her I'd met some servants in church and been invited back to their house for some food. I didn't tell her whose house it was.

'Have you had a pleasant day, miss? Ketch has spent most of it asleep under a tree, he says.'

Molly rolled her eyes. 'Just like you, eh, Ketch? You old slug. Any excuse for a sleep.' She batted his shoulder affectionately. 'I've been out and about, and Joe has *not* been buying me a bowl of punch.'

Sugden shoved his hands in his pockets. 'You get mouthy when you're drunk, Moll, that's all,' he muttered, walking off.

'Tight-arsed bastard,' she called after him. She rolled her eyes and began to pick at a fingernail.

'Well, there'll be work again tomorrow,' said Ketch, encouraging her to sit down. 'Best to have a clear head.'

'Do you think the law men are any closer to finding out why William Simmot killed Lord Hawbridge?' Molly asked Ketch. 'They've had a whole day now. Lizzie here says they don't think it's him, but I bet it is.' She bit the end off the troublesome nail and spat it on the floor.

'I think that's for them to decide,' said Ketch in a soothing tone. 'The likes of you and me are best out of it, I reckon.'

She shrugged, her finger still in her mouth. 'Joe's been jumping about it all day. Wants someone to be had for it. He's been sending me mad.'

Sugden's agitation added to the unease I felt about him.

'He thinks it's Simmot, of course,' Molly was saying, interrupting my thoughts. 'Same as all of us – anyone with sense thinks it's Simmot. He wrote that play, after all, with the hanging.'

I said nothing. It was what most of the actors and stage hands assumed. It suited them that the pompous self-serving Simmot would be the murderer. He was not one of them. They would not believe that one of their own might have done it and would not dare to think that one of Hawbridge's own associates would have done it. Simmot was an outsider.

'Molly Bray, would you come and give us a hand? We're still a man down in the trap room.' Mr Dinsdale's voice, commanding and loud, called across the green room. Tom Firmin was still unable to carry things up and down stairs. He stood, leaning heavily on his crutch, a pace or two behind Dinsdale, looking disconsolate.

'Mr Garrick has put a new after-piece for tomorrow's performance, and I want to bring the scenery up now, before they rehearse in the morning.'

Molly got up, wrinkling her nose. She had been hoping to rest, I think.

'Do you fancy seeing hell, Lizzie?' she said. 'Now's your chance. Come and see how all the little traps and boxes work.'

I did fancy seeing hell. It was possible that someone had hidden there on the night Lord Hawbridge was murdered and climbed out of a secret trap door. I wanted to see how it might be done.

Hell, it turned out, was a lot less exciting than I had imagined. I wasn't allowed to wander about and examine the room. Instead, I was instructed to stand still in the middle of the room, and given a large torch to hold, while Molly and the stage hands retrieved the right scenery pieces from their store. Tom Firmin had discovered that this was my first visit to hell, so he hobbled down the stairs on his crutch and pointed out its features.

The scenery, he explained to me, was painted on heavy wooden boards. The theatre put on many different plays, and there were different sorts of boards to reflect the different locations of the scenes to be portrayed.

'We've got castle walls and palace rooms, forests and cemeteries, gaol cells, city walls and gardens,' Tom said. 'Instead of painting new scenery for every play, the flats required are brought up to fit the play as best they can.'

'Is that easily done?' I said, watching Molly heave a large sack over her shoulder.

He laughed. 'You add a few items of furniture, or props, as well as the actors' costumes to enhance the sense of the scene. The audience imagination supplies the rest.'

He was right. I tried to remember the scenery from *King Lear*, but found that, mostly, what I could recall was the sense of tragedy and betrayal – but nothing particular about the painted boards at all.

Tom limped back upstairs, standing for so long was causing him pain. I stayed where I was, as I had been told, holding my torch high. This was helpful to the men, but it also meant that I could see more of the room. There were a couple of boxes, mechanical pulleys and hoists, located under traps, ready to send the more daring of the actors up through the stage floor. A man might, I mused, wait down here for several hours and, when the stage had been cleared, ease himself up through a hidden door. He could escape the same way too, after he had hanged an earl and cut his throat.

Hell was damp and chilly. Below the level of the street, away from any natural light or air, it reeked like an earthy, wet cavern. I shivered as a rat, nearly as large as a cat, scurried behind a set of castle walls, rocking a pile of stacked wooden planks as it went. There were a few bottles beside the castle scenery. There was a blanket too. I shone the light over to have a better look, wondering whether this was where Sugden kept his stolen spoils. I needed to come down alone and search the floor of this place unhindered.

'Will you hold that bloody torch still?'

Joe Sugden was struggling with a large box. My arm had dropped a little and he could no longer see where he was walking. He was standing with an angry look on his face.

'Sorry sir; my arm's tired.'

'My arms are tired too,' he barked back. 'Lift it up, would you? If you're down here, you'd better be useful.'

I raised the light again, ignoring the ache in my shoulder, dropping it only when he had left the trap room.

When the men had finished, I was allowed to leave. Molly put an arm around my waist as we emerged into the green room in search of refreshment.

'Pay no heed to Joe Sugden, Lizzie. He's been in a temper all day. He'll come out of it eventually.'

'I'm more concerned he'll come at me with his fists before the day's over,' I said. 'He doesn't like me.'

She shook her head, pouring a glass of wine. 'It's not you. He's been fretting about something. Seeing the earl hanging, and all that blood, it's made him afraid – but he don't like to admit it, being a man.' She rolled her eyes, handed me the glass, and grinned at me.

'Aren't you afraid?' I asked, sipping at it. 'I am, a little.'

'Dead men can't hurt you. It's the living you have to watch out for,' she said, pouring another glass for herself, the smile fading. 'Joe's mother was very religious, like I said. She filled his mind with stories about ghosts, dead people, you know. Jumping at everything, he is. And it makes him snappish.' She shrugged and wandered to a chair. 'Just keep out of his way for now. I'll look after him.'

Chapter Twenty-nine

I did not have time to think about Joe Sugden. A new and more pressing problem had arisen. William Simmot had not, as I had feared, dreamed up a scandal about Lady Hawbridge, but he had instead chosen to act on his grudge against Davenport and the men of Bow Street in the light of the murder. He had written about them. Unable to get his malicious piece into a newspaper late on a Sunday, he had, with considerable determination, printed his own pamphlet. He was hawking it about himself in the Garden for a penny. I went to buy one, having heard the thin-nosed spare horse loudly sharing some of the contents with a male companion. I saved my coin – someone had dropped a pile of the pamphlets in the street. I had mine for free.

The writer, who had decided to pen his work, in time-honoured fashion, as '*Anon.*', had made his own investigations. To my relief, he had not spoken with the servants at Hawbridge House, or, if he had, they had not passed on any information about the late earl, the countess or her friends. Instead, he had written about the elegant location of their home, giving a paean of praise to the octagonal garden of St James's Square, and offered – for any that wanted to know – Lord Hawbridge's full pedigree and brief comment about his estate in Gloucestershire. He wrote well, fluently even, if in a rather high and florid style.

Fielding's men were a laughing stock. Some, the pamphlet claimed, were brutish, and barely more honest than the thieves they took, others, despite having an inflated opinion of themselves, were witless idiots. His description of Davenport as vain, arrogant and, essentially lacking intelligence, was particularly cruel. Finally, and with ill-concealed bad blood, he had laid the guilt of Hawbridge's murder at the feet of Garrick himself. He had, wisely, stopped short of claiming that Garrick had strung up the earl and cut his throat, but the reader was left in no doubt that whoever had killed him was, in the opinion of the author, to be found in Drury Lane theatre.

I stood in the piazza, reading by the light of a brazier as the sky darkened to night. Around me, the pavements began to get busier as people made their way to taverns or chop houses to find a bite to eat, a bowl to drink, and a friendly companion for the evening. I let them pass as they jostled, scanning the words as fast as I could, wondering what Davenport made of it. If he had read it yet.

The pamphlet was suddenly snatched out of my hands and thrown onto the fire.

'Hey, I was reading that!'

'You shouldn't waste your time on scandal rags. They slow your wits.'

His face, in the red glow of the fire, was angry.

'I thought I should know what he was saying, Mr Davenport. I was concerned for Lady Hawbridge especially.'

'Mr Fielding is furious.'

He wasn't the only one. I had never seen him so ugly.

'Mr Fielding will recover,' I said, trying to soothe as best I could.

Simmot's words were unkind as well as untrue, but they reflected what many people said of Fielding's men – that they weren't worth what they were paid. If they failed to discover who had murdered an earl, only a street away from the magistrate's house, how could they be trusted to clear the city of crime?

'Mr Simmot has, I think, stopped handing out his sheets.' I said, laying a hand on his arm.

He shook me off, bristling still.

'He ran away when he saw Snowy and me. Dropped a pile of them and ran. He's a coward as well as an evil little bastard.'

I wasn't surprised he ran if Davenport and Snowy showed up, armed and raging.

'And where did you go, after church?' He snapped at me. 'I wanted to speak with you, and you skipped off.'

It would do no good to remind him that I was not a servant at his beck and call – not when he was in such a savage mood.

'I went to Hawbridge House with two of Lady Hawbridge's maids.'

'Oh? How did you manage that?'

'An opportunity presented itself and I took it. I span them a story about being destitute and they took me in.'

He gave a wry smile. 'You're a resourceful little liar, aren't you?'

'Walk me back to the theatre door and I'll tell you about it, if you like.'

He gave me an arm and listened while I told him how I had spent my afternoon.

'You sat sewing for an hour?' He found this amusing. 'I'm glad to hear that you can, truly, hold a needle, Miss Blunt.'

'I received sixpence for my work, I'll have you know.'

'I am extremely impressed by this hitherto unseen domestic ability.'

I forbore the mockery, glad that his humour had been restored.

'I saw Simmot as I was leaving the square,' I said, telling him how I had seen the man scribbling in the garden. 'From what he's written, from what I saw of his pamphlet, it's clear that he didn't find anyone willing to share gossip from the house. Everything he says is common knowledge.'

'About Hawbridge and his family,' he muttered. 'He was less kind to Mr Fielding.'

I ignored this. 'When I was in the house, however, I discovered that the servants' passageways have a few holes in their walls. It is possible to overhear comments from the drawing room, should you wish to.'

He stood still. 'And?'

It pained me to tell him that I had only heard part of a conversation.

'But I would be welcomed into the house again, I know,' I said, as he began walking again. 'And if I can gain Hannah's confidence, I'm sure she'll provide information for me. It'll take some care; she's jumpy, and I don't know what's bothering her. Lady Hawbridge was greatly agitated too. She's hiding something, of that I'm certain.'

We had reached the theatre door. The courts around Drury Lane were coming to life in the darkness. Around us the laughing, barely-clad women were emerging from the shadows to pluck the coats of gentlemen and make their irresistible offers. The sirens of Covent Garden were starting to call. Davenport they ignored, knowing well who he was, and who he worked for.

'I should return to Bow Street,' he said, in a weary voice.

'You're not going home?' I asked.

'No.' He rubbed his forehead. 'Mr Fielding is vexed by Simmot's accusations and vicious comments. I need to be doing something, even if it means walking the streets in the vain hope Hawbridge's killer will fall into my path and announce himself.'

'William Simmot has a lot to answer for,' I said. 'A lost night for you, among other things.'

He growled. 'William Simmot had better not show his face if he values his skin.' His hand dropped to his sword.

The anger had returned. Simmot's slight had cut him deeply. He had played with Simmot in the tavern, certainly, but he had not been cruel. A lesser man might even have taken him to Bow Street and thrown him into the gaol house, simply to unsettle or intimidate him. Yet Simmot had not taken kindly to the way in which Davenport had made him appear foolish and small. Simmot had taken the revenge of a writer: he had accurately described enough of Davenport's features to make it clear who he was speaking of – and then added some snide insinuations that would cause his readers to ponder whether they too were true to character. It was clever, even as it was petty and vindictive.

The fact that Davenport had fared better than Garrick in the attack would be of no comfort: Garrick was always in the press, whether he was praised or pilloried. He expected attention. Davenport was a reserved man and the attention he would receive would be more painful even than the insults.

I reached out to him and put a hand on his chest, wanting to relieve him of some of that pain, wanting to calm him, soothe him, before he walked the dark streets. I thought that I should tell him that I, at least, held him in esteem. I wanted to say that no one, truly knowing him, would take any notice of Simmot's comments, but the words wouldn't come because I did not know how best to say them. He stared at my hand for a moment, and then placed his own hand over mine, holding it firmly against his coat. I could feel his heart beating beneath my fingers. I could feel my own pounding inside my ribs. We stood, neither of us speaking, hands clasped, while all around whirled the yells, shrieks and squeals of men and women finding uncomplicated amusement in wine and one another.

Then he suddenly stepped back, nodded goodnight and turned away towards the Garden, disappearing into the throng.

A feeling that I had not known before rose within me as I watched him go, the warmth of his hand still lingering on mine. The feeling troubled me, so I pushed it away.

Chapter Thirty

Hell was on fire.

The alarm was raised in the early hours of the morning. The day when we were supposed to be opening again. We would not be opening. I had fallen asleep on Lucy Hunter's couch after drinking far too much wine and woke to the shouts from the stage hands that there was smoke pouring out of the trap room.

There were only a few of us in the dressing rooms, but we were all called upon to carry water to quench the blaze. Molly was screaming, running down the passageway banging on all the doors, trying to find extra people to help. Ketch was yelling. I ran, with everyone else, scrambling to find buckets, find water. Market stall holders were prevailed upon to join us and together we formed a chain to pass the water containers hand over hand to Dinsdale and his men to put out the fire.

The fire had been contained in the trap room and it had not spread. Even so, the theatre was a mess. The stage was stained yet again. This time it was blackened by smoke rather than darkened by blood, but, by miracle and by the dampness of the trap room underneath, it had not caught fire. Instead, smoke had drifted up through the trap doors so that the stage area was a filthy stinking fog. Even in the auditorium, the acrid air caught the back of my throat, scratching at it and making me cough.

We learned soon enough that the door to the trap room had been locked. Someone – no one knew who – had smelled the smoke and then seen the dark clouds, pouring underneath the door and alerted Dinsdale. He had rattled the door and, finding it stuck fast, had charged against it with two of his men. It had taken a while to break it down, even with his frame cracking against it. The blaze had been fierce enough, but it was the smoke which had sent them choking into the corridors and out onto the street calling for water and for help.

I saw Mr Garrick, swiftly summoned from his lodgings, throw his coat into the street, roll up his sleeves and call for water. I saw George Hunter, stick tucked under his arm, handling buckets with one hand. I saw Davenport, Grimshaw, Carter and Snowy, pulled out of Bow Street. Everyone who was nearby came to carry water for the men to throw on the flames. When the blaze had been extinguished we all trudged back to the green room where everyone sat, exhausted and stupefied, knocking back cups of small beer that the tavern boy had brought over.

Tom Firmin flung himself into the green room, still hobbling on his stick, coughing, face blackened by the smoke. He looked terrified.

'Body,' he croaked.

Ketch leaped up in horror, eyes wide in panic.

'Oh no!'

We all ran, every person in the green room. It was Fielding's men who got there first. Mr Snow, wrapping a wet cloth over his nose and mouth, then Davenport, likewise protected, followed by Mr Dinsdale.

Someone had been trapped in hell as it burned. People pressed forward to see.

I did not want to see.

Joseph Sugden had not been in the green room with us. He had been in the trap room.

–

Information came to us slowly, and it was a while later that we learned what had happened. Ketch was cradling Molly on his lap like a child. She had said very little, beyond asking for some wine.

The body had not been badly burned, people said; it was recognisably Joe, although his face was black around the nose and mouth. The silver crucifix he wore around his neck had survived. If he had not burned to death, then the smoke had poisoned him.

The magistrate arrived and asked to be taken to the trap room. He was down there for nearly an hour, with his men and Mr Dinsdale. Davenport, I knew, would be examining Sugden's body.

In the green room, members of the company speculated on what he had been doing there in the first place, while we waited for Mr Fielding to return. Someone was sobbing – one of the spare horses. A stage hand called Nat said that he thought Joe sometimes slept in the trap room.

Molly spoke up now. 'It's true. He did. He liked to keep an eye on things, he said. I went with him sometimes. Not last night. Not last night.' She gave a great sigh that turned into a sob.

Molly had been in the mending room last night, she was slumped in a chair when I left her. Sugden had gone to the trap room by himself. He'd had more to drink, perhaps, and knocked his candle over in his sleep. He would have known nothing about it, surely, which was the only good in such a terrible accident.

News of the fire had spread beyond the theatre and beyond Covent Garden. Along with the players and stage hands sat men I didn't know. One of them tried to ask me questions about the fire, about what I thought of Mr Garrick, and Mr Fielding. Scribblers and scandal-mongers, they were hoping for titbits of gossip, even as we mourned. Mr Simmot, perhaps wisely, had decided not to join them. Or maybe he was worn out from yesterday's exertions.

There was a groan from the corner of the room. Garrick sat with his head in his hands. 'Another good man,' he said, his voice raw from smoke and emotion. 'We must remain closed,' he whispered. 'We must respect Mr Sugden, a good and loyal friend to us all.'

The stranger next to me wrote down his words.

When Davenport came into the room, I knew that something worse was coming. I saw it in his face. He was not happy. Mr Fielding arrived with the rest. All of the men drank cups of beer to soothe their throats. No one spoke. We sat, silently, watching them drink.

Mr Fielding wiped his mouth. Then he spoke quietly. 'A large and bloody knife was found under Mr Sugden's body.'

He raised a hand as if ready to prevent anyone from interrupting. No one did.

'Mr Sugden had no wounds on his body and the blood on the knife is not fresh. I believe that he was lying on the knife that killed Lord Hawbridge.'

Now there was murmuring. Davenport, unable to raise his voice, having taken in so much of the smoke, banged his cup on the table to call for silence so that the magistrate could continue.

'It is my belief that Joseph Sugden, who was thought to be in need of money and who had been heard on many occasions complaining about his wages and encouraging others to complain, attempted to rob Lord Hawbridge.'

Molly sat, as if transfixed by what Mr Fielding was saying.

'We know that Joseph Sugden took Lord Hawbridge's snuff box, but he had the sense to hand it to me, perhaps realising that it was unique. I believe that he hit Lord Hawbridge over the head for his purse, panicked at what he'd done and decided to cut his throat.'

Sugden had been an opportunist. He was the sort of man to scoop up dropped coins or pick up a fallen snuff box if he thought no one would miss it, but the idea that he would kill a man for a purse seemed unlikely to me. He had intimidated me – but threatening a girl and stringing up an earl were very different things. His reaction to Lord Hawbridge's corpse had been one of utter horror. He had spent several minutes muttering anxious petitions to the Virgin Mary when he had lit the footlights.

Davenport was looking resolutely at his shoes. He didn't believe a word of it either.

'Overwhelmed by remorse, he locked himself into the trap room, drank a good deal of wine – bottles were found next to his body – and set fire to something, probably newspapers,' Mr Fielding concluded.

'You think he took his own life?' Garrick was incredulous.

Fielding nodded. 'I do.'

No one spoke. Slowly, members of the company turned towards Molly, who sat with silent tears raining down her face. She was shaking her head.

'I can't believe it,' she whispered. 'I can't believe he's gone.'

She looked up and saw every eye on her. She wiped the tears with the heels of her hands and sniffed. 'He's been so jumpy lately. So...' her voice trailed away. 'So lost and angry about something. I don't know what. He wouldn't say. But I can't believe it. I can't believe it.'

'Please sir,' she spoke to Garrick, not to Mr Fielding. 'I need some air.'

Garrick waved a hand, unable to say a word, tears in his eyes.

Her chair scraped as she stood; the only sound as the rest of us held our breath. With a dignity that almost matched Lady Hawbridge, she walked slowly to the door and left us. Ketch followed her, a dark and troubled look on his face.

Chapter Thirty-one

Gradually, the familiar green room noise returned, as each person expressed his or her shock to everyone else. They had no idea that Joe Sugden would kill for money. Yes, of course they had all heard him complaining about his wages. Had he really taken a snuff box? Yes, they agreed he had, as Molly said, been particularly out of sorts since Lord Hawbridge had been killed, but surely it wasn't his doing? And suicide? Setting fire to the trap room? Why, they could not believe it.

I did not believe it.

Mr Fielding, though, had arrived to find a man dead in a fire and discovered Lord Hawbridge's killer. Tragic though it was, the matter was solved. It was neat.

For Joe Sugden, it was more than tragic. To be condemned as not only a murderer, but also a suicide, was grossly unfair. His body would be cast into unhallowed ground; his soul would fare even worse and no one would pray for it.

Dinsdale was wandering the room; there were pale tear-streaks down his blackened face. He looked lost, unable to do or say anything.

The hacks all suddenly needed to be elsewhere and made their apologies, offered their condolences. The newspapers would be full of it later.

Davenport, in deep conversation with Carter and Snowy, must have felt my glare boring holes into his back. He turned, saw me, and glanced over at the door that led out to the Shakespeare. I understood his meaning and went outside.

I didn't have to wait long – for which I was glad, as the morning was turning grey and chilly. I had left my shawl in the dressing room. Out in the daylight, I saw that he was nearly as dirty as I was. The smoke had ruined his neckcloth and his face was covered in a film of black. He was in need of a shave.

'Joe Sugden didn't kill Lord Hawbridge,' I said as he approached.

He gave a heavy sigh and leaned against the wall next to me. 'Mr Fielding says he did.'

'Mr Fielding wants the newspapers to say that it was Sugden,' I said, trying to fight the fury that was rising inside me. 'This is not justice. This is not truth. This is something to keep the hacks happy while Lord Hawbridge's real murderer walks free.'

'Keep your voice down,' he said, his voice still rough. He leaned a little closer, favouring me with the stink of smoke on his coat. 'It's worse than you think.'

I held my breath.

'There was no key in the door.'

The importance of this comment was lost on me for a second. Then, I realised.

'Someone else locked the door? From the outside, you mean?'

He nodded slowly. 'Unless I discover that one of the stage hands has taken the key from the lock, for whatever reason.'

Not a suicide. Not even an accident. A second murder. I felt sick.

'Mr Davenport, I don't like what's happening here. A man with his throat cut hanging on the stage and a second left to burn to death underneath it.'

'I know. I don't like it either.'

'Does this have anything to do with Lord Hawbridge's death?' I asked. 'I can't see how.'

'I don't know,' he said. 'I can't see it either. Someone inside the theatre did this, I think. Someone who knew where the trap room was, knew Joe's habit of sleeping there, knew where the key would be.'

I shuddered. He was right.

'I'm not sure I want to be here any longer,' I said. 'This is more than just scenery falling over and costumes being torn, Mr Davenport.'

He chewed his lip. 'It's useful to have someone here, even now. You're safe. You've not had time to make any enemies.'

I was useful, again. Frightened, but useful.

'If I'm burned to death, or hanged, or found dead in any other way, then you will be responsible. I will haunt you for the rest of your days.'

'Then I'll have to hope that no one will kill you.'

We stood, unspeaking, side by side, leaning against the wall, tired from the morning's drama, glad of fresher air.

'Mr Fielding has asked me to go to Hawbridge House,' he said, after a while. He sounded weary.

I raised my eyebrows. 'You? Why?'

'He's needed at Bow Street this morning, but he wants Lady Hawbridge to know about Sugden as soon as possible, before she reads it in the press. I am to say that her husband's killer has been discovered and that he is dead. He thinks I'll deal better with the countess than Carter or Grimshaw.'

'I am sure she'll be glad to hear the news,' I said. 'There's comfort in lies, sometimes.'

He said nothing.

I eased myself away from the wall.

'You'd better have a wash and a shave first, if you want to appear like a gentleman. And change your clothes. You look grubbier than Mr Dinsdale.'

'I *am* a gentleman,' he said, with a degree of indignation. 'But you're right,' he inspected the backs of his hands, 'I can hardly arrive at Hawbridge House like this.'

'I want to return there myself,' I said, rubbing my arms against the chill wind. 'Whatever the reason for Joe Sugden's death, as I said last night, I'm convinced the answer to Lord Hawbridge's murder lies in his own family, not in the theatre. There are secrets there, and I want to know what they are.'

'Mr Fielding has told the world that Sugden was responsible, and that's how it will be reported, but there's nothing to prevent you seeing whether you can discover anything more from the servants.'

I looked down at my skirts.

'Of course, you're not the only one who needs to find something else to wear...'

He pursed his lips, looking over my gown. 'You're right. It wasn't pretty three days ago. Now it looks as though a dog has thrown up over it.'

'*That* is just about the only thing that hasn't happened to me while I've been wearing it.'

He grunted and reached into his coat. 'I suppose you've no means of paying for anything new?'

I had plenty of means at Berwick Street, but I didn't see why I should pay for it.

He scattered a few coins into my hand, which I inspected with an exaggerated sniff.

'You're to look like a modest servant, mind,' he said. 'You can't go to Hawbridge House decked out in your usual rig.'

I still took all of the coins and then gave him a wink. 'Thank you, sir. I can manage to look respectable.' I slid them into my pocket, knowing exactly which of the many emporia I frequented would offer the right sort of gown, and not question where or how a filthy looking woman had come by these coins.

'I didn't care for Joe Sugden, Mr Davenport, but he does not deserve to be known as a killer. And a person who has sliced one man's throat and burned another alive is not someone who should be walking the streets. We must find out who really killed Lord Hawbridge.'

I turned to leave. I also wanted to know what on earth Joe Sugden had to do with it all.

Chapter Thirty-two

I arrived at the house to find that Hannah had just returned from an errand, and that Mrs Kemp was on her way out. They were exchanging a few words at the back door as I approached. I asked Mrs Kemp if there was any more mending that I could undertake, but she shook her head.

'There's none today. You stitched those cuffs very neatly, though, much better than the laundryman's daughter. If you would like to call again in a few days, I may have more then.' She nodded, as if to dismiss me, and checked the contents of her basket.

This was disappointing. I could not contrive a reason for lingering at Hawbridge House without work.

'You haven't found a new position yet?' Hannah looked at me anxiously, taking in the new clothes. 'Else how do you come to have money for a gown?'

I had purchased a simple blue and white striped affair, a dark petticoat, and a cap, apron and kerchief that were all very nearly white. I thought that I would pass for a servant in my father's house, which meant that I looked decent, honest, and dreadfully dull. Davenport would approve.

I shook my head. 'Best not to speak of it, Hannah,' I said in a whisper. 'I am trying very hard to find honest work.'

Her face fell, and she hugged me tightly. 'Don't worry, Lizzie. Something will come for you. But will you have some food with us?' She released her hold and looked to Mrs Kemp, who was tying the ribbon of her bonnet, making ready to leave. 'Lizzie may eat with us today, at least, Mrs Kemp?'

The housekeeper's mouth tightened slightly.

'You may stay and eat with us for today, Lizzie. The house is not so busy at present. But only for today.'

The household was still in deep mourning.

'I can help, to earn my bread, if any help is required,' I said. I wished to sound like a diligent worker, although the truth of it was that I wished to be back inside the house, to overhear conversations.

Mrs Kemp cocked a head to one side, pondering this.

Hannah cut in. 'There's her ladyship's gowns to sort through, Mrs Kemp. I might make a start on them, to see whether anything needs work before we leave for Gloucestershire. I could do well with another pair of eyes.'

Mrs Kemp nodded. 'Very well. But mind you're not seen, Lizzie, and no unnecessary chattering.' She gave me a fond smile, before set off down the path. 'Perhaps I'll enquire about work for you, while I'm out.'

'Yes, Mrs Kemp. Thank you, Mrs Kemp.'

The last thing I needed was another job. I was struggling to juggle the work I already had.

Hannah and I made our way up the back stairs to Lady Hawbridge's rooms. A small doorway brought us out onto a long corridor that was decorated with paintings. These were mostly pictures of objects or animals – still life with fruit, flowers in vases, studies of butterflies and dogs on cushions. I imagined that these were Lady Hawbridge's own choices. This was the lady's place of solitude and reverie. Here, more than anywhere in the house, she would be herself, undisturbed except by those she chose to admit. Her choices of art suggested simple and unimaginative tastes – or else she had wisely picked the sort of images she knew were appropriate to her status and condition in life.

Lady Hawbridge was not in her rooms.

'I need to take an urgent message to Lady Hawbridge,' said Hannah, with a small sigh of frustration. 'I thought she would be here, but she must have gone to the morning room. Wait for me. I won't be long. Don't touch anything.'

She left, pulling a note from her pocket as she went.

She was barely out of the door when I set to work. I moved as quickly and as quietly as I could, not knowing how long she would be gone. If I was seeking evidence of Mr Astley's part in her life, then I was probably looking for letters. I ignored the dressing table, which I could see was covered only with bottles of scent and boxes of jewellery. The small writing desk held more promise.

The drawer yielded little except a pot of ink, a few uncut quill pens, a knife for cutting them, and a good amount of paper. I spent far too long feeling about for a secret compartment, until I decided that there was none. There were no letters – which meant that either she burned all of her correspondence or that they were hidden elsewhere. I examined the mantlepiece, peering behind vases and under the clock. I took the poker and prodded the fire, just in case she had recently burned anything incriminating.

There were a few books by her bed. None would cause a scandal. On the top was a book of sermons. I picked it up, wondering what she read to help her sleep.

A small folded note was tucked into the cover.

Glancing to the door, I unfolded it and scanned it. The handwriting was not easy to decipher, and it was written in French, but I saw immediately that it was a love note. The words were warm, if lacking in imagination: a memory of tender kisses, a longing to hold her for eternity, that sort of thing.

A floorboard creaked on the corridor outside and I hastily folded it again, not before searching the end of the letter to find a name. There was none – only an initial. '*A*'.

I shoved the note back into the book and stepped away from the table, just as Hannah walked in.

'I haven't touched anything, miss,' I said quickly.

She looked from me to the book of sermons, and then back to me. Her lips tightened.

'Good. I should hope not.' She looked at the book again. I swallowed, wondering whether she had seen me holding it.

'The dressing room is through here,' she said, with a small inclination of her head.

We walked through into the dressing room in silence. Hannah opened up the enormous trunks and began to lift out Lady Hawbridge's gowns. I pondered the note as we laid the gowns on the floor, one over another, and then laid out the petticoats, most of quilted silk, on another pile. '*A*' might stand for Astley, but it might equally be a Christian name, a nickname or even '*amour*'. It might have been a note from her husband, but I doubted it.

We surveyed the gowns. I am used to good clothes, but these were exquisite. We were, as Hannah said, to look over them to see what needed to be mended. Some of them, she told me, her ladyship wished to alter. She became gradually less agitated, and more talkative, as we ran our hands over the fabric and discussed the bead work and embroidery. With my careful encouragement, she began to tell me of Lady Hawbridge, and how she had worked for her since before her marriage.

She admired her mistress, that was clear. I decided to press a little more.

'How did you find the master? Were they very much in love? He was older than her, I think.'

Her face darkened. She hesitated, as if about to say something terrible. Her voice dropped to a whisper.

'I didn't like the way he treated her.'

'Lady Hawbridge?'

She nodded. 'She would come into her chambers in such a state of distress sometimes.'

I wondered what had particularly distressed Lady Hawbridge. After all, a noble wife would expect to put up with rages, ill-temper, and even violence – to say nothing of her husband's inevitable infidelity. But, unlike most women, she could spend most of her time away from her husband, in her own apartments, in a different part of the country even. She could, if she were very careful, find a lover of her own. Having encountered Lord Hawbridge, I thought she would have needed to be very careful indeed. Tucking a note into a book of sermons had been rash.

'You should hear what Martin says about him,' Hannah was saying.

'Martin?'

'Martin Jakes, one of the footmen.' She blushed a little as she said his name. 'Mr Jakes has survived in his lordship's service only because he is so good with the horses. His lordship can't... couldn't,' she corrected herself with a smile, 'couldn't manage without Mr Jakes.'

'And what does Mr Jakes say about the master?'

Any comment that Mr Jakes might make was causing Hannah to glow pink. Poor girl, to be so afflicted in her fancy that it showed on her face. How did she manage to speak to this Mr Jakes without fainting?

'Mr Jakes says that once he tore through the stables in such a temper that some of the hands left.'

I raised my eyebrows. 'It was that bad?'

'He started to thrash one of the stable lads. No one knew why. Nearly killed him. One of the older men pulled him off and got a black eye for his trouble.'

Lord Hawbridge had done the same to my father's stable boy for no apparent reason, so this seemed entirely in keeping with his character.

'You said that some of the staff left. Why did Mr Jakes stay on?'

'The horses. He lives for those horses. And Lord Hawbridge loved riding, so the horses were of the best quality.'

I picked up a heavily-embroidered stomacher and examined it for pulled threads or other damage. It was in good condition, so I returned it to the trunk.

'Lady Hawbridge is better off without him,' I decided.

'Hush,' Hannah glanced at the door, anxious again. 'You mustn't say such things.'

I knelt on the floor again, next to the petticoats. 'Even if it's true,' I whispered in her ear.

We worked in silence after that. I reflected that the more I learned of Lord Hawbridge, the less likely it seemed that his death had anything to do with Garrick and the theatre. He had been a violent man. The manner of his death, strung up like a pig and sliced open from the throat, had also told me that. I recalled the scene of it:

the blood, the stench, the snuff box shining in the candle light.

I gave a start.

'What's the matter?' Hannah asked. 'You just jumped like you'd had a fright.'

'It's nothing,' I said. 'I think my legs have pins and needles, that's all.'

I stood up and stretched, bending to pick up a pink petticoat and taking it over to the trunk.

Joe Sugden had told Davenport that the box had dropped from the earl's pocket. It must have landed on the floor when he had been hanged. But if it had dropped then, why hadn't it been covered in blood? If it had fallen as he was raised up, then it would have been covered with blood when his throat was cut. I remembered that it had stood, pristine in the middle of the lake, as if someone had placed it there. The earl's murderer, knowing how much he loved it, had left it there, as if taunting the dead man. Perhaps made him look at it before slicing his neck.

The thought of this made my own blood run cold.

There was a sound from the room beyond. Hannah leapt to her feet and put a finger to her lips in warning. I rose, arms still full of petticoat.

The door opened, and Lady Hawbridge stood before us.

She was, as I had noticed in the theatre, a beautiful woman. Whatever her life with her husband had been like, he had not cowed her completely. Indeed, she was radiant. Widowhood suited her.

I bent my head as I curtseyed. It was sad that I could not look at her for more than a moment, but, aware of my lowly status in her house, I kept my eyes down.

'What are you doing in my dressing room?' This was addressed to Hannah.

'Sorting your clothes for the country, my lady. We're seeing what needs mending, and you said that some gowns want refitting before we leave.'

I peeped up. Lady Hawbridge was shaking her head.

'I haven't decided yet whether I shall go home with Lord Shand or not. Lord Hawbridge, of course, I meant. Dear Shand is Lord Hawbridge now...' she corrected herself, her voice trailing off. 'I may remain at Hawbridge House a while longer.'

'Yes, my lady.'

The lady smiled weakly. 'But you did well to think of it. Thank you.'

I could see why Hannah loved her. She was generous with her praise.

'Will you help me with my hair?' she said. 'I've just heard that we are to be visited by a man from the magistrate's office. I don't wish to appear dishevelled.'

She wouldn't look dishevelled wearing a sack, I thought, but she was arming herself for what she imagined would be a difficult meeting in the only way she knew how. Davenport, already smitten by her beauty in the theatre, would be happy enough to renew his acquaintance.

Hannah followed her out of the room, not before instructing me to close the trunks and fold the remaining the gowns over the top of them.

'I can sort the rest later,' she said. 'When you've done, go down to the servants' hall and wait for me there.'

I did as she asked.

The door was open, and I could hear Lady Hawbridge talking to Hannah.

'I don't know why he's coming here. All I want to do is bury my husband and have nothing more to do with it. It's up to the magistrate to find his murderer.'

Hannah made soothing noises but said nothing of significance in response while the countess chattered. She sounded nervous.

'Callow is on his way. He'll know how to deal with him. Astley will come too, of course, but he's out with Shand. I think they were going riding this morning. Poor love, he's still in such a state about it all.'

I had finished the folding but lingered for as long as I could without attracting attention from Hannah, just so I could listen. Then I made my way slowly through the doorway, nodding to Hannah as I went and bobbing another curtsey to her mistress.

Chapter Thirty-three

I had no intention of going back to the servants' hall. I was going to investigate the earl's rooms while I had the chance. I made a guess that they would be on the opposite side of the house to his wife's, but on the same floor, and walked quietly but confidently in that direction, invisible and silent and ready to melt into a wall at any moment.

The paintings of flower vases and dogs gave way to images of dead game birds and then Italian landscapes, signs of the earl's interests and his travels as a younger man. The décor was darker in this side of the house. Lord Hawbridge, from what I had seen of him, would have spent little time here. He would have ridden out in the mornings – if he rose before noon – or gone to the Lords when he was required. He might have met friends in coffee houses and discussed the matters of the day, idled away his afternoons with a mistress or whichever fancy harlot was his latest distraction and then gambled and drunk his way into the night. From what I had heard of him, and from the man I had encountered, I didn't picture him quietly reading a book in his salon.

I turned the handle of the door that lay at the end of the corridor.

The room beyond was undoubtedly his. As his wife's rooms had been furnished to be her sanctuary, pretty, light and airy, filled with vases, so this room told me of him.

It was austere, neat and, as I thought, mostly unused. The fire had not been lit in days, so it was cold. The fireplace had not even been cleaned. The walls were lined in dark green paper, the pictures on them were mostly portraits. These were the second-rate paintings of his ancestors. I recognised his features in them, but the better ones would be on show downstairs. The furniture was dark and functional: a writing table, a large chest of drawers, three uncomfortable-looking chairs and a corner table set with glasses on a silver tray. The door to the bed chamber beyond was closed.

I stood still and looked around, breathing in the chilly air, as if somehow, just by standing here, I might discover who had killed him and why. I walked around his writing table. A letter from Astley would offer an opportunity to compare the handwriting with what I had seen in his wife's room. I picked up a bundle of letters and undid the ribbon that held them. They were from a variety of correspondents, and not in any particular order; recently-read letters waiting to be filed away. I shuffled through them, searching for familiar names.

The door to the earl's bed chamber opened suddenly, causing me to jump in alarm. I had not anticipated anyone being in there. The letters dropped from my hands to the floor.

It was the girl I'd met with Hannah at church. Thank God it was only her.

'Oh, Mary, isn't it? You gave me a start. I'm Lizzie, remember me?'

She eyed me with suspicion. This was understandable. Her nose wrinkled.

'What are you doing?'

I bent down and gathered up the letters, still shaking with relief that it was a chamber maid who had caught me and not the earl's valet. If a senior servant had found me, I would be in serious trouble. I could easily con my way around a silly girl like this.

'What are you doing in here?' she asked again. 'You're not supposed to be in here.'

'I was in Lady Hawbridge's room with Hannah just now, helping her to fold some gowns and then when her ladyship came in, Hannah sent me away. I missed the doorway to the back stairs and came in here by accident.'

Even if she worked out that this was a lie, she didn't say anything.

'Is this the earl's room?' I asked.

'Of course it's the earl's room,' she said, brows furrowed. 'Who else's would it be?'

'Yes, I thought it must be,' I said, replacing the letters and gazing about. 'Looks like a man's room.' I needed to divert her attention away from me. 'What are you doing in here?'

She shrugged, lifting up the bucket she was carrying. 'I was cleaning the fireplace. I didn't want to do it before, but Mrs Kemp made me come up today.'

'Why didn't you want to do it?' I asked, walking over to her and making a play of inspecting the pile of ash in her bucket.

She licked her lip and looked back at the door to his bed chamber. 'I was afraid of his ghost. They were all saying he was murdered, and I thought his spirit might be in here.'

I suppressed a smile. 'I don't think ghosts haunt their own homes, Mary. More likely the place where they died.'

Her face was serious as she thought about it.

'You think he'll haunt the theatre?'

'I don't know. I don't know much about ghosts. You're cleaning this fireplace too?' I gestured to the ash in the grate. 'Would you like some help?'

'I can manage it. I always do it.' She still looked anxious, but she was no longer wondering why I was in his room.

'Dead men don't do any harm,' I said, giving her thin shoulders a rub and echoing Molly's words to me. 'It's the living ones you have to worry about.'

At this her face began to crumple.

'Is it so very wrong to be glad that he's dead?' she said, giving a sudden sob. 'Does that make me very wicked, Lizzie, do you think?'

I looked at her. She was fourteen, possibly younger. She had not quite lost her child's face. There were little pimples appearing around her nose and chin. Her hazel eyes, starting to fill with water, were large and appealing, framed by long lashes. She was a pretty thing. He had obviously thought so. She would not have stood a chance against him. She was not intelligent, but she had been innocent. I felt anger rising in my chest.

'No, I don't think it makes you wicked. Men who prey on their maids are wicked, though.'

She looked at me in alarm.

'Don't say anything, Lizzie. Please. She mustn't know, Lady Hawbridge. She mustn't know. I don't want her to be angry with me.'

'You haven't told me anything, so I've nothing to tell.' She had not told me. I had guessed. 'I'd better go to the servants' hall, though, or Hannah will wonder where I am. Show me where the door is?'

She pointed me back to the door I had ignored earlier, and I made my way down the back stairs, as fast as I could.

The life I live in Berwick Street is not the life I chose, but the wealthy men who visit me pay well for what they want. I dug my fingernails into the palms of my hands as I stamped down the stairs. Mary, and hundreds of girls like her all over London – all over England – were living at the mercy of men like Hawbridge, believing everything to be their own fault, cautioned to stay silent for fear of upsetting the lady of the house or losing their position.

His death had brought relief to at least two members of his household: two women who would never know what the other had endured, because they would never speak of their experiences to one another.

Chapter Thirty-four

Hannah had not returned to the servants' hall when I walked in. There was no one present. I sat for a minute or two, waiting dutifully, but quickly became restless.

There was a sound from beyond the doorway. Men's voices. This was Mr Astley arriving with the young earl, I thought.

'What? Why?' I heard Astley's surprise and assumed that he was only now being informed of Davenport's impending arrival.

'Here already? Who's with her? Is Callow here?'

The servant delivering the news had a very soft voice. Even with my ear pressed to the door, I could not make out what he was telling Mr Astley. I could, though, hear Mr Astley's pompous tone very clearly.

'Well, why didn't anyone come and find me? I'll go through now to be with her. No, no, I'll manage. I don't think you need be part of this, Shand, unless you wish to be... what? Yes, of course.'

And then they were gone.

Davenport had arrived then. He was already with Lady Hawbridge. I was cut off, trapped in the servants' quarters. I wanted to hear, but I could not.

I jumped back from the door as Hannah came in with Mrs Kemp. From the look on their faces, I saw immediately that something was wrong.

'There she is,' said Hannah, nodding at me. 'Mary said she was in the earl's room just now, looking at his personal letters.'

I tried to swallow, but my mouth was dry. Silly little Mary might not have been a valet, but I should have guessed that she would be a squealer. Even after she had sobbed over me, she had run straight to Hannah. Shit.

Mrs Kemp had returned from her business and was still in her bonnet.

'Come here, you.' The kindness had vanished.

Reluctantly, I shuffled towards her, outwardly penitent, but ready to run. The back door was open.

She grasped the top of an arm and shook me so hard that I thought my shoulder might break.

'I don't know who you are, or what you are, or why you're in this house, but you are certainly not welcome here.' She shook me again. 'I made some enquiries, while I was out, thinking that I could find an honest girl a new position.' More shaking. This was hurting my head now as well. My teeth were rattling. 'I happened to meet a servant from the Woodmarsh house, and I discovered that Mr Woodmarsh has not dismissed his staff. You lied.' Another shake and a fierce dig with her fingernails that made me yelp. 'Mr and Mrs Woodmarsh did not have, nor ever had, a maid called Lizzie Blunt. And Mrs Woodmarsh,' her voice rose in dreadful crescendo, 'is still very much alive.'

The lying old bastard.

'I can't believe you deceived us, Lizzie,' said Hannah. 'We trusted you. We let you into the house, into her ladyship's rooms.'

There was nothing that I could say. Nothing that I could do, except hope that my shoulder would not be shaken from its socket and that Mrs Kemp might simply order me to leave. She released my arm. I staggered and nearly fell over.

'Pull out your pockets,' she ordered. If I wasn't a servant looking for honest work, then, in her mind, I must be a thief. It was a reasonable assumption. The pockets were empty save for the sixpence she had paid me yesterday.

'That's mine,' I said, grabbing at it before she could take it. 'I earned it fairly. You gave it to me.'

She plucked at the fabric of my sleeve. 'What about this, then? Where did you find the coin for new clothes?'

I could not say, so shook my head. She drew her own conclusions.

'Wicked, insolent girl,' she said, voice rising in anger again. 'Thieving hussy.'

She gave me a sharp slap on the cheek, and then strode over to the corner of the hall, to fetch the stick that was leaning against the wall.

Hannah was not expecting me to run and was not fast enough to grab me as I pushed past her and sped to the open door, unwilling to be beaten as well as shaken to bits. Neither she nor Mrs Kemp could catch me. Through the back door I went, as fast as I could run, knocking over a box on the way, around to the front of the house and out into the square. I turned to see whether they were following, but neither woman had given chase. I was not worth the effort, and I would be unlikely to return. They had not, I was grateful to see, sent any of the male servants running after me.

I leaned against the wall of a house at the top of the square, panting so hard that I thought I might faint or vomit.

After only a few minutes, when my breathing had become nearly normal and the stinging heat on my cheek had died down, I saw the house steward showing Davenport out through the front door of Hawbridge House. He saw me and raised a hand in greeting.

'That's a better costume,' he said, as he approached. 'Less… grubby.'

'Glad you approve.' I gave him a little curtsey, still shaking.

'Have you become a servant of Hawbridge House now, then?' he asked.

'No. Nor would I wish to.' I looked back at the imposing edifice and rubbed my injured arm. 'That's a much better coat.' I nodded to his outfit. 'I rather like it.'

The brown coat, reeking of smoke, had gone. He was dressed in something almost fashionable, as befitted an interview in St James's Square. The rich blue suited him. It was perfectly cut and set with silver buttons, even if it was still rather plain.

'Glad you approve.' He gave me a bow and then grinned. He was a fine-looking man, now that he had lost the old coat and the scowl.

Two stable hands were leading horses to the front of the house. We stood and watched – although I made sure that I was hidden behind Davenport's shoulders, as I was reluctant to be seen by any of the servants. I wondered whether either was Martin Jakes, the man who caused Hannah to blush so quickly. Perhaps the younger of the two, who was talking, not to his companion, but to the horse, stroking its neck as he walked. Poor Hannah would need to acquire a glossy chestnut coat, if she wished to attract this one.

The front door opened again and, this time, the steward was bidding farewell to Mr Astley and Mr Callow. Davenport and I watched as the new earl stood in the doorway and shook hands with his father's friends. Lady Hawbridge appeared next to him. Astley bowed, clasped her hands and said something to her. I watched her nod, serious-faced, at whatever it was. He did not wish to let go of her hands, I thought. It was she who pulled away, glancing down the square.

Mr Callow, by contrast, was lighter in his farewell – much more the old friend from childhood than the would-be suitor. He leaned into her and planted a kiss on the cheek she offered. She patted his face. Whatever it was that he said to her caused them both to laugh – he heartily, she covering her mouth. Astley laid a hand on Callow's shoulder, as if cautioning him to regard that he was out in public. Callow gave a light shrug but moved away. One man had too great a sense of how to deport himself, the other had too little. Callow's flippancy was annoying Astley, but I hoped that the young widow was grateful for the levity he brought. Her smile, although brief, had made her, if it were possible, even more beautiful.

'How was your interview?' I asked Davenport, still unable to pull my eyes from the countess. She had linked her arm through the earl's as Callow and Astley steadied their horses and called their goodbyes.

'Not easy.'

I turned to him as the men passed us. 'She is pleased to hear her husband's killer is dead, I expect?'

'Oh yes.' He offered me his arm and we began to walk back to Covent Garden. 'Yes, that was a great relief. In one sense, the nightmare is over for her. There will be no public trial, no raking over the story in the press. But she will always be known as the lady whose husband was hanged at Drury Lane. She will not escape the gossips.'

I know how cruel polite people can be.

'She had better marry again,' I said. 'And quickly. Take a new name and have done with Hawbridge for good. What did you think of Mr Astley? Will he make her an offer?'

He considered this. 'Mr Astley was warm to her, he was kind. I would say he behaved in a fatherly way. She's still young, after all – young enough to be his daughter. He was the one most keen that she didn't hear details, who intervened when I spoke of Sugden's death. He was… protective.'

'Worthiness can be dull, but she may yet be grateful for his protection.'

'She was grateful for his kindness, I think' he said. 'But I doubt she'll be short of suitors.'

'Ah, the lovely Lady Hawbridge, with her golden hair, beautiful face and large fortune,' I laughed. 'No, they will be forming a queue down to St James's Palace. Sadly, Mr Davenport, she is unlikely to turn to you for comfort, even though you are a gentleman and wearing such a smart coat – I do hope you're not too distressed.'

'I shall try to contain my disappointment,' he said, drily.

'What of the younger man, Mr Callow?'

'I understand that they're childhood friends. His London home is not far. Beyond that, I saw nothing to indicate they were particularly close. She looked embarrassed by his antics on the doorstep. Are you really suggesting that one of those gentlemen would have murdered Lord Hawbridge just to marry her?'

'It's possible,' I said. 'Not only is she extremely fair, she comes with her own fortune. Men have killed for less.'

'They have. But both men are accounted for at the time when Lord Hawbridge was killed.'

'You checked Mr Astley's story?' I thought of the love letter, signed with an *A*.

'I did. His servants are all adamant that he returned home after the first play. He was not in a cheerful mood, one of them said.'

'His mistress had been fondling Hawbridge's thighs all night. I would not have expected him to be dancing a jig.'

'And Molly Bray saw Callow in a tavern, so neither of them was cutting the earl's throat.' He said nothing more for a while as we paced in step with one another. He had slowed his usual brisk pace, content enough to amble with me.

'What about you?' he asked eventually. 'What news from the servants' quarters?'

'I learned that the countess's marriage was not a happy one and that her husband, when not gambling away her money and flirting with actresses, preyed upon one of the chamber maids.'

He said nothing. It could hardly be considered news.

'He once nearly killed a stable boy in a fit of temper. Several of his men left, they were so appalled. I think it must have taken a lot for them to leave such a prestigious house.'

'That matches your own experience of him at your father's house,' he said.

'I thought so too.' I said. It was time to play my best card. 'Oh, and Lady Hawbridge is having an affair with someone who signs his letters with an *A*.'

'Really?' He stopped still, genuinely shocked. 'What on earth makes you say that?'

'She has a note tucked into a book of sermons, of all things, on a bedside table. It's written in French. The declarations of affection are unimaginative, but I didn't have chance to read it carefully, so I couldn't discover who sent it.'

'Ah, I'd forgotten that you were so well-educated,' he said, glancing at my servant's clothes. 'But you didn't have chance to read it properly? That's a pity. You were caught reading it?'

'No, I was not.' I paused, frustrated to admit my failure. 'I *was* caught leafing through the earl's private correspondence in his chambers, though. I didn't find anything there, but I won't have chance to have another look. I don't think I'll be welcome in Hawbridge House again.'

He gave me an enquiring look. 'What happened?'

'There was an unpleasant scene in the servants' hall. I'm sorry.'

We walked on again in silence, each of us digesting our discoveries, presently arriving at the west side of Covent Garden's piazza. Ahead was Bow Street and beyond that, Drury Lane.

'I feel as though I'm wandering about in circles,' he said. 'Mr Fielding is unhappy. He's outwardly content to allow Joseph Sugden to carry the blame for Lord Hawbridge's death, at least for now, but he's a man of principle and he would prefer to know the truth. He's snapping at the men.'

'At least he'll guarantee the funding for their work,' I said. 'The government can't withhold his expenses, if he's found a murderer. Especially when the murderer is conveniently dead.'

'I don't like convenient,' he said in a low mutter. 'I prefer truth. Even if we are forced to put up with the likes of William Simmot making us out to be blundering fools while we find it.'

'You'll find it, I know you will. But perhaps, now that the hacks are off your back, you can go about reaching it without being watched and criticised.'

'Thank you.' He gave me a warm smile. 'And thank you for staying here.'

I pulled my arm from his as we neared the magistrate's house. 'I'd better walk to the theatre without you, Mr Davenport. I have my reputation to think of.'

He laughed at this. 'What reputation would that be, Miss Hardwicke?'

'The one that currently requires me to wear such dismal clothing and live without hope of payment, as Lizzie Blunt.'

He met my eyes, suddenly serious. 'Try to stay out of danger. Whatever the newspapers say, we both know that there is still a killer about.'

Chapter Thirty-five

I left him at Bow Street and made my way towards the theatre. I peered into the Rose tavern on the way, to see if Molly was there, and then looked into the Shakespeare. John, the tavern-keeper hadn't seen her. She was, perhaps, sleeping off her drink in the mending room.

I was about to leave when, in the corner, I saw William Simmot. He was sitting by himself with a small bowl of punch and a pile of papers. He was reading them and, from time to time, scribbling on them, his tiny inkwell and several scattered goose feathers lying next to his drink.

It struck me, watching him, that I had overlooked him as a source of information. He was, it pained me to admit it, an observant man. His description of Hawbridge House, although a little flowery, and written for those who prefer gossip to architecture, had been precise and accurate. His portrait of Davenport had been vindictive, but it had been recognisable – which was why it had stung the man so badly. Members of the company had marked Simmot as Lord Hawbridge's killer because they did not like him, but a charmless man isn't necessarily a murderer. Davenport had questioned him as a suspect, but I wondered whether this puffed-up fool had a talent for seeing and hearing things, when he wasn't writing terrible plays. He could certainly write – I had evidence of that.

I decided that I would favour William Simmot with the one thing I knew he truly desired. Attention.

I sat opposite him at the table.

'Will you buy me a drink, sir?'

He looked up and peered at me, appalled.

'Strumpet,' was all he said, before returning to his papers.

I said nothing but watched him work. His mouth moved as he formed the letters on the page. Again, he looked up and glared.

'Why are you still here? I'm not looking for company. Go away.'

Really, the man was very ill-mannered. A night or two in gaol might have done him good, I thought. Or perhaps a tumble with a decent whore would teach him how to behave. I was very nearly desperate enough for money, but not quite. And he had no money. I hoped that wit and boldness would suffice.

I picked up one of the sheets of paper and read it through, along with his explanatory notes down the margins.

He gave me a scornful look. 'Don't pretend you can read it. Put it back on the table and leave me in peace.'

I did not. I continued to read for a while.

'For the last time, jade, leave my papers and go away.'

'Oh Mr Simmot,' I said, ignoring this and shaking my head with exaggerated despair, 'you've given this character a fine speech, but I cannot imagine any theatre in England able to manufacture a golden bird that would carry her off in its beak, such as you have here.'

He blinked. 'You can read?'

I gave the poor creature a soft smile. 'Your handwriting is almost illegible, sir, and there are too many crossings out, but, yes, I can read it.'

He was assessing my attire, the meanness of my dress and the lack of refinement I had, puzzled that a servant like me could read.

'It's too fantastical,' I said, undeterred by his open-mouthed scrutiny, tapping at the page in my hand. 'However much Ursula's flight from the prison of her circumstance is best expressed by her actually being carried through a small window by a phoenix, such a movement would be utterly impossible to stage. You'll have to find another way around it.'

He coughed. 'You understand the meaning of it? Not just the words?'

'Of course, sir. You've hinted at it in your marginal notes. Ursula is a woman oppressed by her circumstances – I'm guessing a bad marriage, or else she's trapped with her father, step-father, or possibly mired in debt.'

He nodded vigorously. 'Yes. She longs to escape her family. The prison represents this.'

'And the bird is her saviour, carrying her through the smallest window, representing, I think, that the best chance of escape might not be the most readily obvious?'

'How can you know this?'

'The phoenix, I assume, being the bird that rises from the ashes, is somehow connected to a dead hope, a lost love, or something that she thought had been taken from her?'

He was now, I thought, probably in danger of falling in love with me. I was, it seemed, the first person to understand his play. Perhaps the only person. He shouted to the landlord, waving a hand, and a glass of brandy – my request, I don't care for punch – was brought to me quickly, while he sat gazing at me like a puppy.

'You see,' he said, breathless, 'I knew it would work. If you, a girl, dressed... so...' he didn't know quite how to speak of me, concerned now not to be offensive, 'if you can see it, why can't a man like Garrick?'

I put down my glass and laid a hand over his.

'My dear Mr Simmot, I can see what you are trying to do *because* I am a girl dressed like this, a woman trapped by her own circumstance, forced to live in a manner I do not wish, and longing for escape.'

He had no idea how true this was.

He did not quite grasp it.

'You mean, Garrick should be locked up?'

'No, I mean that the people who will best understand your writing are not the gentlemen who sit in the pit at Drury Lane, free to come and go as they please, but the young women like your heroine, Lady Ursula, and possibly young men too, trapped in their family homes and waiting to escape.'

'I don't see it...'

It was obvious to me. 'How might your fantastical, un-performable ideas reach the hearts of impression-able young women, who do not attend theatres, except with chaperones and only then to admire someone else's bonnet or flirt with their fan?'

He shook his head.

'Mr Simmot, it is very simple. You should abandon plays altogether and at once, and instead turn your ideas into novels.'

He sat back, crushed. 'But I do not wish to write novels. Novels rot the mind and corrupt the weak. I want to write for the stage.'

I took a small sip of brandy and let him grumble for a moment. Eventually he stopped pouting and looked thoughtful.

'But, do you think my ideas would work as novels?'

'I would imagine that there would be more money in novels,' I said, cautious now, having only read a page of his work, and knowing the reading public to be happier with simple romances. 'And better a novel that steals into the homes of England and gives courage to every young man or woman who longs to step away from the plans their father has for them, than a dozen plays that are ignored by theatre managers who cannot stage them.'

I watched him turn this over in his mind. He was imagining himself as a novelist now, and not a playwright. This wasn't how he had seen his life as a man of letters. He had wanted to be Dr Johnson, but now he was beginning to see other possibilities for his model – Samuel Richardson, perhaps, or Mr Fielding's late brother.

'You could,' I said, quietly, laying my hand over his again, 'return to your own father's house and behave like a dutiful son. From there, in Lichfield, you could write novels and send them to publishers in London. I would be willing to wager that your fantastical visions will thrill and excite many people. They'll be the talk of all England.'

He did not ask how I knew of his own situation; he was too caught up now in his plans for the future – dazzled by them.

'You may be right,' he said. 'The human imagination is a wonderful thing. And what Garrick cannot or will not put on the stage, I can describe in such detail that my readers will see it for themselves.'

'Exactly so.'

'You are a marvel,' he said, suddenly clutching my hands. 'An angel of God.'

I had never been called that before.

'I can return to my father's house, the prodigal son, and win his approval without ceasing to write.'

'And no longer have to pay rent for lodgings in London,' I said, now fearing for my hands, as he squeezed them tightly.

'You angel,' he said again, although this was the punch talking. He had told Davenport that he did not squander his time on women, being a serious writer of plays. Now, filled with liquor and fresh ideas for making his name as a novelist, he looked to be changing his mind.

I pulled my hands away and finished my brandy.

'What did you see in the theatre,' I asked, 'the night Lord Hawbridge was killed?'

'Eh?'

I repeated my question.

'Why do you ask about that?' He frowned, confusion all over his chubby face.

'Because I am an angel, of course,' I said, taking a small risk with his present good humour. 'Possibly an avenging one. And because I think that a gentleman like you, although blessed with the vibrant imagination that will capture the hearts of many, are also observant and astute.'

'How do you know that I am observant?' He sat a little straighter, intrigued to hear more about himself. Like every man under the sun, he would condescend to listen to his talents being enumerated by a woman prepared to flatter him.

I gestured to his papers. 'You cannot fail to be, sir. It's in your writing. No one could express Ursula's condition as a prison unless he had lived that condition, and seen others live it too.'

'Oh, I see it,' he said, his hand suddenly clasping mine again. 'You're right, I do see it. I observe, I note, I write!'

'So tell me what you saw in the green room, masterful observer.'

He giggled. 'You're mocking me,' he said.

'A little.' I giggled back, as though we were sharing a private joke. 'But tell me anyway.'

He was suddenly serious. He was thinking over the events of that night.

'I was furious,' he said. 'Garrick had rejected another play. I had sent him four – including the one with Ursula and the golden phoenix – and this one, I thought, was my finest yet.'

I had to ask. 'I understand it contained a hanging. An unusual one.'

He nodded, glum-faced. 'Ah yes. That's why everyone in the company believes I killed Lord Hawbridge. I did not kill him, by the way. It was one of the stage hands. A shocking thing. I heard that the earl's blood covered the stage.'

'It did.' I had reason to remember. News of Joe Sugden's part in the murder had spread quickly.

'My hanging didn't have blood. That would be very disturbing. But a man is hanged upside down and dies, suspended between heaven and earth…'

'Is he an earl? This man in your play?'

'No. He is wicked.'

'Ah. So hanging him upside down is… something about overturning evil?' I asked.

'You see? You understand it. You, a mere woman!'

I let this pass without even raising an eyebrow, I needed to keep his account flowing.

'Was Lord Hawbridge wicked?' I prompted.

He sat back.

'I don't know. I didn't know him.'

I leaned forward, stroking his hand very softly. 'But what did you see? He was there with Garrick.'

He was silent for a moment, gazing down at my fingers. Then he closed his eyes. I stopped stroking; he was enjoying the sensation too much and I needed him to concentrate.

'I behaved badly. I know that. I'd spent far too much of my money in here, drinking, reading and re-reading Garrick's letter of rejection and becoming increasingly angry. Finally, I snapped, and marched into the green room, knowing that the whole company would be there, knowing that Garrick would be there fawning over the sort of men who know nothing about plays.'

He was becoming angry even thinking about it. I risked stroking his hand again, hoping to keep him even-tempered.

'Men like my father,' he continued. 'Men like Lord Hawbridge and his friends who turn up to be seen by other people and find flattery when they offer their patronage. None of them ever wants anything but Shakespeare and plays from the last century. Nothing is ever new, except that it looks and sounds like everything that's gone before, or else it is a frippery.'

'And you threw your very new play at Mr Garrick, I believe,' I said, trying to move his account on a little.

'He laughed at me. He *laughed*. Told me to take my "ridiculous little efforts" away. In front of his noble friends he chose to make a fool of me. That was when I decided

257

that if he wasn't going to buy my play, I would tell him what I thought of him.' He rubbed his forehead, now creased at the pain of recalling that moment. 'I probably caused quite a sensation.'

I smiled. 'In a room full of players, a little drama is quite acceptable now and then.'

He pulled a face. 'I did myself no favours though. I threw my play at him and strode out in what I hoped was a suitably belligerent fashion, but then realised I'd left my best work scattered on the floor of the green room. It was my only copy – I don't have much money for ink at present.'

I tried not to laugh and made my face look as serious as possible. 'That wasn't wise.'

'No,' he gave a long groan. 'It was not a wise thing to do at all, in hindsight.'

He had yet to tell me anything I didn't know. I was becoming a little frustrated. I let go of his hand.

'Did you see anything, or hear anything, even in your distress and anger, that was unusual for the green room? Anything at all?'

'It was a riot of players, stage hands and men of fashion, I suppose,' he said. 'As it always is.'

He was quiet, still remembering his embarrassment.

'It was different later on, of course,' he said, biting at an ink-stained fingernail. 'When I went back.'

'You went back to the green room?'

'Of course. When I realised that I had left my best play there, and that it would already have been crushed and trampled on by Garrick and his like, I wanted to rescue it.'

He had returned. I hadn't seen him, so I could only suppose that this was when I was dressing Kitty Suckley, or when the performance was continuing, and all the players were on the stage.

'Were there many people around?'

'No, I was able to slip in and gather up as many sheets of paper as I could. I didn't wish to linger, having been so humiliated earlier – and I certainly didn't wish to encounter Garrick again. I found most of them, although someone had seen fit to use a few sheets as a make-shift plate or napkin. They were covered in grease.' His shoulders drooped a little at the thought of his great play being so ill-used.

'Never mind,' I said. 'I'm sure you'll be able to remember what was in them, when you come to transform your ideas into a highly-praised novel.'

He smiled weakly.

'Did you see Lord Hawbridge?'

He shook his head. 'No, I expect he and his friends were watching the performance. They were into the silly nonsense, *Love's Expense*, by that time, *King Lear* having finished. I saw only the stage manager, Mr Dinsdale, one or two of his crew – that dark whiskery one and a young boy on a crutch. Oh, and Mr Hunter was there. He was speaking to Dinsdale over a drink.'

Joe Sugden and Tom Firmin had been there. It made sense that Tom hadn't moved; he wouldn't go far on his crutch and wasn't able to help. Sugden was probably resting for a moment before the play's end when he would be needed to clear the stage. I would have expected Dinsdale to be nearer the stage, overseeing the movement of scenery or arrangement of lighting, but perhaps he had everything in order. George Hunter having a drink didn't seem surprising, but here they were again, together, talking quietly.

'They are on very friendly terms, Mr Hunter and Mr Dinsdale,' I said. 'They are often talking together.'

He looked surprised. 'Of course they are,' he said. 'They're cousins, I think. At least, they're related.'

'Really? I didn't know this.' They didn't look alike. At least, they hadn't appeared to be alike. Now, I began to wonder whether there was a likeness in the squareness of the jaw and the breadth of the shoulders. Dinsdale's broken nose had distracted me from seeing it.

'Yes, cousins, or something like it,' he was saying. 'They worked together too, years ago when Hunter was acting in the provinces. He was thought to be quite the rising star in those days, but then his temper got the better of him and he got into a fight at Jonny Rich's theatre.'

'I heard about that.'

'Dinsdale was something of a fixer. Sorted things out for Hunter and made sure he got the billing he deserved. I don't know where he was when Hunter had his famous fight, but if he'd been in the same room, you could be sure that Hunter wouldn't have been injured. Dinsdale's always ready to jump in with his fists.'

This was becoming very interesting.

'You've seen his broken nose, I imagine? Dinsdale's face?'

I nodded.

Simmot was warming to his tale now. 'He got that in Lichfield, in a tavern I know,' he said with a touch of pride. 'A theatre manager wanted to put another man above Hunter on the play bill, just because he was a local. Dinsdale went in to sort this out but the disagreement turned ugly – hence the broken nose.'

'What happened? Were they forced to leave? Did Hunter take second billing?'

He laughed. 'Ha. Not a bit. Dinsdale might have got a broken nose, but the manager was so badly beaten that he was in bed for a week. The bills were changed and printed before he was conscious, and the play was a roaring success by the time he was walking. And the drama of it all meant that the theatre was packed every night, with people coming to see the famous George Hunter.'

So Hunter and Dinsdale were related and their history was colourful and violent. I began to wonder what their intentions were in Drury Lane.

'It must pain Mr Hunter a great deal, not to be on stage, I think,' I said to Simmot, who was now rubbing at the ink stains on his thumb with his shirt cuff, dipped in punch. This was having no discernible effect on the stain, and it was not good for the cuff.

'He'd like to be in Garrick's shoes, I'd say,' he said. 'He can't act anymore because of his injury, but he's a theatre man to his fingertips. He might have taken over from Rich at Covent Garden one day, had he kept his fists in check.'

'That is a great pity,' was all I said, now beginning to see that the accidents that had befallen the theatre had been part of a dangerous plan.

'But aside from these people, you didn't see or hear anyone else? You gathered your play and left.'

'As much of it as I could find, as I say. No, there was no one else – apart from a girl who came in to talk to the whiskery fellow. Large shoulders – not my sort at all.'

That would have been Molly.

'She was in very high spirits, laughing a lot. He was trying to make her shut up and calm down, but she was very jolly.'

I rolled my eyes. I hadn't been aware of her drinking in the dressing room, certainly not when we had Kitty and Lucy with us, but she must have found some liquor somewhere. Sugden had tried to stop her from excess.

Thinking of Molly made me want to return. She'd been out with Ketch, drowning her sorrows. I felt a pang of guilt that I had left her.

I reached out and squeezed Simmot's hand. 'I need to go, sir. Thank you for the drink.'

He gazed at me in the way that men often do when they've had a glass or two of punch. I was not dressed like a harlot, but I could see him gathering his courage, ready to make me an offer of a few coins. Any woman alone in a tavern is asking to be bought, after all. I imagined he had little experience of the matter, or how any of it was done.

'Save your pennies, Mr Simmot,' I said, patting his hand. 'Go home to your father and write wonderful stories for young ladies trapped in their gilded prisons. Write their dreams for them and you will be the toast of the literary world. Then find yourself a kind wife to share your ambition. Don't fritter your coins on women like me.'

His mouth gaped a little as I stood to leave. His face turned crimson. 'I didn't mean... I... wait. I didn't ask your name...'

No, he hadn't, and I wouldn't give it. The conversation had been about him. He had much to learn if he wanted to find that wife, but I judged it was someone else's task to teach him. I left him wondering, for the first time, who I really might have been.

Chapter Thirty-six

If Hunter and Dinsdale were conspiring to ruin Garrick and install Hunter in his place, then they would need two things: they would need to demonstrate that Garrick could not manage his company, and they would need the players and stage hands to transfer their loyalty from Garrick to them.

Accidents had certainly happened. Costumes had been ruined with paint or torn beyond repair. Scenery had fallen over at inappropriate moments. A young man's health had been sacrificed to create a nasty fall from a ladder. George Hunter had spoken of candles falling out of the girandole. All of this suggested that Garrick was losing control. I wondered whether Joe Sugden had discovered the truth before me. When I confessed that I was working for the magistrate, trying to uncover the cause of the accidents, he had wanted to know what I had overheard in the dressing room. Maybe he knew that Hunter and Dinsdale were involved. Perhaps he had confronted them – or asked for a share of the profits to keep quiet – and they had silenced him.

Dinsdale had a strong crew among the stage hands. I remembered how, when Mr Fielding had questioned him, they had made noises of support as he spoke. These were theatre people, much more than they were Garrick's people. I saw that now.

Hunter was jovial with the players. He barely spoke with stage hands, the company's servants. He was happiest drinking with the actors, slapping them on the back, helping them learn lines, offering advice gleaned from years of experience. He was not harassing them to turn up on time to rehearsals, as Garrick was. He was the affable actors' friend. He flirted with the actresses – I'd seen him snuggled up in Peg West's bosom – he poured drinks for the men as if he were the one who had bought them wine and beer. How could they not suppose that, under his directorship, the theatre wouldn't be a riot of fun?

And while Dinsdale was with the stage hands, and Hunter was gaining the support of the players, his wife was ensuring that the patrons were not forgotten. It would be crucial, if he were to oust Garrick, that the financial support continued. Hunter could hardly turn to the men of letters, the critics who praised Garrick's attention to detail, and his transformation of the stage. He would look instead to the men of fashion who wanted pretty actresses more than Garrick's elevated sense of artistry. No wonder he had sent her to Hawbridge, rather than Astley. Hawbridge, as well as being an earl, was wonderfully ignorant of theatre. Astley had gone home after the *Lear*, unimpressed by the farce that would follow the serious play. Astley, unlike his companions, thought the play a significant feature of the night out. Hawbridge was, by contrast, something of a philistine. It wasn't his title that attracted Hunter, but his ignorance – and the knowledge that he would draw other, equally ignorant but wealthy men into Hunter's circle. It made perfect sense.

I pushed open the back door and wandered down the dark corridor to the dressing rooms. I had no proof of any of this, of course.

Molly was still out. Or, she was not in the mending room. I made my way to the green room, wondering whether I would find her there. I needed to discover whether Sugden had said anything to her. She did not know that his death had been murder, so I needed to be careful. His death, and the lie that had been told about it, was dreadful enough, without her knowing that he had been locked in the trap room and left to die.

She wasn't in the green room either, but Ketch was back. He was drinking with Tom Firmin. They were talking quietly, the monkey curled up on the table in front of them.

'How's Molly?' I asked. 'Where is she?'

'Gone for a piss. She needs to sleep now, I think. It's been a long and difficult day for my poor little lamb,' said Ketch.

'Is she... has she drunk much?'

Ketch put his head on one side. 'Joe would have had something to say about it, no doubt. She'll be all right by the morning.'

'Poor Molly,' I said. 'Such a terrible thing to happen.'

Ketch looked me up and down, as if only now focussing on who I was. 'You look fancy, Lizzie Blunt. Where did you get your new clothes, eh?'

I had forgotten, for a moment, who I was in this place. 'I found a few coins, you know how it is, Ketch,' I said. I gave him a sly look, as if I had just worked out how women earned their money in the theatre.

He chuckled into his drink. 'And there was me thinking you were being paid by that runner,' he said.

This startled me. 'Paid by the runner?'

He raised his eyebrows, so that the skin on his bald head wrinkled. 'Molly says you told her and Joe that you were here for the magistrate, spying on us all.'

'Spying?' Tom looked up in surprise. 'Why would you be spying on us?'

I rehearsed my story again to them. How Mr Fielding had sent me, a thief, to Mr Garrick, and how I was trying to find out about the accidents in the theatre. 'That was all before Lord Hawbridge was killed,' I said. 'His death put an end to my spying, but by then I was needed, and I like it here.'

Tom shook his head, frowning. 'So when you were talking to me, asking about my fall, you were just wanting to know for the magistrate?'

'In part,' I said, not wishing to be dishonest, 'but I did really want to know about your leg. It looked sore.'

'I'm not sure I like your kind, Lizzie Blunt,' he said. 'I thought you were a friendly girl.'

I said nothing. If he knew the truth, he would be even more shocked.

Molly arrived, releasing us from the awkward silence, and helped herself to the dregs from Ketch's cup. 'Lizzie! Where've you been?'

I struggled to remember where I should have been. 'I went for a walk and found something new to wear,' was what I came up with.

She looked at my gown. 'Suits you,' she said. 'Did you steal the coins for it? Aha, you little trollop, I know what you did.'

I looked suitably guilty.

'I should box your ears for that. No girl from my dressing rooms puts herself about, even if she does need new clothes. You come to me for gowns – I can always find you something.'

'I'm sorry, miss.'

'You spend your life thieving and whoring, you'll end up hanging for something or someone,' she said. Her voice wobbled into a small sob.

'I'm sorry. I didn't mean to distress you,' I said, but her face had crumpled now. She put her head into her hands and ran from the room.

Ketch, giving me a filthy look, ran after her.

'What was that about?' I asked Tom, conscious he was still scowling at me.

'She's upset, of course,' he snapped. 'She was close to Joe Sugden. Very close.'

I knew that.

'Look Tom, I didn't mean to spy on you,' I said. 'I didn't mean to insult you.'

He rolled his eyes.

'Really. You were kind to me. I liked that. But I had to find out. The magistrate put me here to do it.'

He turned his face away. I could see that he was angry.

I stood for a moment, not knowing what to say, aware that I had lost his trust. I recalled the smile he had given me when we had met and felt a pang of regret. Then I remembered what he'd told me. It had been Dinsdale, he had said, who had rushed him, shouted to him to hurry up the ladder.

I made my way to the mending room, wanting to make peace with Molly, but she was not there. Someone was sobbing in Kitty Suckley's dressing room, further along the passageway, so I tapped on the door and entered without waiting.

It wasn't Molly, but Lucy Hunter. She was sitting at Kitty's table, trying to paint her face with make-up. Assisted by the bright afternoon light that was coming through the window, I saw that she was trying to hide not only her red eyes, but the purple bruise under one of those eyes. It was a futile endeavour: not only was her face a mess, she was drinking. I could smell the liquor.

'Oh, I'm sorry, Mrs Hunter,' I said. 'I thought this was Miss Suckley's room. I've come to sort her costumes.'

She said nothing but began to apply rouge to her cheeks.

'You'll not lose that without a dab of comfrey, miss,' I said, not looking at her, but concentrating on the gowns. 'That's what my mother used to do, whenever pa hit her.' It was easier to lie than tell her about Emily's magic salve.

She sat, now poised with the rouge pot and looked at me through the mirror.

'What do you know of it?' she said, taking a swig of brandy from the glass in front of her.

I shrugged. 'Enough to know a shiner when I see one, miss.' My own black eye was still in evidence, after all.

Her shoulders sagged and she dropped the rouge. Then she started sobbing again.

I plucked a handkerchief from my pocket and sat next to her on the bench. She took the offered handkerchief and held it to her face, covering the small white square in the rouge she'd just applied. It was Davenport's handkerchief. He would not be impressed by the rouge.

'Thank you.'

She looked at me with a teary, stained face, the bruise – up close – was ugly and sore, across the top of her right cheek. I assumed it was Hunter who had hit her. The skin had broken, probably damaged by the ruby ring he wore. The back of his hand then: short, sharp and brutal.

Bastard.

'Does he do this often?'

She shook her head. 'No, not often. Just sometimes. When I'm not good enough, or forgotten my lines, or when the man I'm supposed to be with decides he doesn't want me.'

I pricked up my ears.

'Mr Astley?' I couldn't help myself. 'He doesn't want you?'

She frowned a little. 'Oh, it's nothing. He'll come back, he usually does. But he wasn't happy that I was being so cheerful with Lord Hawbridge. He doesn't want to share me.'

'He won't have to share you now, miss, will he? What with Lord Hawbridge being dead.'

She gave a weak smile, as if I had no idea how such things worked. 'That doesn't prevent him from being jealous, silly girl. It's what men are like.'

Privately I imagined Mr Astley was too busy fussing over Lady Hawbridge to spend time with his mistress. Instead I asked, 'Is your husband jealous of Mr Astley, or doesn't he mind?'

She seemed to shrink again at the mention of Hunter. Then she shook herself.

'He likes it that other men want me. But they have to be rich. It's his great plan: one day we'll have enough money and enough support for him to take over a theatre and we'll be the talk of the town.' She scooped up her glass of brandy and toasted herself in the mirror, with something of an ironic lift in her brow. 'Ouch, that hurts.' She put a fingertip to the bruise.

'He'd like to take over this theatre, you mean?'

'Oh yes,' she cast a glance at me in the mirror, believing that she was talking to a nobody. 'He'll be master of Drury Lane one day. That's the big idea. We just need the support, that's all. Garrick's not so popular.' She returned her gaze to herself, swaying a little as she tried to focus.

'Then you'll be the star of the show, miss,' I laughed. 'In the papers more than Mrs Cibber.'

Her face dropped again. 'Perhaps. As long as that spiteful whore Kitty Suckley doesn't steal it all from me. She's after Astley too. That's what George said. And she'll stop at nothing to get herself a rich patron. George said I wasn't doing well enough.' She sighed. 'That's when he hit me.' She mimed the strike, wafting a gentle hand in front of her image in the mirror. George Hunter would have been drinking and probably wouldn't even recall it.

'Where is Mr Hunter now, miss? Can you keep away from him?'

'Ah, thank you for your concern, little one. He'll be in the Shakespeare, or the Rose. I should probably avoid him for the time being.'

I nodded.

'You can keep the handkerchief, miss, but mind what I say: comfrey. A salve or a poultice will help.'

She went back to dabbing at her face. I hoped, for her sake, that she would stay away from her husband – and out of the view of the public – for a day or two.

I went to look for Davenport, and not only to report the loss of his handkerchief.

Chapter Thirty-seven

Bow Street magistrate's court was only a short step from the theatre. I made my way to the house, and not the court, and found the door opened by the young lad whose acquaintance I had made some months ago. He recognised me, bowed solemnly – he was a solemn little creature – and scuttled off to find Davenport. I waited in the hallway which was large, but only minimally furnished with a simple table and a vase of flowers from the market. A magistrate would not want to parade his good pieces when there were thieves about.

A door opened, and Davenport came out.

'I can only assume that you come bearing news?'

'And good afternoon to you too, sir.'

He chuckled. 'My apologies, Miss Hardwicke. Or are you still Lizzie Blunt?'

I gave him my most superior look. 'At the moment, I am, indeed, the archangel Gabriel, the bearer of tidings.'

He ushered me into the kitchen, much to the surprise of the housekeeper, who I recalled was Mrs Priddy. She said nothing as Davenport pulled a chair for me at the table and bade her bring a pot of tea. The boy stared, wide-eyed, at me, before running back to his station by the door.

As Davenport poured the tea, I shared with him all that I knew, beginning with what I'd gleaned from Simmot.

He interrupted me from time to time for clarification but let me tell my story mostly unhindered.

'Have we seen the last of Mr Simmot?' he asked, grimacing, 'or is he still to be found handing out his scandal sheets in the piazza?'

'I believe he will be in Lichfield soon,' I said, 'but if you wish to speak to him, he lodges on Drury Lane, in one of the better lodging houses. I think he's relieved to be saving his funds by going home, his landlord is milking him dry.'

'I'm glad to hear it. You have saved us all from his plays and pamphlets,' he said. 'I am better able to avoid his novels, I think.'

'They'll be everyone's favourite soon, believe me,' I laughed back. 'The talk of the coffee houses.'

'What I want to know,' he said, leaning forward and helping himself to a piece of the cake Mrs Priddy had also set in front of us, 'is how you persuaded him to tell you all that about Hunter and Dinsdale?'

'There are ways of retrieving information from men like Simmot, if you know how to deal with them.'

'Oh God, please don't tell me you took him to bed.'

'Don't be foolish. Of course I didn't. He has no money and there are limits to my charity. I find a little flattery works well on most men.'

'You never flatter me,' he muttered into his cake. 'Mrs Hunter confirmed his speculations, you say?'

I thought of Lucy Hunter, red-eyed and battered. 'I don't think she's living the life she imagined when she married George Hunter,' I said. 'I've no doubt she enjoys the attention from men like Mr Astley, to say nothing of the cheers from the crowds and notices in the newspapers, but I don't think she quite understands what he's up to – there was no deviousness or circumspection in her comments to me. Even so, she said that it was their plan to take over the theatre.'

He chewed for a while, thinking. 'I can well believe that Hunter and Dinsdale are behind the mischief in the theatre. I can imagine them plotting to put an end to Garrick's dominance, although I cannot see how Lord Hawbridge's death fits with their plan.'

'I don't think it does,' I said, remembering the conversation I'd overheard in the dressing room. 'Hunter was agitated about it. Hawbridge was a big prize for him, that's why he was throwing Lucy in his way.'

'Exactly.'

'What about Joe Sugden, though?' I asked. 'Did they lock him in the trap room?'

He pulled a face. 'I can't imagine that either, although, if they thought he would go to Garrick they may have resorted to desperate measures.'

I remembered Dinsdale's face, his bewilderment, and his grief at Sugden's death. He didn't look like a man who was hiding a murder; he looked like someone who had lost an old and trusted friend.

'Besides,' said Davenport, 'if they didn't kill either Lord Hawbridge or Sugden, then all that they have done is cause a few accidents and some damage. Garrick will be at liberty to send them packing, or to claim for the loss, but there's little we can do.'

'And we still have a dead earl.'

'We still have a dead earl,' he agreed. 'You know, I think that your earlier guess was nearer the mark. This has more to do with Hawbridge House than it does with Drury Lane.'

'Hmm,' I said, taking a bite of cake.

'Unfortunately, I can't return there,' he said. 'As far as Lady Hawbridge is concerned, we've discovered her husband's killer.'

'I won't be welcome either.'

He raised his eyebrows. 'Are you sure? You don't think you can use those famous charms of yours and find a way inside? Search for more letters while you're mending neck cloths?'

'I have no intention of being beaten by the house-keeper – which is what will happen if she catches sight of me. She gave enough bruises earlier.'

He didn't respond.

I picked at the crumbs on my plate. 'At least you can deal with Dinsdale and Hunter,' I said.

'I'll speak with Mr Fielding, in the first place, and let him have the pleasure of informing Garrick. It will be a dubious pleasure; I'm sure Mr Garrick believes himself to be held in high esteem by every member of the company. He'll find it hard to hear the truth.'

'He would probably prefer it to being run out of his own theatre.'

'Probably,' he agreed. He stood up from the table and stretched. 'It's been a long day. I'm going home. You'd better return to the theatre for now, before the light fades.' He offered me a hand up from my seat and watched me as I shook cake crumbs from my apron and re-tied my kerchief, trying not to wince at the soreness of my arm and shoulder.

'You don't need to return to Hawbridge House,' he said quietly, noticing that I was in pain. 'You've done everything that I asked of you. Mr Garrick and Mr Fielding will be grateful.'

I started to contradict him, but he held up his hand.

'No, Miss Hardwicke, Lord Hawbridge's death is my business, not yours. I've put you to enough trouble, and I shouldn't have asked more of you. Besides,' he smiled, 'I'm sure that something will occur to me, once I've had a decent night's sleep.'

Chapter Thirty-eight

He was not the only one who needed sleep. I spent the night, unbothered by anyone, on the floor of Kitty Suckley's room, which was about as comfortable as Lucy Hunter's couch, until the light of the morning woke me. I had not realised how exhausted I was after such a long and fretful day.

There was an air of gloom in the theatre that lingered with the scent of smoke. I sought fresher air and space to think. Davenport had told me that he didn't need me to return to Hawbridge House, but I found myself walking in the direction of St James's Square, nevertheless, as if my own feet were determined to walk me into trouble.

It would be risky to enter the house. If I was caught again, everyone would assume I was up to no good and I would have more than Mrs Kemp to worry about. There had to be a way. I sat in the garden of the square watching the front door, knowing that the silent rooms inside were holding a secret – willing the house to give it up to me.

Carts wheeled around the square carrying goods to the elegant dwellings. Some of them turned at Hawbridge House, taking provisions to the back door: baskets of food, milk churns and boxes of wine. The earl's family was not starving itself in grief.

The front door remained resolutely closed.

Having waited for nearly an hour, I decided to give up. Hungry and bored, I scowled up at the house. I could not work out how to gain access. Two stable hands emerged, leading horses. I recognised both the men and the horses. It could only mean that Callow and Astley were inside with Lady Hawbridge. There was a third horse, a handsome grey, that was dancing about. The man I guessed to be Martin Jakes was struggling to hold him along with a more docile chestnut mare.

I shifted my position, interested again. The front door opened, and the house steward stepped out, exchanging a few pleasantries with the hands as they stood with their horses.

Mr Astley came to the door with Mr Callow. The young earl and Lady Hawbridge followed them, and it became clear that the three men were going for a ride. Astley, her protector and admirer, leaned in to kiss her and Lady Hawbridge, still becoming in black, gave him her cheek. There was fondness between them, I thought, but he would need to work harder to win her – now that she was not only a wealthy woman, but a widow with a title. A little less stiffness, perhaps. He was overbearing, and, as Davenport had observed, he was more like a father than a lover.

Callow also leaned in to kiss her. He was more graceful than his friend and his manner was more casual, unconcerned, even, and certainly less like a man looking for rich wife. The men moved to their horses, chatting amiably with the stable hands.

And then something odd happened.

Astley mounted. He was on the chestnut mare. The earl's grey began to jump around as soon as he was up, keen to get moving. Jakes kept a firm hand on the bridle, but the horse was in lively spirits.

Callow was just about to mount when Lady Hawbridge, laughing, dusted something, a speck, a hair, a thread, from the shoulder of his coat.

It was such a simple thing to do, such a small gesture. But it was the sort of intimate gesture that a woman would only make towards a man with whom she was very close. And suddenly I saw that it was not Astley who had her heart, but Callow. And I knew that her affection for him was not recent. He was more than an old family friend, I was sure of it.

Callow jumped up on his horse, which was almost as lively as the earl's. The stable hand let go of the bridle and the horse lifted its front hooves. Callow was strong enough to control him quickly, but it caused the grey to jolt sideways in alarm.

Lady Hawbridge took a swift step back, out of their way. As she moved, her hand lightly, instinctively, touched her stomach. Callow shouted to the others, but their horses had already started out of the square. He reigned his horse tightly and bent down to see that she was unharmed, encouraging her to go inside.

Lady Hawbridge must have spent years in the company of men whose horses were too strong and too spirited for them to control properly. Highly-strung horses, beloved of men who want to show off and race about at speed, have a tendency to jump and strain when they're ready for a ride and feel themselves held back. She was not, I didn't think, a woman to be alarmed by lively animals.

She was expecting a baby. His, I thought. And this put matters in a different light.

Callow, more than Astley, had a reason for wanting Lord Hawbridge out of the way. It was hardly unknown for members of aristocratic families to have affairs – it was all that they ever did, some people said – but if there was a child involved, then it all became more complicated. She would, I imagined, have tried to pass the baby off as Hawbridge's. That would be the most sensible option. But if Hawbridge had suspected the affair, then his temper would have been the least of her worries.

Servants, listening at keyholes or peeping through the cracks in the walls and doors, would have given up the secret eventually, however tightly she had controlled it. Hawbridge, always open to money, would undoubtedly have made the most of her adultery. He would have prosecuted Callow for criminal conversation with his wife, pursued him through the courts – and pressed hard for damages. Callow would have been ruined financially. Lady Hawbridge would have been ruined socially – forced into exile in her parents' home or in another country. The child, if it survived, would be handed over to an obscure family and raised as their own. It would be considered better for everyone if there was no permanent reminder of her ladyship's disgrace.

I wondered whether Lady Hawbridge and Callow had decided to take a different course of action.

The stable hands were still standing outside Hawbridge House, the countess having gone indoors. They were watching the horses in the distance. I wandered over.

'Lively horses,' I said as I neared them. 'The grey especially.'

They turned to stare. The older man was disdainful, but the younger man, red-faced and bright-eyed from grappling with two of the horses, grinned at me.

'You could say. Take a bit of handling, they do.'

'Are they off for a long ride?' I asked. 'It's a lovely day for it.'

The man shook his head. 'Just a short ride in Hyde park, I think. Mr Callow said something about needing to travel home. Shame – his horse could do with a good run.'

'The bay? Yes, I could see he was wanting to go with the others,' I said. 'Is his home far?'

He shook his head. 'Not really. He's over towards Grosvenor Square.'

It had been a long time since I had been out for a ride. I missed it, I realised with a sudden pang. I missed the wind on my face and the freedom of speed. I missed the horse I used to ride. 'It's the grey who needs to stretch his legs, I'd say. That mare won't challenge him.'

Jakes' companion pulled him away.

I watched them go, having gleaned the information I wanted, and made my way to Grosvenor Square. Someone would know Callow's house, I was sure of it.

–

I was even more certain someone would point it out to me when, nearing Grosvenor Square, I saw a familiar figure about to climb into a sedan chair.

'Lucy!'

Lucy Allingham, Berwick Street's finest, was leaving someone's house to return home. She would never go home on foot, believing that to be beneath her dignity. Any man she favoured with her charms had to be rich and discreet enough to send her home either in his carriage or chair. She turned her head when I called her, but then pretended not to know me, hurrying to climb into the chair and pull the curtain.

I trotted next to the box as the two strong-armed servants of whichever house she'd left carried her along.

'Don't ignore me, you old crow. Lucy, stop this chair. I need to speak to you.'

'Will you shut up and go away, little strumpet,' she hissed from inside the box. 'I do not wish to be seen on the street with the likes of you. Certainly not when you're dressed so despicably.'

I pulled back the curtain. 'Lucy, you don't need to leave the chair. I just need your help.'

She gave a loud grumble. 'Very well, but Ma will hear of this and you'll be very sorry. I have a reputation to maintain and it does not include stopping my chair to talk to scruffy servant girls.'

She shouted to the men to lower the box.

'Your chair?' I said, as she scowled at me through the window.

She flustered. 'It is mine while it has me in it. What do you want, Lizzie?'

'Other than to pass the time of day with my dear friend, you mean? I want some information about a man on the square.'

She sighed. 'Not this again. You're running ragged for that magistrate and there's plenty of work at home.'

'Don't remind me,' I said. 'I've got no money and I haven't had a decent meal in days.'

'Be quick about it,' she said, heartless as ever. 'What do you want?'

'Mr Callow,' I said. 'I want to know which is his house.'

She frowned. 'Why? You can't possibly be visiting a gentleman in that sort of gown. Unless he has very strange fancies.'

They would be no stranger than some requests I've had. 'None of your business, Lucy. I just want to know where he lives.'

'I don't know,' she said. 'I don't know every house on this square. I don't know Mr Callow.' Her eyes narrowed. 'Is he very rich?'

That was all she was interested in. 'I've no idea. He must be wealthy enough if he lives here, though.'

I turned to the servant at the back of the chair.

'Do you know Mr Callow? You work here. Which is his house?'

The man looked startled to be addressed so presumptuously by a servant like himself. So startled that he forgot himself and said, 'Yes miss, that's his house there. Narrow one in the corner with the blue door.'

'Thank you,' I said. 'See,' I said to Lucy, 'someone pays attention to their surroundings. Give my regards to Ma and tell her I'll be home very soon.' I drew the curtain back to its place before she had time to retort and patted the front servant on the shoulder and bade him take her away.

My life, when I returned to Berwick Street, would be hell.

I walked nearer to the house. It wasn't especially large, not compared with some of the grand places here, but it was perfectly adequate as the London home of a gentleman of means.

At the end of the square a hackney carriage was waiting, although the driver did not appear to be looking for hire. I wondered why it was waiting here, when everyone in this part of London would have their own transport. I soon saw how it was. The driver was dozing, he'd pulled up for a rest in exactly the location where no one would bother him. I hailed him loudly, reaching into my pockets and bringing out a sixpence. The only coin in my possession.

After a bit of haggling, I sent him over to Bow Street to collect Davenport and return him to me. The gentleman would, I assured him, pay the return fare and anything extra, and yes, he was to drive the carriage, empty, all the way to Bow Street. He grumbled at this, but took my coin and set off. I settled down to wait – either for Davenport or for Callow.

Chapter Thirty-nine

Callow arrived first. His horse had calmed down after a short turn around the park. He was alone. I watched him hand the horse to a stable lad and disappear into his house. He did not leave it again, and I assumed that he was sitting down for a meal. I tried not to think about food.

The hackney did not return. Instead, nearly an hour after I had sent the man on his way, Davenport arrived on his own horse.

'You received my message,' I said as he climbed down. 'Why didn't you come back with the hackney?'

'And have my bones shaken to bits? No thank you, Miss Hardwicke.' He stood, hands on hips, and looked at the houses in the square. 'You have good reason for dragging me out all this way?'

I told him what I'd seen. His eyes widened. 'Callow? I thought Astley was the one we were watching.'

'He was. But I know, Mr Davenport, I know what I saw. If you ask him directly, he won't be able to deny it.'

'He may well deny it. And we have him in the Bedford Head at the time of the murder, so he didn't kill Lord Hawbridge, even if he was bedding his wife.'

'I still think you should ask him about his relationship with her. It may be significant.'

He chewed his lip and said nothing.

'I'll happily ask for you, if you're squeamish,' I said.

'I'm not squeamish. Just… cautious. Mr Fielding does not like to upset these people. They fund his work.'

'Even when they turn out to be adulterers, liars and murderers? He's not so forgiving of the inhabitants around the Garden, though, is he?'

He said nothing. I knew that Mr Fielding's manner of operating did not always sit well with him.

Our conversation was interrupted by the clatter of a carriage. The coat of arms and the blue livery announced that it had come from Hawbridge House.

I raised my eyebrows. 'Lady Hawbridge, do you think? They've been apart for less than two hours.'

'Might be the earl,' he said.

It was Lady Hawbridge, accompanied by her maid.

'It's Hannah,' I said.

'Hannah?'

'The maid. She's been in Lady Hawbridge's service for a long time. She was frustratingly tight-lipped about her mistress.'

He shook his head. 'If you were ever in need of a ladies' maid, you'd want her to be discreet.'

'The things I get up to would make Hannah's hair stand on end,' I said.

We watched as the door opened. Callow's steward answered the door, but Callow himself came out to greet them. He embraced Lady Hawbridge warmly but in a manner that would cause offence to no one. He said something we didn't hear and then glanced down at her stomach. She put a hand to it again and they both smiled.

'There,' I said. 'Did you see it?'

'I did see it,' he said. 'I believe you're right. She's not far gone. A few months, maybe. Not enough to show through the gown.'

He was watching her now with the eyes of a medical man, and as a man whose wife had born a child, before they both died.

'Come on,' I said, 'I think it's time we found out the truth of it.'

'We?'

I pulled a face. 'You can't leave me out here while you tread cautiously around the pair of them.'

He sighed. 'Very well. But you mustn't speak. I'll have a hard enough time explaining your presence.'

'Not a word, I assure you, sir. I only want to watch them.'

He tugged on his horse's reins. 'I'd better see to him first,' he said, and walked off to find the stables.

When we were admitted, Davenport didn't explain me at all. He gave his hat to the servant at the door and I followed quietly. The thing about houses like this, I considered, is that no one will ask questions if you behave as though you were born to be there, and you offer no explanations. Davenport was sitting calmly in one of the high-backed hall chairs, taking in the paintings on the walls and the pleasantness of his surroundings. He, like me, had been born to such a life. He had abandoned it to pursue his medicine, and then his work with Mr Fielding, but that life was still his, if he chose it. I wondered whether his own house was as elegantly furnished. I knew that he lived in Soho, not far from where I did, but our paths only crossed in the grime and the dirt, in the taverns, or in the brothel at Berwick Street.

These days, I only sat waiting patiently in such a fine hallway when I had gone from a tavern to a gentleman's house, rather than to my own place. There, I would wait to be summoned, when he was ready to receive me, conscious of a servant's eyes somewhere, peeping through a crack in a doorway at the painted harlot fidgeting in anticipation.

But I remembered how to sit neatly. I had not lost my good manners entirely when I arrived in London.

I caught Davenport's eye and wondered what he was thinking.

The steward returned and took us through to the drawing room, where Mr Callow and Lady Hawbridge were waiting for us.

The drawing room was small, but exquisitely decorated. Not fussy, but charming enough to contain Lady Hawbridge. She had probably helped him furnish it.

Davenport introduced me simply as Miss Hardwicke and I sat down without a word where I was directed as though it were the most natural thing in the world for a harlot dressed as a servant – who had lately been a theatre seamstress – to be sharing a room with a countess and her lover.

Hannah was standing behind her lady and staring at me as though I had dropped from the sky. I ignored her and fixed my attention on Lady Hawbridge.

Davenport, much better suited to terrifying men like Simmot, decided to play his hand gently. He apologised for the intrusion into Mr Callow's home but said that Mr Fielding now had cause to wonder whether, indeed, Joseph Sugden had killed Lord Hawbridge. He was trying to establish exactly where people were on the night of the murder.

Lady Hawbridge paled at this. She clasped her hands together a little tighter and spoke in a whisper.

'But you told us that this man, Sugden, had killed himself. That he had murdered my husband. What has changed this?'

Davenport cleared his throat.

'We still think that Sugden was involved in some way,' he said, avoiding her puzzled gaze, 'but we are not so certain that we can leave other lines of enquiry untested. It's what the public expects, my lady, that we don't simply jump to conclusions.'

It was a reasonable speech and she appeared to accept it.

'Mr Callow,' he said, turning to her companion. 'You told the magistrate that on the night Lord Hawbridge died, you left the theatre and went briefly to the Rose Tavern, alone, and then had your servants take you to the Bedford Head in Southampton Street. I wondered whether you wanted to confirm this, or whether you've had opportunity to re-think your story?'

Callow blinked. 'Why do I need to re-think it? It's not a story. That's what I did.'

Davenport considered his words carefully, in the light of his gentle audience. 'In the theatre, you suggested to the magistrate that you had not been alone at the Bedford.'

Callow looked uncomfortable. 'Really, man, I'm not sure Lady Hawbridge needs to hear...'

Davenport cut him short. 'I am sure that Lady Hawbridge is quite aware of how her gentlemen friends conduct themselves around the theatres and taverns. But I find myself unable to locate the person you were with that evening.'

Callow coloured pink. 'You told me that someone had seen me there.'

Davenport nodded. 'They said they had seen your coat, but I don't know they will swear to having seen you.'

'Do they need to swear it?' Callow was incredulous. 'Am I under suspicion in some way?'

Lady Hawbridge was becoming very agitated. Hannah was almost more so.

'As I said to Lady Hawbridge, we are now less certain of Sugden's guilt. It's unfortunate, but if I cannot confirm that you were in Southampton Street, sir, then I might suggest to the magistrate that we need to make further enquiries.'

There was a long silence, as the two of them understood his meaning. A look passed between them. Davenport saw it, as I did.

'Lady Hawbridge, I do apologise,' he said, bending his head to her. 'Before addressing this distressing subject, I should have congratulated you on the happier news of your baby. That was negligent of me.'

I was impressed. I had imagined he would leave her out of this.

'My baby?' she said in a little voice.

He nodded to her belly. 'Although I think you have a few months to go, haven't you?'

She gave a tiny cry. 'How did you know?'

'I'm a physician, as well as one of Mr Fielding's men, my lady,' he said in a soothing voice. 'A baby will be a worthy tribute to your husband, and a comfort in the days ahead, I'm sure.'

She turned paler still and shrank a little further into her chair.

'Mr Davenport, I don't think you should be distressing Lady Hawbridge like this. She's been through enough over the last few days.' Callow's face was full of righteous anger now that Davenport had turned his attention to Lady Hawbridge. 'Is this how the magistrate conducts his business? Pestering widows?'

'My apologies, my lady, I meant only to offer my good wishes in a difficult time,' Davenport murmured.

Callow's response had been interesting.

'I think you should leave, sir,' Callow said.

Lady Hawbridge put a hand out to him. 'No, Adam, not on my account. I'm sure Mr Davenport meant no harm.' Adam. She called him by his Christian name. He was 'A'.

Behind Lady Hawbridge, Hannah was struggling to stay still. I could see her out of the corner of my eye, fiddling with her apron strings.

'And I would still like to know where you were on the night Lord Hawbridge died, sir, before I take my leave. And with whom. A description of your companion, at least, would be helpful,' said Davenport, as lightly as if he were asking the name of the man's tailor.

I looked directly at Hannah now. Her face was racked with anxiety.

'I think you're asking the wrong person, Mr Davenport,' I said.

I expected him to scowl at the interruption, but Davenport, perhaps ahead of me, said simply, 'And who should I ask?'

I nodded to Hannah. 'Lady Hawbridge's maid. Hannah knows where Mr Callow was.'

Davenport stood up and walked over to Hannah, who was glancing, terrified, at her mistress, torn between telling us what we had already guessed or seeing Callow taken away to Bow Street with no real alibi for a murder.

'Hannah,' said Davenport, 'if you know of Mr Callow's whereabouts on the night your master died, you must tell me. If you do not, I will ask you and Mr Callow to come with me to the magistrate's office and he will ask you what you know.' He used that slow, coaxing tone I had heard before. Even now it made me quake a little.

Hannah's face was wretched. Her eyes flicked between Callow and Lady Hawbridge. The lady had now covered her face in her hands. She was sobbing softly. Callow looked as though he would burst.

'For the love of God, Davenport, I was here with Harriet, with Lady Hawbridge. She was here with me.'

Davenport had not taken his eyes off Hannah. 'Is that true?' he asked her. She nodded and burst into a great sob.

'You were here too?'

'Yes,' the word emerged in a gurgle. 'She waited for him as arranged. And he came home not long after the clock had struck ten.'

Davenport turned to Callow. 'This was arranged? For her to be here? You were not expecting Hawbridge to return home that night then?' The insinuation was clear.

'He never came home after the theatre,' said Lady Hawbridge from her chair. 'He never came home to me.' She looked up at him, red-eyed but still astonishingly lovely. 'He went from theatre to gaming house to whore-house or to one of his other women. That was his way when he went out to a play. I did not expect him until noon the next day, at the earliest.'

Callow went to her, stood beside her chair and held her hand. He loved her. He was not her husband, but he was the man she had sought.

'Did your husband know about the two of you?' Davenport asked. Their answer was not critical – Callow had not killed Hawbridge if he had been at home – but he wanted to know.

Lady Hawbridge let out a deep sigh. 'I rarely saw him and when I did he was always vile. It was my money that interested him, of course. A steady income – my father refused a single amount, knowing that he was likely to gamble it all in one go – but a regular and substantial income was just what he needed.'

She squeezed Callow's hand.

'And he continued living as he had always lived. But to answer your question, I never told him about Adam, of course. We were always careful. And, in truth, he never took me seriously enough to wonder about my life, my feelings. So I doubt it.'

I didn't imagine Lord Hawbridge had thought of anyone's feelings but his own. He had probably ignored his first wife, except when he required her to produce his heirs. Perhaps she had not minded his absence too much and been content with her lot. I had seen, when she had first lifted up her veil, that the present Lady Hawbridge was endowed with intelligence and strength of character. Under different circumstances, I would have wanted to know her better. Callow's alibi had come at the expense of her reputation, but the only people who knew of it were those of us in this room.

We got up to leave, Davenport murmuring polite words.

He reached into his coat pocket and pulled out Lord Hawbridge's snuff box. 'I haven't had opportunity to return this. It was found near his body. We don't need it.'

She turned it over in her hand and then pressed the catch. The lid sprang up like a peacock's tail.

She gave a wry smile. 'This was how he was, Mr Davenport. So much show, so much grandeur, but full of insignificant dust.' She tipped the contents on to the floor. 'Do you know, he lost this once – just before we married. It drove him into a mad rage, can you imagine? His temper was violent, especially when he didn't get his own way. He beat a servant, a stable boy, believing he had taken it, and then he accused another young boy of stealing it – a lad from a family of passing gypsies, I think he was. He pressed the case so hard that the child was condemned for it.' She placed it on the table. 'And then it transpired that he had simply misplaced it.'

That was even more shocking than the story of him beating the stable boy.

'I am not sad that he's dead, you know,' she said. 'I shall mourn the Earl of Hawbridge in public as is appropriate, but I shall not grieve.'

'And you will have new considerations soon.'

She smiled. 'Mr Callow and I plan to marry, and he will, of course, adopt the child as his own. We must wait, but we know that happiness is around the corner.'

Callow said nothing.

So, it was Adam Callow, I had overheard, wanting to marry her sooner, but she was the stronger of the two and the date of the marriage would be her choice. Her mettle had been tempered already.

Hannah stood, still fretting at her apron. I went to her, as Davenport was taking his leave of Lady Hawbridge.

'You did well,' I said. 'You did the right thing and she won't punish you for it.'

'I hope not,' she said. 'I want to see her happy again.'

I gave her arm a rub and then embraced her. 'Good luck, Hannah.'

She gave me an odd look. 'Who are you? What are you?'

I shook my head. 'As I was before: just a woman trying to make her way in the world, like the rest of us – even Lady Hawbridge.'

She wasn't convinced by this, but it was all I was prepared to say.

Chapter Forty

Davenport led his horse as we walked together. We did not speak for most of the way.

'You were right about Lady Hawbridge,' he said, eventually. 'She was not what I thought.'

I decided it was wise to be gracious in response. 'She has spent a lifetime playing her part, Mr Davenport. A sensitive and clever woman trapped in the prison of wealth and beauty. It's difficult to see beyond how she appears on the outside because she's been so well-schooled in how to behave.'

I thought of Mr Simmot's play about the phoenix. 'I hope that she has found a means of escape in the person of Mr Callow. I hope that he deserves her.'

The horse let out a snort and shook its head.

'Your horse thinks not,' I said. 'I expect your horse is right. But she stands a better chance of happiness with him than she ever did with Lord Hawbridge.'

He stared ahead, saying nothing. He had been enchanted by her, I knew, and even as she had revealed herself to be, in my eyes, a woman of courage and strength, her affair with Callow had diminished her in his estimation. The noble widow was carrying another man's child; she was not the paragon he had imagined.

I changed the subject.

'Who killed Lord Hawbridge?'

He groaned. 'I'm beginning to wonder if we'll ever know. If Callow was with Lady Hawbridge and Astley was at home, as his own staff are united in telling me, then who do we have left?'

'William Simmot, however unlikely a murderer, is still unable to account for his time that night. No one saw him; he was writing, alone in his room. Mr Dinsdale and Mr Hunter are plotting to take over the theatre, as we know. Hunter would not be able to raise the girandole on his own because of his damaged leg, so they must be acting together. I still can't see why they would want to kill Lord Hawbridge, but I wonder whether it was some sort of mad game gone wrong?'

'A game gone wrong?'

'A way of threatening Garrick, perhaps. Dangling one of his patrons over the stage? Yet another strange occurrence to make the company skittish.'

'And then somebody accidentally cut his throat?' he said. 'That doesn't work. It was deliberate. If they meant to frighten Garrick, then they did it by killing a man in cold blood.'

'There's something we're just not seeing,' I said. 'Something about Dinsdale or Hunter that connects them to Lord Hawbridge – beyond the theatre, I think.'

'Hmm.' His pace slowed a little. 'Perhaps I'll gather a couple of men and bring the two of them into Bow Street. Mr Fielding might like to press them about it. He has a gift of getting at the truth, especially if these men believe themselves to be under suspicion. One may accidentally betray the other – I've seen this happen.'

'Ah yes,' I said, 'a man will risk his friend to save his own neck. It's an idea – especially as neither of them is currently aware that we know of their game.'

The plan in hand, his pace picked up and his mood lightened.

'We're nearly there,' I said. 'I can walk from here alone, if you want to go on ahead and find your men.'

'Are you sure?'

I laughed. 'I am perfectly sure. Believe me, Mr Davenport, I am even more hardy than Lady Hawbridge. I don't need an escort from here.'

'Very well.' He climbed onto his horse and collected the reins. 'I'll meet you in the theatre shortly.'

—

I watched him go and walked now with a little more purpose. What was it that connected the two men with Hawbridge? Something, beyond destroying Garrick, had motivated this crime. And what had it to do with Joe Sugden's death, which had been neither suicide nor tragic accident? If the magistrate heard from Davenport that the two men were plotting against Garrick, then he would work harder to discover what had led them to kill. He had his ways, as Davenport said.

Frustrating though it was not to have discovered what was going on, all I could do now was wait for Mr Fielding to do what he did so well and skewer the pair of them with threats and clever questions. I could, at least, be proud of my own part in uncovering their plot, as Davenport had said. I only hoped that Mr Fielding would be generous in the financial reward. I had, so far, earned sixpence in three days, and had lost that to a carriage I hadn't ridden in. And I was yet to eat a proper meal.

I passed the corner of Southampton Street and caught sight of the Bedford Head tavern, where Mr Callow had not, it transpired, eaten a hearty meal with a cheap woman. My empty stomach ached for a good stew or a leg of mutton.

I was struck by a most curious thought. I turned it over and over as I walked towards the theatre. If Mr Callow had not been in the Bedford Head, then why had Molly been so certain that she had seen his coat?

At the back of the theatre, outside the door, there was a small, pull-along cart, the sort a pie-seller would use. There were, sadly, no pies on it, but a few sacks and one small trunk. Molly emerged from the door dragging a larger, heavier-looking, trunk. She reached the cart and then swung the trunk on to it with impressive strength.

'Molly?'

She looked over and saw me. 'Lizzie, you're about to find that you've a new job in the theatre.'

'What?'

She came over and put an arm around me. 'You'll be perfect as head seamstress. I'll put in a word for you with Mr Garrick.'

'I don't understand.'

She rubbed her forehead, wiping away the effort of lifting the trunk. 'I've decided to leave London again,' she said. 'I think it's for the best. I talked it over with Ketch yesterday and I'm going back to Southwark, possibly going from there to the coast. I can find work with travelling players as I go.'

'I can see that life would be hard here, after all that's happened. But you think you'll survive?'

She laughed at this. 'I've survived all my life, Lizzie.' She started to tie the trunk onto the cart. 'Tell Ketch I'm nearly ready, will you? He's in the green room. I'll come and say a proper farewell in a minute.'

The dark corridor into the back of the theatre was brighter for having the door open. It looked so very different now that I could see more clearly. Garrick would need a new seamstress – but I was certainly not going to stay around to fix cuffs and collars in Molly's place. Here was one further irritation for the theatre manager.

I walked, in something of a daze, up to the green room and found Ketch loading a bag with bread and cheese.

'Are you leaving as well, Ketch,' I asked.

'You've seen Molly, then? Yes, I'm going. I never really took to the theatre life. Too much of a traveller, like Molly Bray. We'll head south, I think. Go slow. Stop here and there. It's our way.'

A pattern began to rearrange itself in my mind. A picture started to form. A snuff box and an angry nobleman. A traveller's boy.

'What happened, Ketch? What happened to Molly's mother?'

'What's that?'

'Something happened a while ago and it distresses Molly still, I know. This is about more than Joe's death, isn't it? Her mother died, Molly said. What happened to her, Ketch?'

He looked at me thoughtfully for a moment and put his bag down with a sigh.

'Dear Alice Bray. The loveliest and best of women, she was too. Hanged herself.'

'How terrible. Why would she do that?' I had a feeling I knew.

He shrugged. 'Broken heart. Molly's younger brother Jack. He…' he paused for a moment, recalling something from his own past, as well as hers; pondering what to tell me. 'He was only twelve and he died in gaol. Fever, they said it was. She never recovered.'

The back of my legs began to wobble slightly. I sat down.

'He was in gaol when he died? That's very sad.'

Ketch's brow furrowed as he continued packing the food into his bag. 'It was a travesty.' His shoulders drooped a little at the memory.

'Poor woman,' I said, seeing how it was. 'That must have been a hard blow to bear.'

'It was,' he said, throwing the bag back over his shoulder, avoiding my eyes, his own shining with tears. 'Molly is strong in her body, but she's fragile in her mind, like her ma. She needs to leave this place now and find some peace elsewhere.'

'Are you coming, Ketch?' Molly came in to the green room. Strong, capable Molly, who walked ropes and drank heavily to escape her ghosts. She raised a hand to me. 'Time for us to go, Lizzie. I'll say goodbye, for I doubt we'll meet again.'

I stood up, as if to embrace her.

'Is that why you killed him, Molly?'

She cocked her head to one side. 'Killed who?'

'The Earl of Hawbridge. Did you kill him for Jack?'

'What you been saying, Ketch?' She cast an anxious glance in his direction.

He raised his hands. 'I said nothing, Moll.'

'Some years ago, Lord Hawbridge lost a snuff box,' I said. Molly was rooted to where she stood, a bag slung over her shoulder, her face turning white. 'He, a man with a vicious temper, beat one of his servants so hard when he lost it that half of his staff walked out of his service. The box was not found, so he accused a boy from a company of travelling players. That was Jack, wasn't it?'

She said nothing, but her eyes told me that I was right.

'Jack died in gaol,' Ketch said. 'Gaol fever. I suppose he was waiting for the assizes, which would, surely have condemned him, and your mother, overcome with grief, killed herself.'

She put a hand out to the back of a chair, to steady herself. Then she dropped the bag she was carrying onto a table, as if to ease herself of this added burden.

'You saw the snuff box, didn't you? Hawbridge was carrying it on the night he died.'

She ran a finger across the back of the chair. When she eventually spoke, her voice was soft. 'It was lost, he said. Someone had stolen it. My brother had stolen it, he said and yet, here it was, being flaunted about under my nose. It had never been stolen at all.'

'So you invited him on to the stage?'

'Have a care, Moll,' said Ketch.

She gave a half-smile and said nothing.

Neither of them saw, as I did, the shadow of a figure in the dressing room passageway. He had heard enough already to make him press himself against the wall. He would be listening carefully, I knew. He was blocking their route to the back door, to the cart. I moved to cover their path to the front door of the theatre. My heart began to beat faster.

I looked over at Ketch, who was calmly feeding the monkey on his shoulder.

'You knocked him on the back of the head and tied his ankles together,' I said, a little louder. 'Was that the two of you, or did you do this alone.'

301

'Alone.' She was quick to answer. 'This was my fight, not Ketch's.'

'What happened?'

'I knocked him out with a hammer. There are plenty of tools lying around if you know where to look. It was dark on the stage, but I'd given him a bit of light, to draw him on. And on he came. I got a good crack and he went down. I pulled him under the girandole and strung him up.'

'How did you get him on the stage? Did you send a note?'

'That was easy. I sent a note saying Mrs Hunter wanted to meet him and that he was to come alone.' She laughed. 'He followed his cock, like I knew he would. I took the letter from his pocket. As much as Lucy Hunter gave me grief, I didn't want her to be accused of killing him.'

'You took the snuff box out of his pocket as well?'

She nodded, a wry smile on her lips. 'I wanted to look at it properly. See what Jack had died for. See it up close. The trinket that killed my brother and my ma.'

'You'd already set a rope on the girandole, I think. When you climbed over the beams in the interval.'

She looked impressed. 'You're clever,' she said, quietly. 'Far too clever for a stitcher.'

I was uncomfortable at that. I pressed on, shifting slightly.

'Why did you cut his throat?'

'Because I wanted him dead,' she said, as if I were stupid. 'Why should he live?' She gripped the back of the chair, her voice suddenly rising with a passion I had not seen in her before. 'You know his sort, Lizzie. They get what they want, and if they don't get it, they strike out at the people who can't fight back, or else they take

302

it anyway. Tom Firmin told me what he did to you, you know. Hawbridge. Told me how he'd found you on the floor of the mending room, shaking with fright. You should be glad he's dead. I did it for Jack and Ma, but I did it for the likes of you too. I wanted people to see him for what he was.'

'It was quite a spectacle,' I said, trying to keep my voice even. 'Him lifted up like that. And all that blood.'

She agreed. 'The amount did shock me. I didn't know a person had that much in them.'

'But you didn't take the snuff box?'

'I didn't want it. Why would I want it? I just wanted him to suffer, like we had suffered. I left it under him, like a sign of what he had done.'

I shuddered. I did not wish to know whether he had been conscious when she cut his throat; exactly how much she had made him suffer. Instead I asked, 'Were you covered with blood? I was, and I only stood in it.'

'No, I cut his throat from behind.' Her eyes widened at the memory of it. It had been a moment of triumph for her. Retribution. 'There was some blood on me, but I took off my gown and laid it in a trunk, along with the knife and hammer. I can hide anything in that mending room. It's so full of stuff and no one would have cause to look in a trunk for anything in there, except me.'

Davenport had been more astute than he had realised when he'd said that female servants could walk unnoticed. A female servant could get away with anything, even murder, because she was so far below anyone's notice. Molly had laid her bloodied clothes and the knife that had killed Lord Hawbridge in a trunk in the dressing room – and no one would have thought about looking there, in the piles of theatre costumes.

Another thought occurred to me. It made me nervous to ask it, but I needed an answer.

'Was Joe Sugden a party to this? You appeared on the stage together, when I found the body.'

Something like sorrow crossed her brow. She sat down on the chair and clasped her hands on the table in front of her, in an attitude of prayer. 'You found Hawbridge a bit earlier than I'd expected. I thought the stage hands would find him when they came to open up. I'd forgotten about you.'

'And Joe?'

'No. He knew nothing about it. No one knew. The theatre was empty. I checked. You were the only one about, and you were in Lucy Hunter's room, fast asleep. After I'd done it, I went out to the Shakespeare and found Joe. Told him I'd been looking for him and made it seem like I'd been searching for ages. Then we went back to the theatre and spent a couple of hours in the trap room.' Her eyes softened at the memory of it. 'Then we heard your screaming and came up.'

She had been lying with Joe in the trap room underneath the body. That made me feel quite ill.

'But he found out, didn't he?' Even as I asked, I knew the answer.

She nodded. She sniffed back the sob, but her throat was still thick with it.

'He started asking questions. I told you that I was in Southampton Street, that I saw Mr Callow. He knew it wasn't true. He guessed.'

Callow's alibi had been hers too.

'And then he found the hammer. I hadn't thought about it, but Joe said a hammer was missing. He was such a rule-keeper. Everything had to be back in its place. He knew it had gone. He rummaged in the costume room and found it with the knife. I hadn't dealt with them. That was stupid of me.'

I remembered when Sugden had been angry with me for leaving the theatre, he had been carrying – cleaning – a large hammer when I returned. I had not found it, nor the knife, when I had searched the mending room, but I hadn't been looking for knives and hammers then, and I'd been too fascinated by the false weapons to notice a real one. And Sugden's anger at me had hidden a deeper emotion: fear. He had been afraid of what Molly had done.

'He was trying to persuade me to tell the magistrate about it – said I'd be spared because of what had happened to my family.'

That would have been unlikely, and she would have known it.

'He was getting agitated. Said that every time I had a drink I might say something. Tell someone what I'd done. He was trying to protect me, but all the time, he kept telling me that I'd done a wicked thing, a sin. That was his mother's religion talking. It was making him mad.'

'So, you killed him?'

She groaned. 'I didn't mean to. It just happened. That night, you'd gone to Lucy's room again – you were filthy drunk, I remember. I went to find Joe. Then we were drinking in the trap room and he was badgering me about it. He told me he would go to the magistrate himself. Something fizzed in my head and I went for him. I picked up a plank of wood that was lying nearby and I hit him with it. He went down so hard, and I panicked. I thought I'd killed him. And then I saw a way to make it work to my advantage. I went and found the knife, put it under him, gathered the bottles together and made it look like he'd been drinking. I set fire to the newspapers and watched them catch the scenery. Then I walked out of the trap room and turned the key.'

In cold blood, she had made sure that her lover would never tell her story. She had laid him on the bloody knife and made it look like he had committed suicide, and then let Mr Fielding spread the lie to save herself.

Ketch picked up his bag and walked over to her, put a hand on her shoulder.

'Come on, Molly. I think it's time we went now.'

She looked up at me. 'You can tell my story to the magistrate, if you like,' she said. 'But wait until I'm over the border to Southwark, won't you? I can disappear into the mist once I've crossed the river.'

'It's what travellers do,' said Ketch. He was looking out for her. He had promised to protect her, and he would.

There was a sound from behind her. Davenport emerged from where he had been standing. He was on his own.

'I don't think you're going to Southwark,' he said.

Molly sprang up from the chair, eyes wide with fury. With lightning speed, she pulled two pistols from her bag, aiming one at Davenport and one at me.

'Shit.' This from Davenport.

I took a step back.

'Molly, be careful,' said Ketch. 'We don't need this.' His voice, the voice of her protector, was soft and gentle, as if he were talking to a child.

I took a second step back.

'Lizzie,' Davenport said, with quiet urgency, 'stay very still.' He raised his hands to Molly and nodded to where I stood. 'Don't shoot. Don't shoot her.'

Molly cocked the pistol in her right hand – the one aimed at him.

From behind me a door opened, and, of all people, William Simmot came in.

His face, at first amiable and even cheerful, turned to horror as he saw what was before him. His eyes widened and, without thinking, he cried out. No word; an animal cry of alarm.

She swung around, the pistol in her left hand now pointing at me, and then at Simmot.

'Get back,' I called to him.

But he stood transfixed, unable to move, staring at the weapon.

Molly jerked her head to Ketch, her eyes wild, her head flicking between me and Davenport. She cocked the left pistol. The one aimed at me.

'Get out of it, Ketch,' she said. 'Go to the cart.'

'Molly, this isn't a good thing,' he said. 'Put the pistols down, eh?' He walked towards me and stood, the monkey on his head, blocking her aim.

Simmot gave a short laugh. 'They're not real!'

I kept my eyes on Molly. 'What?'

'Those duelling pistols. They're not real. They use them in the theatre all the time when duels are called for. There are no bullets in them. All of the smoke and bang from the powder, of course, so you get the effect, but nothing harmful.'

A half-smile appeared on Molly's face as she listened.

'She's bluffing you, Mr Davenport,' Simmot called in a sing-song voice.

I had seen the actors playing with pistols only three days ago, on the night Hawbridge died. I had watched Garrick play with one, pretending to shoot Kitty Suckley.

I had seen her swoon, dramatically, with all applauding her. But something in Molly's eye made me unsure.

'Molly, put the weapons down,' said Ketch again, a stronger hint of warning in his voice.

'There's no bullet, I tell you,' Simmot was laughing now, giggling like a silly schoolboy. 'Why are you standing there like a coward, Davenport? Why so faint-hearted? Take them from her.'

Davenport relaxed his shoulders a little, but kept his hands up, his eyes still on Molly's right arm. But he was readying himself to move, I knew it, spurred by Simmot's taunting.

There was something about the curve of the handles. Something that was wrong. The pistols I'd seen Garrick toy with had a rounder curve and were ornate in the silver tooling. These were plain; straight and smooth, without fancy detail.

These were not stage props. These were the pistols that I had seen in her costume room, down in the bottom of the wardrobe. These were Molly's own. Or Ketch's. To keep them safe as they travelled.

And I had no idea whether they were loaded.

Then everything happened very quickly.

Behind me, behind Simmot, Fielding's men, Grimshaw and Snowy, came in through the door at the front of the theatre, expecting to collect Dinsdale and Hunter, or at the least, to wait for them with Davenport.

Molly, distracted by the sound of them, dropped her right arm a little and Davenport, believing it to be unloaded, moved to grab the pistol.

I launched myself at Davenport, running in front of him with a shout and pushing him back as I heard her shriek in anger, and at the same moment, Ketch leaped towards her, the monkey clinging to his hair.

There was a very loud explosion, a gust of wind and smoke, and the monkey screamed.

Ketch tumbled to the floor.

'Ketch!' I yelled, abandoning Davenport and running to him.

His shoulder was a mess. There was blood beginning to seep from his chest into his shirt.

'Molly, what have you done?' I could not believe that she had shot him.

Neither could she. She stood, horror on her face, the smoking gun dangling from her left hand.

She dropped the spent pistol and now stood with the other, swinging about, aiming it at all of us, any of us, a wild look on her face. No one wanted to go near her. I held Ketch in my arms, on my lap, still gasping in fear, clutching at him, willing him to live, knowing that he would not.

Ketch groaned, as he raised half-closed eyes to Molly.

'Oh God, Molly. No.' He was not crying for himself. He cried for her.

I looked from him to her and saw that she had turned the pistol up under her own chin.

'Time to go now, Ketch,' she said, and, with a twisted smile, squeezed the trigger.

It wasn't just the monkey who screamed this time.

Chapter Forty-one

There was a good deal of confusion. The sound of not one but two loud reports brought people running; players and stage hands. I had no idea where they had all come from. I only knew that I was covered in blood. I didn't even know whether it was mine or Ketch's or Molly's. It was just more blood.

I sat on the floor, cradling Ketch in my arms, while the little monkey ran around the green room squealing. Ketch was trying to call him, words cracking in his throat. The tears ran down my face as I half called, half sobbed for him too. His name, I learned only then, was Jack. Like Molly's brother.

The monkey calmed down, finally, and sat on Ketch's lap, snuggling into him and crying like a tiny baby.

Ketch put a hand on the monkey and stroked his head. He gave a small judder. And then he was very still. I started screaming again, but no sound was coming out of my mouth.

The runners were standing around Molly's body. They had come, believing that they were escorting two men to Bow Street, but had, instead, witnessed a woman blow her own head apart. There was blood everywhere – over the floor, over the tables and up the walls. There was blood on the ceiling and even a great splatter across the mirror.

Everything in this room would need to be replaced. Snowy and Grimshaw were covered in blood as well.

The room was beginning to throng with people and their cries of horror and surprise filled the place.

I sat with Ketch's body, unable to make any more sound, his blood on my hands and all over my gown and apron.

One of the stage hands came to me and, kneeling, gently rolled Ketch's body off my lap. Someone took the monkey. Strong arms lifted me from behind.

'Come on, up you come,' said Davenport in my ear. 'Come away now.'

He turned me around to face him. Then he pulled me to his chest and held me tightly, stroking my blood-streaked hair and hushing me like a child as I began shaking.

When the shaking stopped, I eased myself from his shoulder. His arm was still about my waist.

'I've made a mess of your lovely coat,' I said, putting a hand on it, making it worse. 'And your shirt. I'm sorry.'

He glanced at my hand on his chest, as if seeing the blood for the first time. 'As long as it's not your blood, I don't mind,' he said. 'You ran in front of me, you know.'

'What?'

'When she aimed at me. You ran in front of me. I thought she'd shot you.' He took hold of the bloodied hand and squeezed it tightly. 'It was a foolish thing to do, you know.' His voice was very soft.

'Yes,' I said.

He pulled me a little closer still and brushed a damp strand of hair from my forehead. His face was nearly touching mine.

Someone ran past us, jolting my shoulder, and we broke apart. I put a hand to my cheek, to wipe the mess of tears. This was a bad idea, because the hand still had a fair covering of blood.

'I don't want to look in a mirror before I've washed,' I said. 'I need a wash.'

He didn't have chance to respond. The magistrate was now in the room and was calling for him. He apologised, gave me a little bow and went over, and I saw him begin to explain to Mr Fielding what had happened in the room. I staggered over to the side table and leaned against it, pouring myself a large glass of wine. I felt as though I had been battered by a storm. I wanted to sleep.

Instead, I was called to join Mr Fielding, Davenport, and with them, wild-eyed and desperate with shock, Mr Garrick.

I sat at a table and told them what I knew, while all three men listened carefully. Simmot, who still looked badly shaken, eased himself into the circle and pulled out a pen and some paper. As I spoke, he wrote. It all came out: the accidents in the theatre, Lord Hawbridge's history, Molly's brother, and how we had been wrong to suspect Joe Sugden. With a glance at Davenport, I carefully omitted Mr Callow and Lady Hawbridge from my report, aware that, beyond the intimacy of the table, the whole room was listening. No one needed to know their part. I told my story simply and without embellishing it. It needed no ornamentation, no dramatic flourish.

'She killed Lord Hawbridge because she wanted justice,' I said. 'Some will call it revenge, but to her it was a kind of justice.'

'She evaded justice herself,' said Garrick, wiping a handkerchief over his face.

'On earth, perhaps,' Mr Fielding said. 'But not ultimately. She took her own life, as well as the lives of three men.'

Simmot wrote the words.

I said nothing. Hawbridge meant little to me: he was a man who had used or abused many around him without sparing them a thought. But Joe Sugden and Ketch had tried hard to protect Molly, each in their own way, and she had killed them both. They had been good men. She would not, I thought, fare well in eternity.

There was a rustling among the company. Dinsdale had come into the room. He was staring about him in bewilderment, taking in the blood and damage and the mood of the gathering. The company parted a little and he found himself in the eyeline of Mr Garrick.

As if on cue, George Hunter limped in behind him, only to discover that he too, was centre stage in the green room.

Garrick rose from his seat, as if he, now, were the almighty, about to deliver judgement. A hush descended on his audience.

'Get out of my theatre,' Garrick said, with a voice of doom. 'Get out, you snake, you Judas, you betrayer. You, Dinsdale, and you Hunter, are worms of the worst kind. You will never work in this city again. I will see to it. No one will trust you, no one will touch you. You, who were once my friends, are forbidden from entering this place for as long as I am manager here. And I intend to be here for a very long time to come.'

There was a cheer from the back of the room. The cheer was taken up by everyone else and the two men – who must have wondered what on earth had happened – were pushed roughly back through the door.

Garrick sat back in his chair, spent by his most personal performance to date.

'Very fine, my dear friend,' said Mr Fielding. 'I'm sure that the bard himself will be cheering with everyone else.' Garrick, too exhausted by everything, missed the light touch of humour in Mr Fielding's voice.

Davenport laid a hand on the magistrate's arm and spoke a few quiet words in his ear. I saw him nod and then he turned in my direction. The eyes were hidden behind his band, but he smiled.

'Miss Hardwicke, I think your part has been played. And what a performance it has been.'

'Thank you, sir, but I would be grateful to return to Berwick Street soon. I am not cut out to be a seamstress, after all, it appears.'

'You may go as soon as you would like,' said Mr Fielding.

'I would like a bath most of all,' I said to Davenport, as he helped me up from my seat. 'And some sleep. And a decent meal and a gown that is clean and brightly coloured and not covered in blood, and someone to dress my hair—'

William Simmot appeared in front of us, as we made our way to the door. Davenport stiffened.

'Mr Simmot,' I said with a small curtsey.

He clutched at his papers, fingers still black with ink, and made a bow.

'An avenging angel. That's what you said. You were right.'

I gave him my best smile. 'So it appears. But are you returning to Lichfield, as you planned?'

He pouted and stared at the papers in his hand. 'I am. I came to tell Mr Garrick. I'm not cut out for London life. It's too…'

'Bloody?'

The skin was beginning to crack on my cheek as the blood dried, so at least he was no longer gazing at me in adoration. I had been right about the pistols and he had been wrong, and the puffed-up little man was sore about it; I could see that in the tight set of his jaw. He was not so observant after all and he knew that I knew it.

'I wish you well with your novels, Mr Simmot,' was all I said.

He stepped aside to let us pass.

Davenport took me as far as Covent Garden. Refusing to let me walk home in the state I was, he called a carriage and paid the driver to take me all the way to Berwick Street. Neither of us spoke beyond saying goodbye. He could not linger, he was needed in the theatre.

The carriage jolted me all the way, denying me the peace of body and mind that I craved.

When the carriage turned into Berwick Street, I steeled myself for the joy of home: Mrs Farley's sharp words, Sydney's disapproval, and the girls who were adorable and spiteful and annoying all at once.

I needed to be earning again. If I wanted to be independent, as free as Mr Simmot's heroines, free to choose how to spend my days, I could not depend on a golden bird to rescue me. Only gold.

Chapter Forty-two

A week later

'Mr Fielding's kind regards will not pay my bills,' I said.

Davenport was in my room, in my best chair, trying to explain why he was not carrying a fat purse from the magistrate.

I was furious.

'Have you any idea how Ma has been working me these past few days? She says we've lost the moment to capitalise on my notoriety and she's taking out her disappointment on me. I've barely slept; and I needed to sleep.'

His face contorted.

'I'm sorry, truly I am sorry. It won't help you, but you should know that I spoke on your behalf, but Mr Fielding said that, having already paid Simmot, he couldn't spare anything more.'

Simmot had witnessed everything, and he was the sort of man who might weave fantastical stories for pamphlets if left unchecked. So, he had been specially commissioned to write the exclusive and true story of Lord Hawbridge's murder for the press. He had been paid to write what Fielding wanted. What Garrick wanted. But he was a greedy little toad and had demanded a shockingly large sum of money. At least Fielding had made sure that the men of Bow Street emerged from the story with full honours.

I had not been mentioned in the piece, which I did not mind at all.

I had not been paid. Which I minded a great deal.

'That's the last time I let you persuade me to do your work,' I said, shaking my skirts. 'Unless Mr Fielding pays me before I begin.'

The edges of his mouth began to crinkle.

'Then you'll not completely rule out working with me again?'

I glared at him. He had made himself comfortable in my favourite chair and was toying with a glass of wine. He had removed his wig as well as his coat and hat. He had arrived in the blue coat I had admired, not the old brown one, I noticed. He'd had it cleaned. It was no longer covered in blood.

'You enjoyed the adventure, even without the coin, admit it.'

I didn't want to admit it.

'It would have pleased me more if you had brought some with you. You've no idea how grasping Ma can be.'

He sipped his wine, smiling into his glass.

'I called on Lady Hawbridge yesterday, by the way, I thought you'd want to know.'

'And how is the countess?' Even though I was cross, I was still keen for news.

He considered the question. 'Physically, she is blossoming, as only a woman in her condition can.'

I expected this meant she was even more beautiful, but he didn't say that.

'But she is in a fragile state. I told her about Molly Bray, about Jack. It caused her some pain.'

'It didn't cause her pain when she told us that a child had been condemned for stealing her husband's snuff box. She was quite calm about it then.'

He shrugged at this. 'I expect that, when she told us, it was just another example of how he behaved. Now his behaviour has been revealed as the root of his death, the heart of it. And perhaps,' he said with some greater effort, 'as she is about to become a mother, she has a deeper appreciation of what the death of a boy might mean.'

I said nothing. He was speaking from his own grief, still fresh, and I did not wish to contradict him. But I did not need to be a mother to feel the injustice of Hawbridge's accusations. Jack Bray had been little more than a child; the earl's vain attachment to a trinket had robbed him of his life.

'It's Joseph Sugden's plight that causes me pain,' I said. 'I didn't like him, but he was wrongly accused, too, you know. What is being done to restore his name?'

He drank another mouthful of wine and laid his glass on the table. 'You'll be glad to know of this,' he said. 'Here, at least, I can bear good news.'

'You can?'

'I took this upon myself. Mr Fielding was busy with the journalists and busy in court. I went to find out where Sugden's body had been taken. I expected that it would have been cast in a common pit, certainly that no church yard would have taken him in – a murderer as well as a suicide.'

'Where was he?'

'It appeared that there had been some delay at the undertakers. One of their men was sick and they were dealing with a family where two daughters had died the same day. Sugden's body had been wrapped and even put into a plain coffin, but it had not been buried. I arrived in time to make sure that he was buried decently – and in a church yard.'

'That is good news.' Now I smiled, pleased that one small act of mercy had taken place – glad that Davenport had found the time to do it. 'Thank you for that. Perhaps we might find a priest of his sort to pray for him. It's what they do, I know.'

'I'll try my best.'

'Thank you.'

He looked over at me, returning my smile.

'How are your own injuries? I see your bruise has disappeared.'

I put a hand to my cheek.

'Yes, thank goodness. Mrs Farley was not impressed at the state of me when I returned home.' For some reason, my battered and bloodied appearance had been entirely my fault, as far as she was concerned.

'You wouldn't tell me what happened, when we were in the Rose,' he said. 'It was Hawbridge, wasn't it? Did he hit you?'

He had heard Molly's words, when he'd been standing in the passageway.

I told him the story. He was impressed to learn how I'd outwitted the earl, but when I described how Hawbridge had thrown me against the wall I saw his hands clench.

'I was saved from any further ill-treatment by Mr Garrick's cuff. I have cause to be grateful to that silly strip of lace,' I said, making light of it. 'Tom Firmin arrived to tell me that Garrick needed me to repair it just as the noble gentleman was about to kick me in the head.'

'I'm sorry,' he said, aghast at this. 'I didn't mean to place you in such danger.'

I shrugged.

'I can handle myself, Mr Davenport.' I looked around my room. I had learned how to keep myself from too much harm. 'The little chamber maid in his house was less able. I hope that, for a time at least, she'll be free to go about her work untroubled.'

From the room next door, I heard familiar sounds. Polly was entertaining and she was in a noisy mood. He heard it too. He ran a hand over his hair and looked away. Brown curls, in need of a cut.

'Has Mr Garrick found a new seamstress yet?' I asked, ignoring Polly's encouraging squeals.

He cleared his throat. 'Ah, I believe so. Although, the theatre is still closed. It's in need of redecoration. I doubt Garrick will open again before the next season.'

'Blood, fire, smoke damage and yet more blood,' I said, pulling a shawl firmly across my chest. 'I'm not surprised. I hope that the new season will bring better luck for him. He'll be looking for a fresh crew as well.'

'Dinsdale has disappeared,' he said, turning his head away again as we heard the unmistakable thumping sound of a bed in use, increasing in tempo. 'Hunter has gone too. Although Mrs Hunter is still in favour. They are no longer together, it seems.'

'I'm glad of that,' I said, becoming amused at his discomfort. 'She might even flourish as an actress without him. I doubt she'll ever be good at reciting lines, but I'm sure Mr Astley will be generous to her.'

The sounds next door reached a spirited, and clearly satisfactory, conclusion. Davenport reached for his glass and knocked back his wine with what I thought was relief. I was tempted to make a lewd comment, but then he turned his head and looked at me.

I know that look.

It's the regular source of my coin.

Seeing it on Davenport's face made me tremble.

I had told myself that he wasn't interested, that he didn't think of me in that way. But there it was. I had half-guessed it, but now I knew.

Someone was coming along the corridor. The shuffling sound of a foot dragging told me that it was Meg, our maid with the bad leg. Davenport's expression changed and he was his usual self again.

Meg tapped on the door and entered at my call.

She rolled her eyes when she saw Davenport.

'Ma says you're to come downstairs, miss. She says she doesn't want you up here gossiping all afternoon, and that there's a gentleman to see you.'

'I told you,' I said to Davenport with a grimace, 'she's not let me have a moment's peace. Who is it, Meg?'

'It's Mr Dudley.'

'No, no, he's one of Emily's. Ma's got it all wrong.'

'He's asking for you most particularly. Ma wants you downstairs.'

I groaned at this unwelcome news. 'Tell Ma I'll be down in a minute.'

She favoured Davenport with one of her sauciest looks. 'Mrs Farley says she'd like you to leave, sir. Mrs Farley also says that if you want to return in an hour or two and bring your purse, you can have a go with Lizzie.' She giggled. 'We all know you want to.'

'Get out, Meg!' I threw a cushion at her. 'I'm on my way.'

She clattered out, chuckling, with me chasing her down the corridor, chiding her for embarrassing my guest. By the time I had returned, Davenport was ready to leave.

I met him in the middle of the room, clear in what I needed to say. Before he could open his mouth, I placed my hands on his chest – wanting to touch him, to hold him close, but needing to push him away.

'Don't come back with your purse, Mr Davenport. Not tonight and not ever.'

He said nothing. He only looked at me, his brown eyes steady. I could not meet his gaze so stared at his coat, trying to keep my voice strong.

'Don't… don't become just another man to me. Please.'

'No.' He had his hands on my shoulders now.

'I don't want you to be another gentleman bringing his coins to my room. I would rather have you as a friend, a brother even, than for you to become just one more like Mr Dudley and the others.'

His hands tightened a little.

'I know that.'

'Will you be a friend to me? Nothing more?'

'I will.'

We stood for a moment in silence. He understood me, I was certain of it.

'Besides,' I said, finally daring to look up at him now, 'in this room I have some choice in who I entertain. If you come here brandishing your guineas, I'll kick you down the stairs.'

'That doesn't sound like the action of a friend.'

'Well, don't give me cause to kick you, then.'

He leaned forward and kissed the top of my head, inhaling my scent. I pushed him away gently, indicating that it was time for him to leave.

Not wanting him to go.

'Goodbye for now, friend,' he said, opening the door.

'Until the next time you require a seamstress, or house maid, or some such, you mean.' I forced myself to give him a wide smile.

'Until then.'

He was gone. I stood alone in my room for a while, breathing slowly. There was a man downstairs waiting for me. I would do what needed to be done, claim my coins and build up my funds. Plan for my retirement.

It would only be later that I would climb into the chair that Davenport had vacated, wrap my shawl about me and imagine his lips on my hair. This would be an indulgence, though. A folly.

I would only do it once.

Historical Note

As with the previous Lizzie Hardwicke novel, *Death and the Harlot*, this one blends historical facts with fiction. The magistrate John Fielding (1721–1780) was a real person, but the men who make up his team, including William Davenport, are all my own creation.

David Garrick (1717–1779) was also a real person and much has been written about him. In his lifetime he was painted by some of the most famous artists of the period; you can see those wonderfully expressive eyes in works by William Hogarth, Joshua Reynolds, and Thomas Gainsborough, as well as others. It is generally acknowledged that he played a significant part in making the works of Shakespeare so central to English (and world) theatre. Despite his great love and respect for Shakespeare, Garrick did, indeed, rewrite his words, and altered the ending of *King Lear* to make it more acceptable to audiences of the eighteenth century. Samuel Johnson, for example, claimed to find Cordelia's death unbearable. Garrick worked with Nahum Tate's 1681 version, which gave it the happier ending to which Lizzie Hardwicke alludes. Much of Garrick's character in this novel has been drawn from what has been written about him: he was notoriously stingy in paying wages, and obsessively drawn to disputes with critics – which he played out in the newspapers.

Susannah Cibber and Frances (Fanny) Barton were real actresses. In 1759, when this novel is set, Fanny Barton married James Abington, a music teacher. The marriage was not a happy one, and they parted, but she retained his name. Susannah Cibber – also unhappily married – was a singer as well as an actress.

The Theatre Royal at Drury Lane opened in 1674. It suffered several fires and was rebuilt between 1791 and 1794. Audience riots were not uncommon and audience members did not behave as politely as they do these days. Shouting, singing and throwing food were part of the evening's entertainment.

If you would like to read more about the history behind this novel, here is a section of the books I have found helpful:

Beattie, J. M., *The First English Detectives. The Bow Street Runners and the Policing of London*, 1750–1840.

Benedetti, Jean, *David Garrick and the Birth of Modern Theatre.*

Brewer, John, *The Pleasures of the Imagination. English Culture in the Eighteenth Century.*

Brockett, Oscar, *History of the Theatre.*

Buck, Anne, *Dress in Eighteenth Century England.*

Cruickshank, Dan, *The Secret History of Georgian London.*

Cunningham, V., *Shakespeare and Garrick.*

Gatrell, Vic, *The First Bohemians.*

McIntyre, Ian, *Garrick.*

Parsons, Florence, *Garrick and his Circle.*

Picard, Liza, *Dr Johnson's London. Life in London 1740–1770.*

Porter, Roy, *English Society in the 18th Century.*

Pringle, Patrick, *Hue and Cry. The Birth of the British Police.*

Rubenhold, Hallie, *The Covent Garden Ladies. The Extraordinary Story of Harris's List.*

White, Jerry, *London in the Eighteenth Century. A Great and Monstrous Thing.*

Williams, Clifford, *Theatres and Audiences. A Background to Dramatic Texts.*

Acknowledgements

I owe a continuing debt of gratitude to my agent, Laura Macdougall (at United Agents). I am extremely lucky to have someone so hard-working, cheerful, patient and enthusiastic rooting for me.

Thank you, once again, to the team at Canelo for their expertise and encouragement.

Thank you to all the writers I've met since embarking on this series. I have gained a brilliant collection of new friends, which has been the most wonderful by-product in the otherwise rather isolated world of novel writing.

Thank you to my 'old' mates too, especially those of you who have only now discovered my secret life and embraced it with joy, laughter and pledges to buy all of my books. I love you. I will make sure that you buy the books but promise not to talk about them all of the time.

Thank you to Tim, my husband, who talks to me even when my eyes have glazed over and he knows my mind has wandered in another century, and who bought me an eighteenth-century snuff box (and some snuff) to help me wander along.

Finally, my son Sebastian, the performer to whom this book is dedicated. He is still far too young to engage with the vocabulary or the subject matter. His need to entertain started at his christening when, aged only three months, he lifted his head up high and spent the service smiling and cooing at the congregation. I suspect I will spend many hours watching him performing in the coming years. I am looking forward to this enormously.